Praise for
The Lace Makers of Glenmara

"Barbieri's deft writing style is charmingly wry yet evocative, with details and descriptions both telling and vivid.... A sweet summertime yarn [that] . . . provides a lovely, leisurely escape to the bucolic charms of the Emerald Isle."　—Karen Campbell, *Boston Globe*

"*The Lace Makers of Glenmara* is richly peopled and beguilingly charming, but what ultimately makes it so moving is Heather Barbieri's deep understanding that no life is immune from sorrow and difficulty. I read this wonderful novel with enormous pleasure."　—Margot Livesey, author of *The House on Fortune Street*

"*The Lace Makers of Glenmara* is a charming, moving story, written with a delicate touch."
　—Joanne Harris, author of *Chocolat* and *The Girl with No Shadow*

"Barbieri's world generates convincing warmth and emotion, making it worth a look for *Friday Night Knitting Club* fans between sequels."　—*Publishers Weekly*

"In her second novel (after *Snow in July*), Barbieri puts a graceful spin on the theme of a young woman influenced and aided by a group of older female friends.... A delicately handled romantic subplot featuring a somewhat shy and emotionally wounded Irishman named Sullivan rounds out a compelling and charming story line. Readers who have enjoyed the novels of Maeve Binchy and perhaps Rosamunde Pilcher will find this book equally entertaining."　—Margaret Hanes, *Library Journal*

"[An] unforgettable tale of love."　—*National Examiner*

"She has created an interesting story using exceptional characters and the dynamic backdrop of Glenmara, a traditional town trying to balance old world values with modern practices. Barbieri weaves together stories on life, love, friendship and family to create a multifaceted novel, where personal histories define her characters and influence their decisions. In her affinity for literary patchwork, Barbieri has created an entertaining novel by blending a thoughtful story with a light read, perfect for this summer's vacation."
—Kari Edgens, *BookPage*

"Devastating loss gives way to new life in Heather Barbieri's charming novel *The Lace Makers of Glenmara*, about a heartbroken American designer who discovers inspiration, comfort, and friendship in an intimate circle of lace makers from a quaint Irish village."
—*Parade Magazine*

"Barbieri examines with searching intelligence Kate's personal resilience and her quest for creative fulfillment. . . . Barbieri's rendering of the details of lacemaking seems impressively authentic. The novel features insights into human entanglements both current and from the past."
—Katherine Bailey, *Minneapolis Star Tribune*

"Expect fresh starts, romance, intrigue, sudden tragedy and redemption."
—Allen Pierleoni, *Sacramento Bee*

"The novel is steeped in folklore and tradition, and Barbieri writes with a sweet, lilting tone that serves the subject matter well. . . . This hopeful, comforting novel is a testament to the power of taking changes and starting fresh and a reminder that life can bring joy after sorrow."
—Hannah Sampson, *Miami Herald*

"The author . . . paints a vivid picture of Ireland in her immensely readable novel. . . . Heather is note—perfect in her depictions of Irish people and places in the book." —Brian Campbell, *Irish News*

the
LACE MAKERS
of GLENMARA

Also by Heather Barbieri

Snow in July

the

LACE MAKERS
of GLENMARA

A NOVEL

Heather Barbieri

HARPER PERENNIAL

NEW YORK • LONDON • TORONTO • SYDNEY • NEW DELHI • AUCKLAND

HARPER ● PERENNIAL

HarperCollins books may be purchased for educational, business, or
sales promotional use. For information please write: Special Markets
Department, HarperCollins Publishers, 10 East 53rd Street,
New York, NY 10022.

FIRST HARPER PERENNIAL EDITION PUBLISHED 2010.

Designed by Emily Cavett Taff

Library of Congress Cataloging-in-Publication Data
is available upon request.

ISBN 978-0-06-177246-7 (pbk.)

10 11 12 13 14   OV/RRD   10 9 8 7 6 5 4 3 2

For my family

Life itself is a thread that is never broken, never lost.

—Jacques Roumain

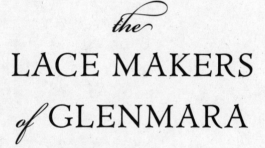

the

LACE MAKERS
of GLENMARA

Learning to Sew

What you need:

    A *sewing machine,* your mother's, yes, the sky blue Singer, its hum a lullaby from infancy, you in a Moses basket at her feet, grabbing bright threads

    Notions (tools and thoughts in equal measure), such as

    Scissors, three to six inches long, sharp pointed, pinking shears, thread clips, buttonholers, seam rippers—there will be edges to neaten, material to cut

    Tissue (dressmaker's and Kleenex)

    Tailor's chalk and *tracing wheel,* for dots, dashes, cutaway marks, arcs, outlines, traces, what has been and what will be

    Pins, for forming attachments

    Needles—sharps, betweens, milliner's, darners, tapestry, embroidery, beading, for all that must be pierced and adorned and joined together

Pin cushion, apple-shaped, with a felt stem, to keep pins from
   getting lost
Thimble, your mother's, gold, on a chain, a tiny loop soldered
   to the top; wear it on your index finger so you won't prick
   yourself, or around your neck, to remember
Measuring tape, for determining shape and size, yards, inches,
   centimeters, the distance from here to there
Thread—mercerized, nylon silk, textured, floss
Fabric, swatches and yards and bolts, wool, silk, linen, net,
   whatever will come next, whatever will be made
The pattern?

Will it come from a drawer at the fabric store—McCall's, But-
terick, Simplicity, names from your childhood, the instructions in
an envelope, the outcome preordained? Or will you make it up
as you go, letting the spirit guide you, trying to pick up the loose
threads, fix the holes, make something new? Each step, each dia-
gram, fig. 1, fig. 2, fig. 3, revealing itself in time?

You hesitate, thinking of past mistakes, when you threw
the pieces across the room in a fit of anger because nothing was
coming together the way it should, and you cried over a misshapen
collar or sleeve, lying prone in your lap as an injured child.

And yet you must press your lips together, pick up the thread.
Don't be afraid. You'll find your way.

This is a place to start.

Chapter 1

That Irish Rain

Kate had been traveling the road for hours, the rain her sole companion. It was an entertainer, that Irish rain, performing an endless variety of tricks for her amusement. It blew sideways, pounded and sighed and dripped. It hailed neat little balls of ice that melted off her hood and shoulders. She did her best to ignore it. She knew the type. She was from Seattle, after all, the city of her birth, life, and heartbreak. She'd left a few days after the separation on a day much like this nearly a month ago. She didn't know if she'd ever return, but the rain, or its cousin, followed, along with the memories that had driven her from that place.

The story was simple enough, or seemed to be, on the surface, as stories often are. She adopted a deadpan delivery in the telling, an amusing shtick, as if she were a warm-up act at a comedy club. She'd told the story on so many occasions, drawing laughs and knowing nods and sympathy, that she had the timing down pat.

Three minutes. Three minutes was all it took to dissect the end of a five-year relationship.

It came down to this, she said: Ethan ran off with a model. A girl with black hair and pale skin and aquamarine eyes and a sizable trust fund. A girl who would have been courted by princes and lords if she lived in another time and place. A girl thin and angular as a praying mantis, who wore Kate's designs at her failure of a fashion show and claimed to be her friend.

The model spoke five languages, was a champion fencer and violin virtuoso. Kate lacked such impressive qualifications. She knew enough French to order three courses in a café or ask directions to the train or toilet, so long as accents and dialects weren't too strong. She could run a seven-minute mile. She thought of herself as pretty, not beautiful. Petite, not tall. She tended to be lucky at cards, though little else relating to games of chance. She loved Fellini movies and popcorn and chocolate cake. And she loved Ethan, still, after everything that had happened.

She couldn't stop thinking about him, imagined making arguments far more winning than she was capable of in real life. Real life was empty rooms. Real life was eating and cooking for one. Real life was less laundry and a cleaner apartment. (He was a pack rat and a piler—he should have come with a warning.) Real life was waking up alone. Which was all right, because she was furious about the betrayal. Furious, yes, though still in danger of succumbing to the impulse of forgiveness, as she had before. No more. She was resolute, intent on enjoying this sojourn as much as possible, keeping sorrow at bay. The road lay before her, plain and simple, offering two ways to go, forward or back, no forks or splits or detours, just wide-open fields of lumpy, foxglove-strewn green. The road made no excuses or apologies. It didn't have to. It was what it was. It went on, walls of moss-bearded stone hemming in the narrow lane, past ruined farmhouses with half-collapsed roofs and blackened eyes. She'd been walking and hitching for nearly a month, in the far western part of the country now, one of the few areas in which signs of civilization were slim to nil. She liked it that way. She'd toured Dublin in four days. Dublin, both grand and gritty: the halls of Trinity, the Book of Kells, the Georgian streets, the museums, with glass-encased mannequins and mummies with tattered clothes and bad teeth and marble eyes; heroin addicts stealing her backpack (she gave chase, recovered the bag, she could be swift and fierce when she wanted to be); housing estates and suffocating smog. There were two sides to everything. Two sides, if not more. She'd taken one bus, then another, heading for the mythical west, buses that didn't take her as far as they were supposed to, missing connections, finally breaking down entirely, the station agents saying new vehicles would arrive within the hour, then two, then three, claims that took on the air of fairy tales. In the end, she grew tired of waiting and set off on foot, eventually winding up here, exhaustion making the scene all the more surreal.

Each step she took left a mark, some visible, some not, marks that said, *I was here, I exist.* That was one of the reasons people went away, wasn't it, to forget, to reinvent themselves?

She'd been a quiet person at home, had let the gregarious people in her life—Ethan, her friend Ella, even her mother—take the lead, happy to be the soft-spoken sidekick who offered the occasional sage remark, witty aside.

She was on her own now. It felt strange, yes, but she was ready for something new, to be someone new.

The air smelled of grass, damp, dung, and peat smoke from a distant fire, though she saw no indications of life in the immediate vicinity, other than cows and sheep. They weren't the sheep of her dreams, white and pure and fluffed, but dingy and yellowed and matted. *Maa*, said the sheep. *Maa*, she replied, the exchange bringing her to the point of tears, because it was something Ethan might have done, when they were easier together and kindnesses and clowning were possible. *Maa?* as if the animals had lost their mother, as she had done, that February.

No crying, she told herself sternly. She could keep herself in hand, smile in spite of everything. It wasn't so hard, really. *You can choose to be happy.*

She didn't mind the rain, not usually, but this was too much. I should have picked some place drier, she thought ruefully, like Spain. But even Spain had its challenges that year, with legions of stinging jellyfish, blackouts, and a plague of voles consuming crops and gardens; she'd read about it in the paper.

Shouldn't the weather be nicer by now, so close to the first of May? She took shelter under a rhododendron, its blooms surrounding her with pinked fragrance, and nibbled on an energy bar, which tasted like sawdust in the best of circumstances, and these, assuredly, were not. She wasn't hungry—she was never hungry at the beginning or end of a love affair, this one, especially, this one that was supposed to last. Everyone had been so sure she and Ethan would get married, that she would catch the bouquet at the medieval wedding they attended that March (the couple being devoted not only to each other but to the Society for Creative Anachronism), the event at which he left her, if not at the altar, just southwest of it, next to an ice sculpture of a knight in shining armor that had begun to melt, a moat of water at his feet, his sword soon no more than a toothpick.

"I can't breathe," Ethan said as they filed out of the room after the minister pronounced the couple man and wife. The turreted stone house in Seattle's Denny Regrade neighborhood had been transformed into a castle, festooned with tapestries, standards and heraldry, the wooded grounds a miniature Sherwood Forest, a formidable scene, especially after multiple flagons of ale.

"I know what you mean," Kate whispered in a mock-English accent. "This corset is an iron lung—though you do look rather comely in those tights." The scent of prime rib and roast vegetables drifted from the banquet hall. She wondered how she'd manage to eat, wished she'd brought a change of clothes. She would have liked to slip into something more comfortable, but it wasn't that sort of wedding. It was a theme party, and the bride was determined to have her way, mutton sleeves and all. Kate felt, by turns, amused and ridiculous.

"No." Ethan avoided her gaze. "I mean, I can't do *this* anymore."

"This?" She didn't let her smile falter, wouldn't let him spoil the evening. "We can leave if you want, but Sean will be disappointed you missed the joust." And she, too, because she'd hoped they could dance afterward. The bride's parents had hired a pipe band, already skirling away. A jester tumbled down the great hall, narrowly avoiding a priceless Ming vase, jingling his bells. Fire eaters gulped flames on the balcony. She wondered if they ever burned their tongues.

"No. *Us.*" He let the words sink in a moment. "It's over. I'm sorry." He moved away, tottering slightly, loose from his moorings, though others probably put it down to drinking. Before he reached the exit, a friend reeled him in, clapped him on the back, and he allowed himself to be caught in this way, obviously grateful for the distraction. Within moments, he was raising toasts and laughing. He was, among other things, resilient—and clever enough to know Kate wouldn't follow and make a scene.

She stood there, speechless, her expression not unlike that of the roast pig in the center of the feast, mouth agape, minus the apple. At first she'd wondered if witnessing the exchange of vows, the pledge of fidelity, the till-death-do-us-part, had unnerved Ethan. She could understand that. She could wait. She wouldn't pressure him. She got a ride home with Ella, figuring she and Ethan would kiss and make up later, as they always did.

She was wrong. That night, he moved in with a friend, saying he needed the time and space to think. He left most of his things behind. Whenever she called, he was out. She wondered if he was even living there, but where else could he be? She waited two weeks, counting the days, until his friend finally took pity on her and confessed that Ethan had been seeing the model for months, that they were, in fact, soon to be engaged. Instead of Ethan and Kate moving to Manhattan to pursue their dreams (he in finance, she in fashion), it would be Ethan and The Model. Kate was left with no boyfriend and few buyers for her debut line. The concept hadn't "clicked," her rep, Jules, said; she needed to try something more "high concept"—never mind that she thought she had already, following his advice against her best instincts. The only takers were two small local boutiques, the money she earned hardly enough to pay her expenses, meaning she would have to start doing alterations. She was sick of letting down hems, making allowances, mending buttons and holes, tasks people could have done themselves if they'd only taken a few minutes. Less than it took to bring the garments to the vintage clothing store, Ella's, owned by her best friend, where Kate tried to make ends meet. Her fingertips were rough from the work. Seamstress hands. Her mother had them too.

"I have to get out of here," she'd told Ella. Not just the shop— the city, the state, the entire country. To Ireland. Land of her ancestors, land of the green, of rainbows and magic and pots of gold.

She and her mother had intended to go together, but her mother's cancer had accelerated, taking her before they made the trip; she made Kate promise to travel on her own, left her a small inheritance to finance the venture. Then Kate and Ethan meant to visit, as part of a European tour, which Kate had thought of as their future honeymoon, and Ethan, she now realized, probably hadn't.

There she was, halfway around the world, heading down this potholed, split-lipped road that went God only knew where. Trying to forget the way Ethan's hair stuck up in the morning, the way he made her coffee and burned the toast, the way his eyes held so many colors—flecks of green and gold and brown and blue. She'd never seen eyes like that before, had been seduced by them the first time he'd asked her a question in a college literature class seven years ago. They had been studying Thomas Hardy that term. Had that been a bad sign? They were friends in the beginning. She watched him date a succession of people, waiting to be chosen, waiting for the night she and Ethan would drink too much, fall into bed, and become inseparable.

She'd be more careful next time. She'd only date men who chose her first, when they were sober and sure. She'd only date men with solid, reliable eyes, eyes that had settled on being one color, say brown. Yes, brown. If she ever trusted herself enough to date again.

Bells. There on that Irish road, she heard bells. Had she frozen to death? Were they rung by angels? Fairies? The wedding jester, returned to mock her? Or was it a beast of a man wielding chains, who would murder her in the ditch, the news of which would eventually reach Ethan, plunging him into paroxysms of guilt?

No, she wasn't famous enough to rate the media coverage, though she'd dreamed of being known for her designs, once; she would be a footnote on the *Seattle Post-Intelligencer* obituary page, "Local aspiring fashion designer dies on lonely Irish lane."

She shrank into the bushes, waiting for whatever it was to pass or put her out of her misery.

A horse snorted, hoofbeats plodded. A wagon appeared, painted with exuberant flowers, an ode to Peter Max in mod red, yellow, and green, canvas stretched over the top. A stocky traveler held the reins to the portliest equine she had ever seen. The man and his colorful cart looked as if they'd stepped out of a fairy tale or the Beatles film *Yellow Submarine*.

She stared at him through the leaves in surprise, and he, at her. "Haven't washed away yet, have you?" he asked.

She shook her head. The branches showered her with water, drops pattering on her hood in hollow applause.

"Where are you headed?" He wore a canvas coat, vest, jeans, and, rather incongruously, brand-new sneakers, his skin tanned as cognac and heavily lined. There was a natural openness in his face she rarely encountered at home.

"Someplace dry," she replied with a half smile, dipping her chin slightly.

"You won't find it standing there—though those leaves are rather becoming on you."

She fingered a length of honeysuckle vine. "The arboreal look is very in this season." She felt her cheeks begin to color.

"Is it now? You're giving the wearing of the green a whole new meaning." He tipped the rain from the brim of his hat. "Would you like a lift?"

She brushed the lichen from her jacket, hesitating. Instinct told her to trust him. Besides, she had to consider her options, her present situation. There was nothing but the road and the sheep and the *drip-drip-drip* of rain. And then there was him, offering her what could be a pleasant alternative. Perhaps it was time to take a chance. He looked harmless enough.

"Can't stay out in this weather, that's for certain," he continued. "You'll catch your death."

She imagined herself expiring in a field like a tragic heroine in a Victorian novel. "Or drown." She held out her hand, palm up, catching raindrops, letting them fall.

"Come on then." He patted the seat beside him. "Hop up. I could use the company."

Chapter 2

William the Traveler

In all his days of wandering, William the Traveler had never seen a face so wistful, hope and sadness intermingling. Her skin had the delicacy of fine porcelain, her eyes luminous too, the sort of eyes that revealed every emotion, by turns pensive and filled with mirth. Her hair had a bit of chestnut in it, a wave too, teased by the mist. She'd pulled her hood forward as if to keep the elements and the rest of the world at bay, but a few tendrils crept out, tentative curls clinging to her cheeks, reaching for the light. She hadn't been eating much, he guessed. Her bones were already too close to the surface, angles pressing against pale skin, which only added to her aura of fragility. And yet she had strength too, apparent in the intensity of her gaze. Nor had she lost her sense of humor, bantering with him there by the road. He spread a plaid blanket across her legs, draped another over her shoulders to ward off the chill. (He was glad he'd cleaned them that week, so they didn't smell of travel and horses.) It would take a while for her to warm up. Her teeth were still chattering. He wondered how long she'd been out in the weather, if she knew where she was going. From the bewildered look in her eyes, he doubted it. She put on a show of being sure of herself, but the shaking of her hands (he was sure it wasn't just because of the cold) gave her away. He offered her a sweet damson. They weren't local, too early in the season for that. He'd bought them in Galway as he was passing through, unable to resist. He liked a good plum.

She thanked him and took a bite, juice dribbling down her chin. She swiped it away with the back of her hand. No ring, though there had been once, a faint tan line all that remained of the promise.

She traveled light, with only a small backpack and sleeping bag. Judging by her expression, there were other things that weighed her down, not that she let them, not completely. There was fight in her yet. He saw that in the sense of wonder with which she took in her surroundings, in the way she looked at him with those sparkling green eyes.

"Where are you from?" the traveler asked.

Kate told him.

"My nephew went to Seattle once. He was mad for the music scene. Can't stand the new stuff myself, though I don't mind a good *craic*." The man paused. "Pipes and the fiddles are more my speed. You been to one?"

She shook her head.

"Not much for crowds, eh? Don't like them myself either," he agreed. "But *craics* are different. The music brings everyone together, so no one is a stranger."

"Yes, the music." The Irish tunes called up something in her. She felt them in her veins, a deep place that moved her to tears. It wasn't sadness, not entirely. It was everything at once—joy, pain, hope.

"I see you know what I mean," he said as she blinked back tears.

"I'm sorry," she said, dabbing her eyes with her sleeve. It was the tiredness, that was all, lowering her defenses.

"No need to apologize. It's a gift to feel things keenly."

"There's something about being here, about the songs . . ." Her voice trailed off as she tried to explain.

"How long have you been in the country?" he asked.

"Three weeks or so. I don't even know what day it is anymore. I've lost track of time."

"That can be a good thing," he replied, adding, "but it's the first of May, in case you're wondering."

"Already?" She pushed her bag under the seat with her foot. She hadn't brought much: a pack stuffed with clothes and toiletries, a sketchpad and pencils; a digital camera, the memory card filled with timed self-portraits taken next to various tourist attractions. Frame after frame showed her smiling determinedly in front of the entrance to Newgrange, the Blarney Stone (she couldn't bring herself to kiss it, and a gang of boys cheered her escape, shouting that one of their da's had wee-ed on it after drinking with his pals). A day here, a day there, taking in the major sights of central and southeast Ireland, traveling by bus and on foot, each morning promising a new adventure.

But her most prized possession was the golden thimble that had once belonged to her mother, Tallulah. Her mother had asked a jeweler to solder a loop to the top, so that it could hang from a slender ribbon, like a charm, attached to the top of

Kate's bassinet when she was a baby—and now to a chain around her neck.

"People spend too much time chained to the clock anyway. On holiday, are you?" the traveler asked.

"Yes," she said, "and looking for inspiration."

"I thought you might be an artist."

"What gave me away?"

"I can see it in your hands."

She glanced at her fingers before tucking them in her pockets. "I wouldn't make much of a hand model, would I?" she said.

"No need to be. They're lovely hands, small, but capable. A callus here and there to let people know you mean business."

"I used to." She wasn't so sure anymore, though she kept telling herself things would get better. "Tomorrow is another day," her mother used to say, right up to the end.

The traveler handed her a handkerchief. "Thought you might want to dry your face a little, not that there's much point until the weather stops carrying on like this." He paused a moment, seeming to sense she was holding back. "You're too young to give in to disappointment. The joy will come again, and when it does it will be all the better because of what you've suffered. Love is life, you know."

Ethan had read that line to her, when they were studying for a test in their second English class. "Tolstoy," she said faintly.

"The very one." The traveler kept his eyes on the road while he talked, but it felt as if he were looking right through her.

"So you're a reader of books—and people?" she asked.

"I like a good story."

"It looks like you could run a mobile library with the collection you have back there." She gestured to the stacks of books underneath the canvas cover, hardcover and paperback, well thumbed, by the look of them: Edna O'Brien, William Trevor, John Banville, James Joyce, Roddy Doyle, Samuel Beckett, and Thomas Pynchon, among others.

"I have time for extensive reading. It improves the mind."

"I love Edna O'Brien's work, *The Country Girls Trilogy* in particular."

"Of course you do. And Joyce?"

"Yes, though my mother was his biggest fan."

"She must be a fine woman, your mother. Few are up to the challenge of taking him on."

"Yes." She gazed at the surrounding country, as if to see it with her mother's eyes, the colors saturated as an oil painting, the sky dusky pearl over fields of foxglove and lupine and wild narcissus, the textured brushstrokes of velvet mosses and tussocks of shaggy green and gold, brilliant in the sun. And then the rain started again, extinguishing the light, the chill settling over her once more.

They sat in silence for a while. Kate listened to the tap of the rain on the canvas, on her hood, the traveler's hat; the beat of the horse's hooves, the jangle of the reins and bridle, the creak of the wheels, the wind in the grass. "I feel as if I've gone back in time," she said.

"There's a magic here, it's true. That's why I can't leave this place. Not for long."

"How do you make a living?" she asked.

"Other than as an amateur philosopher? No pay in that, that's for certain." He laughed. "I get by fixing things. There's always something broken that needs to be fixed."

They journeyed for hours, swaying to the rhythm of the wagon, tracing one of the minor routes taken by farmers and soldiers and pilgrims and seekers and famine survivors over the centuries. Kate dozed, dreaming of Ethan again. This time, he was hand in hand with someone new. She tried to call after him, not caring how she humiliated herself, but the sound wouldn't come. As she struggled to speak, her body turned inside out, nothing left of her but a scrap of cloth, which a homeless woman picked up from the littered sidewalk and used to patch a hole in her jeans, a large needle in her roughened hands.

Get out of my subconscious! she wanted to shout. Instead, she woke, mouthing air like a beached fish, cheek pressed against a sack of grain.

"Bad dream?" the man asked.

She rubbed her eyes and sat up. "But only a dream." She would not let it get the best of her. She shook off the dust of sleep and took in the scene at hand. The sky had cleared again, a gilded blue now, terns circling overhead. "It looks like heaven," she said.

"Sometimes. Others hell, all gray and miserable. Never can tell what the next day will bring. At least it keeps things interesting."

"Do you ever get tired of traveling?"

"Me? No. I was born to it. It's not for everyone, though. Most people need to settle."

She heard cheers coming from over a rise to the west, rising and falling in waves. "What's going on?"

"The Saint Brendan's Festival," he said. "They've got activities planned for two weeks, I hear. The feast day is coming up later in the month."

"Saint Brendan. Which was he? Not one of those who met a horrible death?" Her mother had an encyclopedic knowledge of the saints, her parents Irish, education parochial, a book of saints among her belongings, handed down through the generations, the stories of martyrdom scandalous and lurid enough to make the modern tabloids.

"No, he had it good, compared to some. Brendan the Navigator," the traveler said. "Set off to discover the world with a band of monks in a coracle. Patron of boatmen and travelers."

"A coracle. Aren't those small boats for traveling by sea?"

"Yes, with ox hides stretched over a wooden frame."

"Doesn't sound sturdy enough for the ocean," Kate said. "Did Brendan and his crew make it?"

"So they say. Takes someone with a strong stomach and conviction to venture out in a coracle, that's for sure, but Saint Brendan and the monks had faith and God on their side. The boat had some sort of power in it—drop the *c* in *coracle* and you have *oracle*, as my grandmother always said. That must have been true for him too. I suppose he and his men fared well enough, though they didn't find the paradise they were looking for, and the sea, no doubt, presented its challenges. It can be wicked, that sea."

"I don't think I could have managed a trip like that—I'd need a bigger boat and a life preserver," she said.

He laughed. "A smart girl you are—or at least a careful one—leaving little to chance."

The land looked greener there, if that were possible. A green that vibrated in its very intensity. A green of dreams. "Where are we?"

"Near Glenmara. The end of the road. Can't go more west than this, unless you take wing or boat. I'll drop you here." He pulled on the reins. The horse stopped, tossed his head, eager to move on. "You need to get warm. The town's just over that hill." He pointed in the direction from which she'd heard the cheering. "Why don't you stay awhile? See what happens."

Kate hopped down from the wagon and stretched, muscles sore from the ride. "Is it so special?"

"It could be, if you let it."

She shouldered her backpack. "Aren't you coming?"

He shook his head. "I'd best be getting on."

"I could go with you." Already she missed the rhythm of the wagon, the ease of his presence.

"You don't want to do that," he said. "It's not as romantic as it seems, this traveling. It's dirty and hard, but it suits me."

"Where are you headed?"

"Another camp on a beach somewhere. I like to hear the sound of the sea. I'll know when I get there. So will you, maybe sooner than you think." He clicked his tongue and the horse set off, the pace slow, yet steady. She could have caught up with him easily if she tried.

"Wait," she called after him, standing at the crossroads beneath the weathered sign with its faded lettering and arrow pointing the way: *Glenmara*. "I don't even know your name."

"William," he said over his shoulder, before turning to face the road again. "William the Traveler."

Chapter 3

A Village at the End of the World

The turnout hadn't been what Bernie hoped for. She'd done all the right things, advertised in the regional papers, sent press releases to the tourist boards, to no avail. Tour buses bypassed Glenmara in favor of towns with museums, workshops, and more significant histories. Their village, like so many other dying Gaelic hamlets, possessed an obscure narrative, the kind that mattered, if at all, to those who lived there, not that many remained. It was a run-down little place that tried to put a bright face on things—despite there never being enough money or jobs, especially now that the fishing industry, if one could call it that, had collapsed.

To be sure, the ruined abbey off the coast counted for something—not much left now except the limestone foundations, where the nuns had died of fever, or, more likely, the residents joked, sheer boredom. The town didn't have a holy shrine, Pictish fort, or standing stones nearby, though someone once floated the idea that a particular boulder in Declan Moore's field was blessed, which worked for a time, until the priest called them on the lie. Father Dominic Burn-in-Hell Byrne was forever ruining their fun. The seventy-five-year-old priest made note of everything, kept close watch over his flock. He considered Bernie one of the devoted. And she was. Up to a point.

"Did you notice the chip man is using the newsletter to wrap the kippers again?" asked her friend Aileen.

"He is not," she said, aghast. She was the sole editor and writer of the four-page paper, the *Gaelic Voice*, having taken over the duties from her husband, John, after his death last year. The crime blotter, which she'd added recently at Aileen's urging, was especially popular:

> Man calls Garda, complaining his neighbor won't stop playing Frank Sinatra at 2:00 a.m. Garda tells him to be patient. The woman is suffering from a broken heart.

> Woman calls Garda, says there's a rat sitting on her couch, watching the football match; would he please get rid of it? Garda asks if the rat is a fan of Manchester United.

"Is," Aileen said with a pin in her mouth. "What's the circulation now?"

"One hundred, including the surrounding villages," Bernie said. "If I had my way, all the towns up and down the coast would have their own Gaelic papers. A Gaelic newspaper empire."

"Careful. You're starting to sound rather Machiavellian." Aileen laughed. "You going to have an English edition too?"

"That's cheating."

"More like subtitles, you know, in films? It's a known fact the language is dying out. There's no getting around it, sad though it may be."

"I've never been much for known facts, and it's my mission to keep the language alive. John would have wanted it that way. I do too." They could go on like this for hours, debating the merits of the village, the people, themselves.

But another day was ending, not much different from the last. The vendors were packing up for the day or nodding off in their chairs. The only people wandering the streets at that hour were a group of restless teens and a couple of aging pub regulars—Denny Fitzpatrick, their friend Oona's da, and Niall Maloney, dressed in trousers, jumpers, and caps. They weren't the sort who'd be interested in the lace.

"If we had a beer garden or an espresso stand, people would come," Aileen said. "My son's got an espresso bar in Galway. Keeps the bookstore open. He couldn't run it otherwise. The shoppers go for coffee first, he says, Yeats second."

"What's the world coming to, that Yeats should come second to anything?" Bernie loved poetry. She and her husband had read it to each other every night before bed. She hadn't imagined she'd forget the sound of his voice; she would have given anything to hear it again. "We can't sell espresso," she added. "It would spoil the lace. People are forever spilling things."

"I suppose you're right, though I could use a shot of something right now. I didn't sleep well last night. The Change, you know." Aileen had been having hot flashes. She was a striking woman, and if she didn't keep bringing the matter up, people would have thought she was younger. Not that there was much chance of fooling anyone in Glenmara, where everyone knew everyone else's business, or thought they did.

Aileen had never felt comfortable with her looks, not real-izing that her flaws—the slightly too large nose, the gap in her teeth, and her whippet-thin figure—were part of what made her interesting. She wouldn't listen, no matter how many times Bernie reminded her of that. "You're my friend, Bee, it's your job to tell me what I want to hear," Aileen would say.

"Try valerian tea," Bernie suggested. "I heard that helps."

"Probably causes cancer."

"These days nearly everything causes cancer, or so they think, for at least five minutes. Try to enjoy life and not worry so much. You only live once." That had been her mantra since John died, especially in the beginning, whenever the inertia descended and she sat at the table in the morning and found that hours had passed as she stared out the window, the cup of tea by her elbow gone cold, her Labrador, Fergus, whimpering at her feet, his brow wrinkled with worry.

"I'm not programmed that way—especially when I can't get any damned rest. I'd kill for a good night's sleep. I used to be such a good sleeper—"

"Yes, I remember," Bernie replied. Aileen had slept like the dead when they were girls. "You snored something awful."

"It was the adenoids. Been better since I got them out, though now I think I'm getting a nose whistle."

"Maybe you should form a band." Bernie smiled. They were forever teasing each other about the good and the bad. Bernadette Anne Cullen and Aileen Mary Flanagan had been friends for forty-four years. They couldn't believe how quickly the decades had gone by, the loves and disappointments and fights and mar-riages and deaths they had witnessed. And there they were, sit-ting at that collapsible table with the stiff little legs that could be snapped up or down—an exact replica of the one at which they'd sold lemon ices on the road during the summers when they were girls—together, after all that time. Nothing could keep them apart for long. They were like family, Aileen said, without the excess baggage.

"Ha. Ha. Should we go, then? Everyone else is throwing in the towel." Aileen tossed a dish towel, its edge embroidered with lace, into the basket at her feet for emphasis.

Someone let out a whoop down the road that died quickly, not enough voices or enthusiasm to sustain it. When Bernie was a girl, there had been coracle races in the bay and hurling matches in the fields and dancing all night long. Now, the few young people in town hung around the bar. They were the glowering sort of teenagers indigenous to many a sleepy village, seemingly angry about everything. Aileen's daughter Rosheen, too. Sixteen-year-old Rosheen had recently announced that she was changing her name to Jane, muttering something about Gaelic shite. She'd gotten another tattoo and pierced her nose and was at that very moment smoking cigarettes with her friends nearby. She and Aileen tried to ignore each other.

"Bernie? Did you hear what I said?" Aileen asked.

"Just a little longer." Bernie was in no hurry to return to the empty cottage. She and John never had children. She only had Fergus, the brown Lab, resting now at her feet, for company. Fergus, who'd been young once, his fur lustrous and thick, who ran through the lanes and over the hills, chasing rabbits and robins and foxes. Fergus, dear boy, aging too.

"Why? Are you expecting a visiting dignitary?" Aileen asked.

"You never know who might come down the road."

"Nothing interesting has come down that road since Cromwell's soldiers attacked in the 1600s. And they nearly killed everyone."

Bernie was about to admit defeat when she saw a young

woman cresting the hill. "There," she said. "What did I tell you? A tourist."

Aileen squinted in the direction Bernie indicated. "It's a miracle—though she might have had the decency to bring a friend along. Who travels alone? Do you think she's a criminal?"

"You can't be serious. She hardly seems the type." The girl looked like a sprite, with great dark eyes and pale skin and a tangle of long hair down her back, steam rising from her shoulders like mist.

"They never do."

"You watch too many crime shows."

"What else is there to do around here in the evenings except play cards and make lace?" Aileen said. "Don't get your hopes up. She's not going to stop here. Why should she? There's nothing of interest. No clubs, no posh shops, no gourmet restaurants, no Internet cafés. She'll move on. Everyone does."

"No, no, no. . . ." Bernie imitated Aileen's grating voice. "Let's say yes to everything, just this once. This will be the week of yes. Let's try it and see what happens."

"I said yes to Rourke, and look where that got me." Aileen snorted, adding, "I told you. She's going."

The girl glanced back in the direction she'd come. Second thoughts, perhaps? Understandable. They had them every day, or at least Aileen seemed to.

The visitor turned toward them again, and Bernie exclaimed. "Ha. See? She's staying, of course she will."

"Only because there's nowhere else to go at this hour."

Bernie nodded with satisfaction. "Here she comes. Don't scare her away."

Chapter 4

The American Girl

Along the main street, if you could call it that, tents sprouted like white-capped mushrooms. There was a bar, naturally, and a hodgepodge of squat buildings, none higher than a single story, that braced each other up for a block or two before the boulder- and heather-strewn fields took over, tumbling down to the sea, a single cottage here and there among the barrens. Some structures had been given a fresh coat of whitewash in honor of the occasion, the smell of lime lingering, and doors had been brightened with an application of red, blue, or green lacquer, the peeling, faded parts painted over. In the distance, atop a gentle rise, stood the parish church, spire pointing heavenward, whiteness so bleached and pure it hurt the eyes.

The wind blew off the sea, bending blades of grass, snapping the canvas tents. One tore clean away, a man swearing in pursuit as it flapped down the narrow street like a great bird.

"Look! It's the holy host!" a pair of tottering men, caps askew, cried out. They fell on their knees—prostrated by religious fervor or the effects of Guinness or mirth—as it careened past. "Praise the Lord. Someone get the priest."

The fugitive tent continued its merry rampage, knocking over a bicycle and snagging on an aerial before taking flight again. The kids hanging around the pub in a cloud of smoke jeered at the scene, which passed all too soon, the long, dull evening returning. Soon night would fall, only the glowing ends of their pilfered cigarettes visible in the failing light, darkness sending them into the fields where someone had hidden a cache of ale, so that those who desired oblivion could find it again. There was little to do in Glenmara, few livings to be made, no matter how much praying to the saints anyone did. "Fecking saints," one of them said, too young to know better, too belligerent to care. Their faces hadn't lost their softness yet, though the teens made a show of hardening their edges with black makeup and clothes, indulgence in the bad, denial of the good. They wouldn't miss their innocence until it was gone.

Kate shivered from the chill, a hint of a smile on her lips, seeing an old version of herself in the kids (though never so rough as that), entertained by the shenanigans of the man and the tarp, entranced by the beauty of the landscape. She wondered if her ancestors had stood on a spot very like this, miles north, in Donegal, looking down on their abandoned crofts. Her mother's family had few stories of those early days. They were too busy becoming American, forgetting the past. The tale they chose to tell began with laboring in the coalfields of Pennsylvania, then boarding the trains west, to Montana, to wield pickaxes in the copper mines of Butte,

Montana, because they were run by an Irishman named Daley, one of their own, who would give them a fair chance, or so they thought. They came in waves, the Irish, the dusty streets ringing with Gaelic, the bars blaring the music of the pipe bands and fiddles, ale flowing freely, the inhabitants drinking disappointment away. As the years passed, their accents weakened to a mere hint of a lilt. Day after day, they disappeared into the earth—some said it was like going into the grave; others, the gates of hell—and, eventually, for good.

What came before, in Ireland, Kate didn't know. There were gravestones somewhere, she supposed, imprinted with her ancestors' names, perhaps another headstone that read "Tallulah 'Lu' Robinson," like her mother's, the letters worn away by the passage of time. Or, more likely, a simple wooden cross, decayed long ago, since there'd probably been no money for formal burials, only a series of small mounds, overgrown with brambles and grass. Kate sifted through what might or might not have been, seeking a reference point, a place to say: *This is the beginning.* A spot on the map: *You are here.* Or were here. Or might be here. *You belong.*

She reached for the golden thimble on the chain around her neck, the only tangible link to her mother she'd brought along, because she treasured the notion, remembered playing with it as a little girl. How precious it had seemed then—now, more than ever.

Her neck was bare. She searched the road, frantically at first, then more slowly, in growing resignation. It would have gleamed, caught the light, if it were there.

Like her mother, the thimble was gone. No amount of searching would bring it back.

Kate set off down the half-cobbled lane again, over stones that had been there since the road's birth over three hundred years before. She felt the vendors' eyes on her, the coming attraction. First, she bought fish and chips from a man who greeted her in Gaelic, *Dia duit*, Hello. She'd learned some of the language when she took Irish dancing lessons as a child, but she'd forgotten all but a few of the steps. Her mother had kept one of the costumes—the green jumper with the Celtic knot embroidered in gold thread on the bodice. Kate took first place at the *feis* that year. She didn't know where the garment was now—shoved away in a box in the storage facility, most likely. The sum of her mother's life contained in that dark rectangular space, a vault filled with echoes. (Lu insisted on packing her things before she went into the hospital for the last time, knowing she wouldn't return. She hired someone to do it to spare her friends and Kate the trouble. She did it without telling them. That was her way.) Kate couldn't face opening the cardboard cartons and trunks, letting the memories escape. She had left the key with Ella, saying she would be in touch to tell her what to do.

"Mind the grease. It adds to the flavor but can stain your clothes." The seller wrapped the fish—so fresh it still had fins and tail, though thankfully, not the head—in a page from a newsletter written in the local dialect.

Kate took a bite, closing her eyes as she savored the morsel. She hadn't eaten since that morning, and then only a biscuit and tea.

"Good, eh?" he asked.

"The best." She pressed on, studied *claddagh* rings and jasper bracelets at another stall, slipping them on her finger, then off.

As the wind skirled up from the sea and down the lanes of Glenmara, Kate stopped at the next stand. She considered lengths of linen and lace, perfect for a hope chest. She took a deep breath. She'd traveled this far with her perseverance and sanity relatively intact. She would not, under any circumstances, have a nervous breakdown over a towel embroidered with shamrocks.

"May we interest you in some lace, miss?" asked a lilting voice, a voice that soothed and calmed and drew her away from the edge of wherever it was she'd been going.

Miss. The perfect form of address, as if she'd lost something—which, of course, she had.

"Miss?"

Kate nearly thanked the women and walked away. She'd never gone for frills or ruffles, but the quality of the work made her reconsider. She'd never seen such intricate stitches. Some pieces were adorned with crocheted lace, others bobbined, or with appliqués applied to net. They were extraordinary: flowers, Celtic dragons, nymphs, fish, saints, king and queens, come to life, rendered with almost painterly skill.

"I'm Bernie Cullen," the sweet-faced woman with curly dark hair said, trying to put her at ease. "And this is Aileen Flanagan."

"Nice to meet you," Kate said. "Did you make these yourselves?"

"No, we imported them from China. The boat left the dock a moment ago," the woman called Aileen said, everything about her, even her voice, angular, sharp.

"Aileen has a fine skill with a needle, doesn't she?" Bernie said, giving her friend a nudge with her elbow. "No, these are local.

We're part of a guild, you see. Most of us learned from our mams and grans."

The lace would have delighted Kate's mother. She'd been a costume designer for the theater—she made eighteenth-century ball gowns, 1950s circle skirts, tentacled sea monsters, futuristic space suits; nothing was beyond her skill or imagination—and a devoted craftswoman during her time off, a string of beads or needle and thread at hand. She'd taught Kate to draw and sew. "You have a gift," she often said, believing in her dreams, the Singer sewing machine bobbing its head in agreement as they stitched lengths of black and orange cloth, attaching rickrack to sleeves, joining bodices and skirts: mother-and-daughter witch costumes with capes and pointed hats and brooms. Kate was four, her mother twenty-seven that year. Kate carried a plastic pumpkin bucket for the candy. Her mother held Kate's hand, taking her from house to house. That Halloween, it had been a clear night, the moon bright as they traversed the shadowed streets with the other ghosts and goblins.

What would her mother say now? *Take up the thread and start again. You can always start again.*

If only it were that easy.

"You're one of those artsy types, aren't you?" Bernie asked. "You've got style, even in that mac."

"That's kind of you to say—especially when I'm such a mess," Kate said.

"Indeed," Aileen said, giving Kate the once-over. "See anything you like?"

Kate tucked a damp strand of hair behind her ear and pretended she hadn't heard Aileen's critical aside. "My mother would have loved these things," she said. She and Kate should have been taking the trip together, but instead of traipsing along the Cliffs of Moher last fall, Lu had been in a hospital bed. Kate visited daily, the nurses exclaiming over the resemblance—they had the same hair and eyes, gestures and laugh.

The same bad luck with men.

"She's artistic too?" Bernie asked.

Was. Kate didn't correct her, didn't want to deal with sad-eyed looks and murmurs of sympathy.

"She must miss you, being so far away," Bernie said.

Farther than they knew.

Bernie whipped a hook in and out of the crocheted lace. "Would you like to learn?" she asked.

"It doesn't seem like something that can be mastered in a few minutes," Kate demurred, "though it's kind of you to offer—if I had more time . . ." Even now, her fingers itched for a needle, old habits dying hard.

"Surely, you'll be stopping awhile," Bernie said. "You've been on the road too long, haven't you?"

Yes, she had. "I only planned on staying the night," Kate said, thinking of Killarney and the Ring of Kerry to the south; all the places she and her mother intended to go, so much left to see. "Is there a B&B in town?"

"Whatever you do, don't go to Dooley's," Aileen warned. "The place suffers from the damp something awful. The last person who lodged there wore all the clothes in his suitcase fighting to stay warm and he still got the hypothermia, didn't he, Bernie?"

"He did indeed, poor fellow. He almost had to go to hospital. I could have sworn his skin looked blue."

"Weren't the owners bothered by the cold too?" Kate asked.

"Lord, no. They're used to it. It would take a blizzard to kill them. They'd probably wear bathing suits in Antarctica, though it might scare the penguins," Aileen said.

A Labrador emerged from under the table and nudged Kate's hand with his nose.

Kate bent down and scratched his ears. "I didn't see you there. What a handsome fellow you are."

The dog woofed and looked at Bernie expectantly, as if he had something to tell her.

Bernie patted his head. "It's his way of saying he wants you to stay with us," she told Kate. "He's a good judge of character, my Fergus."

Aileen rolled her eyes.

Bernie ignored her. "Your timing couldn't be better," she told Kate. "I was just thinking about renting out the guest room—and then you came along. It's nothing fancy, mind. But we have plenty of space. And I can promise you we keep the windows closed and the blankets dry, so you won't catch pneumonia." She had the sort of laugh, deep and full, from the belly, that made others smile to hear it.

"I don't want to put you to any trouble." Kate considered the empty road, twilight settling over the landscape, another day almost gone. Clearly, she couldn't keep going that night. She had her trusty sleeping bag with its 10-degree rating. She could have slept under the stars again. She'd done it before, under bushes, among the weeds, in empty barns, abandoned buildings, when she was trying to save money (she still had enough, though it wouldn't last forever), but the idea held little appeal, what with the state of the ground, the weather, and her clothes. She should have brought a tent. As it was, she needed to dry out, and the thought of a roof over her head, a hot shower, and a clean, warm bed was irresistible. She'd stop for the night, then the next day, she'd be off.

"It's no trouble at all." Bernie pressed her hand and smiled, the night full of sighs and murmurs, as the vendors collapsed their awnings and loaded their cars, like a circus leaving town.

Chapter 5

Absences and Visitations

At home, the same scene greeted Bernie day after day, a place of echoes and loss: John's suits in the closet, his shoes lined up below, his underwear in the drawer. Bernie would slip his socks over her fingers, hands knit into stumps, smooth, digitless, then bend fingers to thumb, making a toothless mouth. "Hello," she said, "fancy a show?"—a puppet without an audience. She pressed the navy cashmere to her cheek, hard, against the bone, and wept.

This was what had awaited her until she met the girl at the market, offered her a room: his pipe on the desk, the tobacco pouch nearby. She'd tried smoking it, because his lips had touched the mouthpiece, but she couldn't get it right and choked. He would have laughed if he'd been there. Maybe he was. *John?* Sometimes she felt him, looking over her shoulder, and she turned to face the bare room, the absence of him that forever altered the space they'd once shared. The dust showed more now that he was gone. The worn spots on the carpet. Knife marks on the dishes. The smoothness of the pillow and sheets on his side of the bed. She stretched diagonally across the mattress, searching for him in sleep.

His poems were stuffed in the drawer with the broken lock. He'd never written about her. He didn't write about people, even those he loved. He wrote about the land, the sea, what it meant to be Irish. He carried the history of his family on his shoulders, the deaths from the Famine and the purges, when those who wouldn't say their names in English were struck down, his grandfather and great uncle among them. She went through the pages, thinking she might make them into a book one day, if only she could decipher the handwriting. (Even he couldn't always make it out.)

He'd written in the evenings by the window overlooking the garden, where the snowdrops and grape hyacinths emerged each spring, murmuring the words to himself, finding the rhythm, the meaning for his purpose, while she sat by the fire, making the lace. They didn't speak, but it was a companionable silence, the only sounds the click and pop of her needle twisting threads, piercing cloth, and the scratch of his pen against paper.

She missed that sound. She missed the smell of him—all grass and wool and tobacco. She missed his voice, the mellow timbre, the music of it, when he spoke. She missed his touch, sought it in everything he had come in contact with, wouldn't give anything away, not yet, maybe never.

She could keep these things. His things. There was room. There was too much room.

Stacks of dishes rested on the shelves he had built for her. They didn't need so many plates, no way of knowing that in the beginning, when they were receiving wedding presents—when they thought they'd have a family. That there would be more than just the two of them.

Now she didn't have to worry about a broken cup or dish. There were plenty of replacements. The dishes were the sort of opalescent porcelain that caught the light, sprigs of lilac and gold along the rim. The manufacturer had discontinued the pattern; she'd checked the shops when she went to Galway on the annual trip with Aileen. They'd go again that fall. She looked forward to it, a change in the routine, the going and the coming back, even if it meant a return to loneliness too.

This past year, she'd become aware of the bones of everything, the structure underneath. The hard edges, the flagstones, the frame of her home. Her own skeleton. She hadn't noticed before, when his presence filled the home, but things were different now. *She* was different, part of a shrinking world: the Gaelic, John, so much fading away.

She went on long walks in the mornings to help her sleep, to help her feel better. She kept her boots and jumper by the door, a reminder that she could open it any time, let herself out, let someone in, if the occasion arose. It worked, up to a point.

She couldn't imagine being with anyone else. She was happy enough with things as they were. Content. The years could go on this way, and she'd be fine, fine. She picked up a photograph, ran a finger down the glass, closed her eyes, as if she could climb inside the frame, into his arms, a likeness on paper all she had, one that would fade with time, that could be lost or torn, memory another fragile thing.

If Fergus hadn't been with her in those first few days, when there didn't seem to be anything tying her to the earth, she didn't know how it might have ended. But he was by her side through it all. He slept at the foot of the bed, followed her around the house, licked her hand. He didn't want her to go, communicating with her in a soft whine when she seemed on the verge of slipping away: *Stay*.

The rooms would not be so empty now. The girl had come. Kate. Kate Robinson. She would break the silence, even if all she did was breathe.

"Now, there's a sight for sore eyes," Denny said as Kate and Bernie passed the bench by the pub. He and Niall could be found there most evenings after playing darts and drinking ale. They'd ruled the bench for the past ten years. No one, not even Rosheen's gang, disputed their right of ownership. Denny's face had grown more gaunt of late, his lungs wheezing like an accordion. Niall's doughy paunch continued to swell against his belt buckle, evidence of a lifelong sweet tooth. He knew he should cut down on the rhubarb pie and orange cake but figured he'd lived long enough that he ought to be able to eat what he wanted, calories and cholesterol levels be damned.

The bench had been occupied by the elderly men of Glenmara for as long as anyone could remember. Denny and Niall achieved seniority after the deaths of the previous benchwarmers, Eamon and Greeley, a decade before. The bench was the local equivalent of box seats at a football match, offering the best view of the goings-on, such as they were. Niall lived on his own, his cottage too quiet now, his wife having passed on some years ago; Denny liked to have some independence from his overly attentive daughter, Oona, with whom he'd lived since his own wife's death. And so the two men spent a great deal of time on the bench, hailing whomever walked by, offering a running commentary on everything from the weather to the latest rugby standings.

Bernie carried the basket of lace on her arm, having only managed to sell a couple of pieces. (It would have to do. At least she had the income from John's pension.) She traveled relatively light that evening. Aileen had loaded the larger items—the canopy, table, and chairs—into the back of her car and driven home, still shaking her head over Bernie's openness with a complete stranger. "I hope you don't get murdered in your bed," she'd whispered.

"Two pretty ladies taking the evening air," Niall greeted them.

"And two old flirts making the most of it," Bernie replied.

"What else is there to do on a night like this but tip back a Guinness and admire the view?" said Denny.

"These two were right terrors in their day," Bernie told Kate. "Drove like maniacs and broke a lot of hearts, they did."

"Sounds exciting," Kate said with a winsome smile.

"Would still, if my daughter didn't take the car from me." Denny brought his watch close to his face (he refused to wear glasses, saying they ruined his looks), the timepiece small in his arthritic paw. "She'll be here any minute to take me home. She's always ruining my fun."

"If we were only a little younger." Niall dabbed his nose with a plaid handkerchief. He was missing his little finger, lost in a fishing accident when he was a boy. Nine-fingered Niall, they'd called him ever since. "Oh, the times we had. The dancing. The singing." He broke into a tune, a deafening baritone version of "Irish Rose."

Denny winced. "Jaysus, man, what do you want to do, take what little hearing I have left?"

"You're jealous, because I should have been on the stage. The girls have always gone mad for my voice."

"Mad, yes, but not in the way you suppose. Your serenade won't win the ladies; it will frighten them away."

"You have no appreciation for the arts." Niall sniffed.

"The arts? You sound like a foghorn. You could plant yourself on the pier and bring the boats in on misty nights."

"If I weren't so old and drunk, I'd pop you one for that." Niall waved a shaky fist.

"We agreed it would never come to that."

Their last fistfight had occurred eleven years earlier, during which the Garda had to be summoned. Niall broke his dentures, Denny his nose. It had started over Denny accusing Niall of cheating at darts. After that, they swore to never hit each other again. Increasing age and infirmity helped them keep the promise.

"He has a voice only God would love," Denny told Kate. "He's been tormenting me with it since we were boys. You'd think he would have figured out he can't sing by now."

"Anyone can sing," Niall said.

"Well, yes, if you mean forcing air in and out of one's lungs," said Denny. "The question is, should they?"

"Can I help it if I know how to impress the ladies?" Niall winked at the women.

"And here I thought Irishmen were supposed to be shy." Kate laughed.

"Don't believe everything you hear about the Irish," Denny said. "We're full of contradictions."

"And ale." Niall belched. "Excuse me."

A Mini bumped over the cobblestones, the driver beeping to get their attention.

"Here she comes, my daughter, the infamous Oona," Denny said. "She drives like a crazy woman."

"Like her da," Niall said.

Oona had flaming red hair and a long neck and startled eyes somewhat reminiscent of an ostrich, yet pretty in her way. "The taxi service has arrived, gentlemen," she called through the open window, snapping her fingers. "Hurry up." A silver-haired woman sat in the passenger seat.

"Hurry, hurry, fuss and flurry," Denny muttered. "Always the same story."

"Unless you want to spend the night on that bench, I suggest you move your legs as fast as your tongue, mister."

"Aren't you a smart thing? What a way to talk to your da."

"Hiya, Bernie. And you must be Kate." She waved, ignoring the jibe. "I'm Oona, and this is Colleen. I see you've already met the Glenmara welcoming committee." She gestured to the men. "The COOFs."

"What does that stand for?" Kate asked Bernie.

"A couple of old farts," she replied in a stage whisper, as Kate stifled a laugh.

"How about you meet us here on Monday?" Niall said to Kate. "It's bingo night. You know I've got your number."

"We'll see," Kate said.

The men piled into the back of the Mini, folding themselves with the slow deliberation of a pair of rusty-jointed lawn chairs. Oona urged them on. "Really, I'm already late enough as it is. Can't you move any faster?"

"No need to be such a nag. You give me the gas, you do."

"You're full of hot air without me having anything to do with it."

"These girls of Glenmara, they're right feisty, they are," said Denny.

"I'm a grown woman now, Da."

"You'll always be a girl to me," he said. "You and Colleen and the rest of your friends."

"I swear you two are worse than teenagers." Oona tapped on the steering wheel as the men got settled.

Denny leaned out the window as the car roared away in a cloud of exhaust, calling, "Oh, I almost forgot, I dropped the column in your letterbox this afternoon."

"He writes a piece for the *Gaelic Voice*, called 'This Old Geezer,'" Bernie explained as she waved in reply. "Been doing it for years. Sports and gossip, mostly. Maybe he'll do something on you next."

"Really, I'm not worth the ink. I'm hardly a celebrity."

"Oh, yes, I suspect you are."

As Kate and Bernie headed west, leaving the village behind, the hedges rose high on either side of the lane, the air smelling of primroses and moss. Cigarette butts and shards of glass from broken side mirrors and bottles glittered in the grass, the grime of the cities present, to a certain degree, even there.

"So are paparazzi lurking in the bushes?" Kate smiled.

"Not yet. You're the first foreigner to stay the night here in ever so long. The villagers will be dying to know everything about you." Bernie was too.

Kate smiled but didn't take the bait. "Here," she said, holding out her hand. "Why don't I take the basket for a while?"

Bernie had been switching the basket from arm to arm to distribute the weight; it wasn't that heavy, just awkward, and her muscles had begun to ache. If they'd sold more lace, it would have been easier to manage. "Oh, heavens," she said. "I'll be all right. You've got enough to carry with that backpack, and besides, we don't have far to go now. But thank you just the same."

The girl had a kind soul. She was thoughtful, observant.

Bernie could see that in the way she contemplated the landscape and listened attentively to everything she said.

Fergus stopped and snuffled in the bushes. Bernie snapped her fingers, urging him along. "Come on, boy!" He was too old to chase rabbits now, but still possessed the memory of pursuit. She knew how hard it could be to let the past go.

"Have you been traveling long?" she asked Kate.

"Just under a month." Kate stopped to shake a rock from her shoe, steadying herself against a stone wall. Her boots were worn at the heels. She probably tended to come down hard on them, marching when she walked, a woman with a purpose.

"What a joy to go wandering like that. There's so much to see in the world. I've never been beyond Galway. Lived here my whole life. There've been Cullens in Glenmara since the beginning. People don't move around much. The only time was during the Famine. Nearly everyone left then."

"But your people stayed."

"They did. Don't know how they managed to survive. I guess they were too stubborn to die. Oh, the stories my great-grandmother used to tell. Scared the life out of me when I was a little girl. The walking dead, she called the ghosts. Some people say the roads are still haunted by those who fell and never got up again. Black ooze everywhere, the blight on the earth, their tongues and eyes." She shuddered. "There's a village nearby where the dead supposedly speak, needing to be heard. No one goes there anymore. I get a fright just thinking about it."

Bernie knew she was chattering, but she couldn't stop. She was so pleased. *So pleased* to have Kate there. Fergus sensed her joy, ran ahead, doubled back, wriggled from head to foot.

They passed a shrine to the Virgin Mary on the corner, a few scraggly violets and heartsease at her feet. Bernie crossed herself.

Kate did too.

"Are you Catholic, then?" Bernie asked.

"Sort of. I'm afraid I've turned into one of those Christmas and Easter types, though I'm partial to the pomp and pageantry," Kate confessed.

"Aren't we all?" Bernie didn't ask for a detailed explanation, though it was hard to resist the temptation to pry.

"Is this it?" Kate asked as they turned up the lane, exclaiming, "Oh, it's delightful—"

"Welcome to Casa Cullen." Bernie unlatched the gate. If she had known a visitor was coming, she might have neatened the garden, but no matter. A few weeds never hurt anyone. The shriveled state of the daylilies was another matter. She'd never trimmed the old leaves in the fall and they were in terrible condition, all stringy and brown, though the green shoots were fighting their way through, the old and the new commingling, struggling for supremacy.

Bernie opened the front door to the waiting house, passing through the sitting room with its book-lined shelves and overstuffed velvet couch and chairs, to the blue-and-white kitchen beyond. The cottage itself seemed to reflect Bernie's growing anticipation, even the furnishings poised to receive their guest, the chairs edging closer, as if the saucers and cutlery might leap from the cupboards of their own volition, eager to serve her: someone from Seattle, Washington, in America had come to visit.

"Would you like a cup of tea?" Bernie asked. Tea, the ultimate gesture of hospitality and comfort. She wished she had a greater assortment to offer. She rummaged in the drawer: Earl Grey, Darjeeling—the English got their names on everything, didn't they? If only she had a Gaelic tea—mint.

"It's been a long day," Kate said, a note of weariness in her voice now, a hand on the table, as if her legs might give out any moment. "I think I'll just take a bath and go to bed, if that's all right. I'm so bedraggled I'm surprised you even let me in the door in the first place."

"I've seen worse," Bernie said, teasing her a little, adding, "Of course you need to settle in, especially after being out all day—such nasty weather we've been having—but it will change for the better soon, you'll see. I'll take you up to your room, shall I?" She led the way upstairs, trying not to let her disappointment show.

She opened the door to the chamber at the end of a short hall, lined with John's framed watercolors of seascapes and crofter's cottages. "Here are the guest quarters. The bath is across the hall. Are you sure I can't make you something to eat?"

"No, I'm fine. I had some fish and chips at the market earlier."

"Oh, that's right," Bernie nodded. "Well, let me know if there's anything I can do to make you more comfortable."

"Thank you. Thank you for everything," Kate said as she closed the door.

"Sleep well," Bernie called.

"You too," replied Kate.

Bernie smiled to herself as she went downstairs, funny how two simple words could make one feel so happy. She wasn't ready to turn in herself, still filled with a nervous energy. She puttered in the kitchen, refolding tea towels, sponging the counter, washing the single cup she'd left in the sink before going to the market.

No one had occupied the guest room since Aileen stayed with her for a few nights after John died. The room that had been meant for a child all those years ago, over a quarter of a century now. Bernie listened to the sounds above, Fergus too, his head cocked to the side.

"Isn't it grand, Fergus?" Bernie said as she wiped the counters again, making the white tiles shine.

He barked.

She put a finger to her lips. "Inside voice, Fergus."

He smiled and panted, reveling in her delight.

A guest had come to stay. A guest had come, and they were no longer alone.

Chapter 6

Cliff Walk

By the time Kate woke, the sun was already high in the sky and shadows stretched across the quilt, rebuking her laziness. She rubbed her eyes, taking in the lace curtains, the crucifix on the wall, the bouquet of lily of the valley and stack of books Bernie had placed on the nightstand the night before while Kate was taking a shower. Kate hadn't paid much attention to the room's decor that evening, so road-weary she fell asleep the minute her head hit the pillow. She still hadn't unpacked her bag. What was the point? She wouldn't be staying long. The room at Bernie's cottage didn't belong to her, nor she to it. She was only a tenant, their association temporary, and yet it felt, in a peculiar way, as if the room had been waiting for her.

She couldn't remember what day it was at first. Yes, Sunday. Early Sunday afternoon, she guessed. She parted the lace curtains, tatted edges intricate as snowflakes. Her clothes flapped on the line below, the arms of her coat waving. *Hello. Good-bye. Help.* Bernie's garments hung alongside: a sweater, blouse, and the sorriest excuse for lingerie she'd ever seen, high-waisted panties and an industrial-strength bra that might have doubled as a Valkyrian breastplate. Both nylon, flesh-colored, broadcasting *the woman who wears these isn't getting any sex.*

Off to one side were neat rows of lettuce, carrots, and peas emerging from the earth, stick teepees ready to receive the first tendrils; clumps of parsley, rosemary, and chives flourished in a kitchen garden; bees buzzed drunkenly in the pansies. Early tulips bloomed in green-glazed planters, red petals matching the front door. In the distance, where the land dipped to a small bay, Kate glimpsed the sea, glazed pewter and teal. Was it from the precipitation? The quality of the light?

The air was full of moisture, from the sea and the ever-present promise of rain. Kate saw Bernie dart from the house in a pair of Wellingtons and pull the clothes off the line so the damp wouldn't undo a morning's work. Her hostess glanced up, smiling when she saw Kate, and began folding the garments into a wicker basket.

Kate managed a wave—she'd never been much of a morning person, not that it was morning any longer—then pulled on the aqua-colored chenille robe hanging from a hook on the door. She washed her face and brushed her teeth in the bathroom across the hall. Evidence of Bernie's handwork was everywhere—in the lace doily atop the low cabinet and the violets embroidered on the towels, the stitches tiny, precise. Kate gave herself a quick once-over in the mirror, neatening her hair—the weather made it wilder than usual—then padded downstairs in her socks. She hoped Bernie didn't notice the heels were almost worn through.

Fergus rose from the hearth and tottered toward her. "Hello, boy," she said. He rubbed his graying muzzle against her hand before settling by the fire again. Kate studied photographs on the mantel: a young Bernie with a mass of curls and sparkling eyes; a wedding picture of the young couple touching foreheads, smiling; a portrait of Bernie's husband, years later, striking a pose on the cliffs. Kate wondered where he was. Off on a job? Fishing with friends?

"Good morning—or should I say afternoon?" Bernie set the laundry on the counter, her cheeks pink from the breeze, matching the color of her sweater. She slipped off the boots, set them by the back door, and smoothed her skirt. "Had a nice rest, did you?"

"I'm sorry I overslept." Kate stifled a yawn. "I had no idea how late it was."

"It's not as if you had an appointment to keep. We take our time around here," Bernie said. "You know that trend in cooking—what's it called—slow food? Our version is slow living. Mostly because we don't have a choice in the matter. Nothing goes fast, even when we want it to."

"I didn't mean to impose on you—I meant to be off early today," Kate said.

"The bus doesn't come until next week," Bernie told her.

"Next week?" Kate couldn't hide her surprise.

"We don't get much traffic here, especially on a Sunday, so the service tends to be irregular," Bernie explained. "Do you have someone waiting for you?"

"No. It's just that there's so much to see—" She had a plan. An itinerary. Following it, checking places off the list, let her think there were things she could still control, the design of her life a pattern that could be set, worked. And yet ever since the bus broke down and she'd started walking, met William, and ended up here, in Glenmara, it felt as if the map by which she'd been navigating was being gently pried from her hands.

She considered her options: she could try hitching again. Or perhaps there was a farmer heading to the next village, though as Bernie said, it was Sunday, and since Glenmara seemed to be a Catholic village, it was doubtful anyone would be making the trip.

"The good news is, the road isn't going anywhere," Bernie added quickly. "It will be there when you need it. There's stew on the stove if you'd like some, since it's nearly lunchtime—I put it on before I went to mass this morning, though I can make eggs, if you prefer."

"Please don't go to any trouble. Stew is fine."

"Oh, and here are your clothes. They smell of the sea, but at least they're dry." A pair of Bernie's panties, tangled in the sleeve of Kate's jacket, fell to the floor. The older woman snatched them up. "Aren't these the most god-awful things? Not fit for the light of day. Elephant drawers, I call them."

Kate smiled, in both sympathy and amusement. "They must be far too big for you."

"They do bag a bit in the bum, not that there's anyone around to see," she said. "The nearest town doesn't sell much in the way of fashion, especially when it comes to intimates, even if I wanted to get something fancier."

"Don't you? You deserve to have beautiful lingerie," Kate said. Already, a new garment began to take shape in her mind. "Every woman does."

"I'd never thought of that." Bernie ducked her head. "Well, I'll just put these away. Let me know if you need anything else." She hurried from the room, basket in hand. "And don't forget to help yourself to the stew."

Kate hoped she hadn't embarrassed her hostess. She ladled stew into a ceramic bowl. The bowl had an almost iridescent drip glaze in shades of blue that captured the colors of the sea, the shape and form reminiscent of 1930s-era Beswick pottery, but uniquely its own. She checked the maker's mark, taking care not to spill the contents: "SD." Local, probably. She wondered where the studio was. She wouldn't mind taking a piece home.

She took a bite of the stew, a traditional sort, heavy on the beef, gravy, potatoes, and carrots, light on the spices, nothing fancy, comfort food in the truest sense. It reminded her of the meal her mother made on Saint Patrick's Day, though she used more vegetables and less meat; it was one of the few recipes into which she didn't try to sneak some tofu.

Bernie reappeared. "There's plenty for seconds," she said. "It was my husband's favorite. That's him on the mantel. He was a handsome fellow, wasn't he? He passed last May. Had an aneurysm, they said, while walking Fergus. Nothing anyone could do."

"I'm sorry. I didn't—" Here she'd gone saying the wrong thing again.

"It's all right," Bernie assured her, stirring the pot. "The stew brought it to mind, that's all. Things have a way of doubling back on themselves. It gets better with time—both the stew and the grieving. More tea?"

After lunch, Kate put on a shapely brown fleece jacket (just because it was utilitarian didn't mean it couldn't have style), a pair of jeans, and hiking boots, and set out, eager to see the countryside. She brought a sketchpad in the hope inspiration would strike, as it often did when she went for a walk. The beauty of the place was overwhelming, wrapping her in a velvet cloak—such purity of color, texture, and scent. It was everywhere, in the belled petals of foxglove, the rawness of the earth, even the handful of broken window glass she scooped up from the side of the lane, sparkling like diamonds. She let the pieces fall in a glittering cascade, admiring how they caught the light. She felt the stirring of creative impulse, but didn't act on it right away: she must coax it from its hiding place, like a fox from its den. She wouldn't force anything; it didn't work that way. She took her time, picking daisies for a bracelet, slipping it on her wrist as she crossed the meadows. The air smelled of grass and wildflowers.

A half hour later, she reached the cliffs, the sea raging below. Waves rushed the rocks, recoiled, hurled themselves forward again. She sat down and closed her eyes, let the sound fill her— the sensation of power was thrilling—and opened her notebook in anticipation. Nothing happened. She clutched the pen, the nib hovering in the air. The blank page stared back, daring her to make the first move. She pressed the point of the pen to paper, let it flower into a blot, ink saturating the fibers. She filled the page with a doodle universe, splotted with tears, turned the page, and tried again. None of it was right.

Don't think. Play.

Could she remember how?

After more false starts, a line danced across the page, then another, twisting, turning, tangoing. She laughed, surprised at what came forth: new-and-improved versions of Bernie's underwear. She'd never attempted to design lingerie before, having focused her efforts on what she'd hoped would develop into lines of couture. She loved Audrey Hepburn, Gigi Young, Suzy Perette, Jerry Gilden, but her timing was off; the hottest looks were 1970s-inspired, with banded hips and thighs, blouson tops, and

undefined waists. "People aren't buying these styles now," Jules
had said while reviewing her sketches over lunch at the Two Bells
Tavern last summer. (He'd taken her to the Palm Court at the
Four Seasons Hotel when he'd first signed her.) He was impec-
cably dressed, as always, in a handmade suit by Gian DeCaro. He
kept glancing at his watch. He had appointments to keep, appointments with people whose designs were selling, who were on the
rise. She tried to smile, radiate positive energy, take his advice, but
inside, she felt as if she were drowning. She noticed, later, that she
hadn't turned down the collar of her jacket, that her vintage scarf
had a stain.

"You have to decide who you want to be," he said. "What you
want to be known for. What your signature is. Hot concepts sell."

He'd probably shake his head in disappointment if he could
see her perched on the precipice of those remote Irish cliffs, embellishing bra straps and panties. "I'm giving all my clients a reality
check, Kate," he'd said. "I have to be honest with you—" No, she
wouldn't think about him now. She wouldn't let doubt spoil her
fun. To hell with viable projects and ex-boyfriends, this was real:
the ink on her fingers, the callus on her finger, the weight of the
pen in her hands, the rhythm of dashes, dots, and lines.

The sea crashed and sighed against the rocks. The wind curled
the pages. Her lips tasted of salt. The sun, while not exactly warm,
shone in a clear blue sky, the mist having moved off to the north, a
momentary gift after the clouds and rain. Minutes, hours, passed
as she filled the pages. She lost track of time, not moving until the
sun slid toward the horizon and she realized she should return to
the cottage, or Bernie would get worried and send out a search
party. The thought of a chorus of Irish voices hallooing her name
amused her.

She stuffed the supplies in her bag, shifting the detritus of old cough drops, Kleenex, a dry-cleaning receipt for Ethan's work shirts—which she wadded up and threw off the cliff, the wind bearing it aloft, as if it was something worth keeping, before letting it fall into the spray below (*Get your own fricking light-starched shirts, Ethan!*); a leaky pen, soft plum lip gloss, cover-up, a Chinese fortune ("You will travel far"—well, it had that right) from the dinner she'd had with friends before she'd left town. "I'll be fine, really, I'll be fine," she'd protested, an edge to her voice that warned them not to probe too deeply, to stop exchanging glances of concern and pity when they thought she wasn't looking.

"This is far enough," she said, nearly convincing herself. It ought to have been, and yet grief was a stowaway, coming along for the ride, undetected by airport security. She had to keep the bag zipped, or it might escape and spoil everything.

With a start, she realized she didn't know the way to Glenmara. She'd never been good with directions. *Think.* She retraced her steps, ending up on a lesser path that descended rather precipitously to the valley. No, that wasn't right. She considered going back and trying again, but she couldn't spare the time, the sun an orb of liquid glass, pouring itself over the end of the world. Oh, well, she didn't mind an adventure. She'd take this new route. The trails probably connected at some point. There were only so many ways she could go.

The path descended into a steeper section, which, if she could negotiate it, would save half a mile of backtracking. She reached out a hand, a foot, one hold to the next. *Careful.* She didn't want to sprain an ankle. She'd left her cell phone in Seattle, packed in a box. Perhaps that hadn't been such a good idea, but it felt right at the time, when she was throwing things into crates, putting her life on hold.

She breathed steadily to calm her nerves. *Don't think about the drop*. It went well enough at first, and she felt proud of the progress she'd made. At this rate, she'd reach the bottom in no time. Then she made the mistake of looking down and had the frightening realization that she was clinging to a near-vertical section of rock. How had she gotten herself into this? The main path was just below, if only she could get to it. A flock of sheep snickered from the grass on the lower slopes. "Oh, shut up," she snapped at them. The sheep *maa*-ed more loudly. She was getting tired of sheep and their stupid remarks.

She pressed her stomach against the rocks, breaths coming shallow, fast. People made poor decisions every day, though they usually didn't die from them. *Take it slow and easy*. She crabbed along the shelf on a descending diagonal, only progressing a foot or two. *Jesus*. Would she ever get off that wall?

"Looks like you've found one of the more challenging pitches in the area," a voice called.

She glanced down, fighting a wave of dizziness, and glimpsed a man with unruly black hair. He was tan for an Irishman. She supposed he must have spent a good deal of time outdoors. Handsome too, so handsome she stared at him for a moment, entranced— those dark eyes, square shoulders, a grace and strength in the way he carried himself, the scar on his cheek lending an air of mystery or roguishness, she couldn't be sure which—before regaining her composure.

"Need help?" he asked, his smile broadening, as if pleased she'd been studying him.

"No. I'm fine," she said, embarrassed now at having a witness to her predicament, at having stared at him so openly. She'd never been much of a flirt. She supposed it showed. "I know what I'm doing."

"An expert rock climber, are you?"

Was he mocking her? "I do all right," she replied, on the defensive now, even though in truth, she didn't, at least not the last time she'd tried rock climbing at the Vertical Club in Seattle with Ella. "How come you look like a dominatrix in that harness and I just look like an idiot?" she'd asked, laughing so hard she'd turned upside down and had to be lowered to the ground on a cable.

But she wouldn't think about that now. She couldn't afford to lose her balance, no safety net here.

"You're not exactly dressed for it," he observed. "Jeans are tough to climb in, especially if they're tight."

He was beginning to irritate her. If she fell, she might squash him. The thought had some appeal—and besides, she needed someone to break her fall. "Don't need a uniform, just legs and hands and rocks," she replied through gritted teeth.

"You've got those, that's for certain," he said, "though I wasn't aware a sharp tongue was required too."

"Only when necessary."

"A dangerous weapon, that tongue of yours."

"If you don't mind, you're breaking my concentration."

"Sorry. I didn't mean to interrupt your tête-à-tête with the limestone," he said. "You sure you'll be all right?"

"Positive." Her muscles burned.

"I almost forgot: is this yours?" He held up a page from the sketchbook, covered with sketches of bras, camisoles, and panties. "I found it over there."

The paper must have fallen from her bag when she was clutching for handholds. "Yes," she said, immediately wishing she'd denied it. She couldn't think fast enough. No doubt he'd make some crack about the designs, which was the last thing she needed right then.

"I'll anchor it with this rock, so it doesn't blow away." He sauntered down the path. "Good luck with the descent—and the knickers."

Her cheeks felt hot. Why was she blushing? What did she care what he thought? She averted her face, waited until he'd rounded the corner before lowering herself down, one shaky leg at a time, the rush of adrenaline and annoyance giving her the push she needed to reach solid ground. When she finally set foot on the path, she nearly collapsed in relief and exhaustion. She held her side, trying to catch her breath. Now that she looked back at the cliff, she realized it wasn't so treacherous after all. From this different—and safer—vantage point, she could see that if she'd lost her grip, she wouldn't have fallen to her death, though she might have—what? Broken a bone? Sprained an ankle? Pulled a muscle? Scraped her knee? Injured her pride?

The drawing fluttered, still pinned under the piece of granite. She tucked the page, now smudged with dirt, into her bag and kept the stone, round as a miniature globe, for a souvenir. It was rare to find rocks of such symmetry. The man stood on the opposite rise, the wind ruffling his hair, hers too, in the same long breath. Before he disappeared from view, it occurred to her that he might think she'd kept the stone as a memento of their encounter. When really, if asked, she would have explained—skirting the truth—that she liked the shape, which fit perfectly in the palm of her hand.

Chapter 7

Holy Orders

The next day, Kate rode Bernie's bicycle along the hills of Glenmara. The seat squeaked and the chain needed oil, chattering away like a set of false teeth. It was a woman's bike, an old-fashioned one-speed, red, with a straw basket in the front, the sort of conveyance associated with elderly men and women all over Europe, though Bernie was far from elderly. Kate guessed she was about her mother's age. Jerry-rigged panniers held the newsletters that Bernie had run off at the post office, home to the only printer in town.

The week's crime blotter:

Man calls Garda, says his wife won't stop swimming in the bay; he fears she's a selkie. Garda says he's a lucky man.

Woman says a faerie has enchanted her well; when she tries to bring up a bucket of water, the rope breaks.

Garda says she's usurping the faeries' property rights and should pay a usage fee. One euro is the going rate, the faerie economy not being immune to inflation.

When Bernie mentioned she needed someone to help with deliveries that week, there being too much to do in preparation for the rest of the Saint Brendan's festivities, Kate offered to help. It was a fine day, the azure sky hinting at better things to come. Kate lifted her face to the light, felt the warmth on her eyelids and cheeks.

As she passed the turnoff to Kinnabegs, a band of children launched mud balls at her from behind a wall. "Hey, stop that!" she cried.

"Hey, stop that!" they mimicked. "Fecking foreigner!"

Kate dropped the bike and chased after them. "That was a rotten thing to do!" she cried, only causing them to laugh all the harder. Perhaps they sensed she didn't have it in her to punish them. They eluded her, rail-thin urchins scampering over the heath and disappearing behind another series of walls. She knew what children were capable of, the thousand mischievous acts that could occur when boredom set in. She supposed she deserved payback for the crimes she'd committed in her youth—the prank phone calls and dingdong ditching and random acts of vandalism (such as beheading the neighbors' dahlias)—though she definitely could have done without a border collie shooting out of a gate a short distance down the road, snarling and nipping at her heels as if he'd like to take her foot off at the ankle.

"Stay," she said firmly, then, when that didn't yield the desired result, went through the litany of commands she knew: "Leave it. Stop." Nothing worked.

The dog refused to give up the chase—maybe he only knew

Gaelic?—until his owner, sporting the ubiquitous tweed cap and sweater, called, "Go on then, Jack, back to work with you, leave the girl alone," and to Kate, "Sorry about that, guess he mistook you for a sheep."

Thanks a lot, she thought. The dog was Fergus's opposite, the sort of mutt that no doubt took pleasure in sinking his teeth into the calves of unsuspecting victims. She could have sworn he gave her a malevolent grin as he trotted back to his bovine charges, snapping at their haunches for good measure.

The landscape was breathtaking, but full of perils such as these at unexpected turns, hidden burrs among the beauty. Much of the terrain remained uninhabited, too rocky or far from the sea to attract development, as hamlets closer to Galway had. She let her mind drift, thinking about new lingerie designs, wishing she'd brought along her sketchpad. Inspiration could strike at the most inconvenient times—in the shower, in the car, on this road—but she was grateful it was with her again, an old companion with whom she was getting reacquainted, pleased to find they could take up where they left off, as if there'd been no estrangement at all.

She was racing downhill, considering curved seams and embellishments, the wind drawing her hair into a flame, when the tire hit a pothole, nearly wrenching the handlebars from her hands. She felt her weight go forward—oh, God, she was going to end up in the ditch—but somehow she jumped free at the last second, escaping with a lightly scraped knee. She got up shakily, brushed off her clothes, relieved to see she'd lost no cargo in the mishap. The newsletters were still tied in neat bundles, scattered across the road, awaiting retrieval—and eventual delivery.

She took a moment to catch her breath—she'd certainly had her share of minor misadventures that morning. She should have kept her eyes on the road. She would from now on. She gathered up the newsletters and pushed on, stuffing the papers into mailboxes, some painted with flowers or fish, others a less-imaginative regulation silver or hazard orange. She paused at a crossroads and consulted Bernie's list: two more to go.

A van seemed to come out of nowhere, careening around the corner, passing close. A horn honking, hand gesturing, conveying irritation she'd stopped there. She caught a glimpse of a face, the look of surprise they shared: it was the man from the cliffs.

"Maniac," she fumed, her frustration spilling over. He'd almost hit her! And to make matters worse, he didn't even stop to make sure she was all right.

In his wake, there was only the empty road, a long sigh of dirt and green and crumbled walls and her small, furious self, hurtling through a place so much bigger than she was. She stood up on the pedals, going uphill now, heart beating hard, until her legs were unable to carry her forward. She had to hop off and walk, catch her breath, calm down. Sparks of temper flared, flickered out. The stranger would be in her past soon enough—he already was, wasn't he?—a character in a story to tell her friends when she went home.

"When are you coming back?" Ella asked in her last e-mail, which Kate had read at a Dublin café over two weeks ago.

I don't know. Despite the kids and the dog and the driver, she was beginning to like it there. Perhaps it was just as well she'd missed the bus after all.

She'd crested the hill, but others lay ahead, one after another, as far as she could see—and a colorful wagon on the next rise: William. He'd been traveling along a walled lane, so she hadn't noticed him at first. Her spirits rose. She'd been hoping to see him again. He raised a leather-gloved hand in greeting, recognizing her at once. She glided down the incline, coming to a stop by the wagon.

"I see you've graduated to a bicycle," he said, as if they'd only stopped speaking moments before, adding, when he noticed the dirt on her elbows and knees, "Took a tumble, did you?" He rummaged in his bag and handed her a cloth and water bottle.

She told him what had happened as she cleaned herself up.

"And who said the countryside is dull?" he said, his amusement tempered with a note of caution. "Though you should take care on the roads. Will you be traveling by cycle now?"

"No, I just borrowed it from a friend," she told him.

"So you've made friends in Glenmara? I'm happy to hear it. I thought you might spend some time there. Who are you staying with?"

"Bernie. Bernadette Cullen. I'm helping deliver the *Gaelic Voice*."

"A fine paper. Good someone is trying to keep the language alive."

"Do you know her?"

"I used to come through town and play at the dances," he said. "She and the other Glenmara girls were fine ones for dancing."

"Come back with me—I'm sure they'd like to see you."

"No. I'm just passing through. That's my way. But I'm glad I ran into you again for another reason too: you dropped this." He held out the golden thimble. "I found it on the floor of the wagon after you left. Must have come loose when you stepped down. Had a bad link. I fixed it for you."

"Thank you." She put the chain around her neck, feeling the reassurance, the metal cool against her skin. "I thought I'd never see it again."

"You sew, do you?" he asked.

"I used to. Not so much anymore." She thought of the new designs. And yet they were only sketches, a few marks on a page that probably wouldn't amount to anything.

"A thimble like that is meant to be used. The time will come. Perhaps sooner than you think." He snapped the reins. "I have to push on if I'm to make the next village before nightfall. But I'll be back on market day to see how you're coming along."

"Soon, then." She waved until he crested the next rise and was gone.

Kate had to summon the energy to make the day's final delivery. She coasted along the road to the church. Apparently the local priest was a subscriber to the *Gaelic Voice*. As she approached, Kate thought she saw movement in the cottage next to the chapel, a shadow in the window by the door. No one came out to greet her, but she was sure she was being watched.

She had mixed feelings about her faith. She prayed every night, out of habit, and because some small part of her still believed. She hadn't gone to mass in a long time, keeping her faith, such as it was, in her own way. She wondered if the priest was as conservative as people said. "Hello?" she called.

There was no answer, not that she expected one. God worked in mysterious ways, if he worked at all, sometimes the men who served him more so. What good had prayers done her mother? What good had faith? Kate still hadn't made sense of it. Maybe she never would.

She tossed the newsletter up the walk. The rolled bundle hit the door and landed on the porch next to a pot of purple pansies. The door opened partway, and the stern-faced priest appeared at the entrance. He wasn't a particularly large man, but his expression was formidable, his features set in such a way that suggested he rarely, if ever, smiled.

"You aren't Bernadette," he observed, his eyes an overcast gray.

"No. I'm Kate. Kate Robinson. I came into town Saturday night—" She couldn't complete the sentence. He was the sort of person who could make you feel as if you'd done something wrong just by looking at you.

"I am Father Byrne," he said, adding, "I didn't see you at mass Sunday morning."

Mass. Yes, she'd overslept, branding herself a heathen. Was excessive slumber a cardinal sin? Bernie had gone to the service while she'd been in bed. Not that Kate would have attended anyway. She couldn't remember the last time she'd been inside a church, not that she'd tell him that. Next he'd be asking her when she made her last confession.

"What brings you to Glenmara?" He didn't advance beyond the threshold. Didn't offer his hand or name. He stood as if he had a metal rod in his spine, she below him on the path, holding the bike by the handlebars, wishing to be gone, but not wanting to be rude.

"I'm traveling," she said.

Such a statement usually prompted questions about where she was from, where she'd been. Not from him. "Traveling," he repeated, turning the word over in his mind like a stone on a beach, searching for what lay beneath. "And somehow you ended up here."

"I did." She felt as if she were being cross-examined, damning herself with everything she said.

"There's little in the way of public transport in the area," he said. "How did you arrive?"

"On a traveler's wagon." She decided it would be best to keep her answers short, in keeping with the brevity of his remarks. She sensed he'd already formed an opinion of her—and that it wasn't good. Maybe it was her slightly disheveled appearance from the fall she'd taken. She tugged the hem of her skirt, pushed her hair out of her face, to little effect.

"Indeed," he said, taciturn as ever.

"His name is William. Perhaps you know him?" She was annoyed for letting herself be cowed by him, yet felt helpless to change the dynamic between them. He'd made up his mind about her—and a keen, unbending mind it was.

"No, I don't. He isn't one of my parishioners." He squinted at her. "I surmise that this traveling doesn't involve attending mass. Or perhaps you're not Catholic?"

The sky was a brilliant sort of gray that afternoon, the kind backed with steel, matching the priest's eyes, as if heaven itself were frowning on her. "I slept in—I'd been on the road for so many days—"

"Yes, I suppose you were."

She shivered.

"Our climate takes some getting accustomed to," he said. He did not invite her inside.

"I come from Seattle. I'm used to the rain," she offered with a smile, trying to charm him.

It didn't work. "I guess that's some sort of qualification."

A silence fell between them, a rook sounding an alarm from the copper beech near the front porch. The priest bore some resemblance to the tree in the uprightness of his carriage, the thin rigidity of his limbs, the creases on his forehead and bracketing his mouth. It seemed to Kate as if both of them, tree and man, towered over her, magnificent, glowering, immovable. She couldn't bear the scrutiny any longer. His coldness stunned her.

She didn't understand what she'd done to make him so mistrustful. He didn't even know her, and he'd already passed judgment. "Well, it was nice to meet you," she said finally. "I'd best be getting back. To Bernie's. She's expecting me—"

"Yes, of course." He picked up the paper, knocked it against the palm of his hand, once, twice. "I heard she'd taken in a boarder."

Nothing, those gray eyes seemed to say, as he gave her a long look, escaped his notice. Nothing at all.

Chapter 8

A Cup of Tea & Jealousy

Aileen always went round to Bernie's for tea on Mondays at 2:00 p.m. Ginger biscuits or shortbread (sometimes both) served on the Carlton Ware plates Bernie found at a secondhand shop in Galway. Aileen had been there when she bought them last year. The Mikado pattern in cobalt blue. Gorgeous, they were. Orange pekoe brewing, scenting the room, the conversation flowing. She and Bernie never ran out of things to say.

Remember the time we tried to build a raft and it sank in the bay and we screamed for help, thinking we were drowning, but Richie Greene saved us—and then we realized it was only knee-deep? Knee-deep!

I thought I'd die of embarrassment.

Richie Greene always had a thing for you, Ailey.

Oh, well, that was over and done a long time ago.

If you say so—

Remember when you put a mud sandwich in your brother's lunch, Ailey, and he bit into it, thinking it was chocolate?

I should have put a worm in it too. Would have served him right. He was a bastard back then.

Remember when we ran naked down the lane in the middle of the night when everyone was asleep?

And we jumped into the hedge, because Mrs. Mullen opened her door, thinking she heard a prowler.

I thought I'd never get the thorns out of my backside.

Remember when—

They had their own special history, knew each other better than anyone in the world, better than their families, even, because when it came to families, there were roles to play and expectations and arguments. Bernie didn't have siblings, only a mother and father who doted on her, the longed-for child, until the day they died. Aileen's childhood had been more fractious. Once her brother shoved her against the wall in a fight over the radio—he wanted to listen to the football match, she to music. Her mother didn't come out of her room, let the battle rage, numb to everything in the dark silence of that curtained space. It had been her older sister who pushed them apart: "What are you on about now?" A bruise had already been forming on Aileen's back. She cried, and not for show. He'd scared the life out of her; he'd grown that summer and they'd both forgotten what a difference that made, the advantage it gave him. Her sister thought they might have to take Aileen to the hospital. "And how will we explain that? How?" her sister asked him. "She spat in my face," he said. "Right in my face." And Aileen had. But she never said so.

She and her brother got on well enough now, well enough to see each other for the occasional major holiday. She and Moira were the only ones left in Glenmara. Moira. Well, Moira was another story. Moira, who resented her and loved her all at once.

It was easier with Bernie, a lifelong friend who accepted Aileen as she was, who laughed at her jokes and sympathized with her problems, large and small. Aileen could be herself with Bernie, her other self, the self that wasn't a mother or a wife, just Aileen, Ailey, a girl once more, Bernie the link to her past. Aileen depended on those Mondays, on Bernie.

She noticed the table was set for two, not three. "Has she gone then?"

"Kate? No. She's delivering the paper."

"If I'd known you'd needed help—" Aileen sometimes pitched in with the deliveries. She couldn't believe Bernie hadn't asked her first. She knew the routes, the customers.

Bernie poured the tea. "I thought it would do her good to get to know the place better."

"Why would she want to do that? She said she was moving on."

"Yes, but there's no bus for a week, is there?"

No, there wasn't.

"The poor thing needs a rest anyway," Bernie continued. "She's been traveling too long."

"You make her sound like a stray animal. Next, you'll be feeding her Fergus's dog biscuits."

"I can do better than that. No offense, Fergus," Bernie said, adding, "I wonder if she's running from something."

"I could think of a few things: the police, Interpol—"

"There's no need to be so suspicious. I meant memories, not criminal acts."

"I was joking," Aileen said, though she wasn't entirely. She was beginning to find everything about the girl annoying. Just because her great-grandparents were born in Ireland didn't mean she could instantly belong here. She was an American, American to the bone, pushing her way into their lives.

"She's not a bad person."

"It's hard to say what she is. We don't know her, do we?"

"I'm beginning to know her. She's a good soul, always willing to lend a hand." Bernie laid the words down carefully as a silver place setting, heavy, shining, true. "We have a connection. We like the same books—"

"If I'd known she needed a lift out of town, Rourke could have taken her," Aileen said. "He was off to Galway this morning."

"I didn't think of that." Bernie glanced away, her voice light, evasive. She was too good at making arrangements to have over-looked the possibility.

Aileen regarded Bernie over the rim of her cup as she sipped the tea, the distance between them larger than the span of the table, its oversize damask tablecloth brushing against her legs. Why was Bernie using the damask anyway? She never used the damask. It was for special occasions, christenings and weddings and funerals. Was she trying to impress the girl? Why? What was wrong with the everyday cloth, the one with the faded cabbage roses she put out whenever Aileen came to call?

Bernie didn't seem focused on anything she had to say, but Aileen tried to push the conversation forward. "Sile took first in the *feis.*"

"She did?" Bernie asked as if she'd never heard about it before.

"Remember, she was upcoast, performing in the invitational?" Aileen's prodding had an edge to it. Bernie should have remem-bered—Sile was her goddaughter, for heaven's sake. Granted, it wasn't one of the majors. If it had been, Aileen would have been there herself. She'd stayed home to keep an eye on Rosheen.

(Bernie could have asked about that too. She knew how difficult things had been for Aileen lately.)

"The *feis*. Oh, that's right." Bernie's mind was elsewhere. "Will Rosheen be dancing for the Glenmara title?"

"She's not dancing now, remember? She specializes in carousing."

"Yes. I've seen her around town."

"Smoking, no doubt. The girl will blacken her lungs as sure as she's blackening our name."

"It's not as bad as that, is it?"

"Bad enough."

"She's nearly old enough to be on her own."

"So she keeps reminding me. To be honest, her outlandish behavior lets me consider the possibility of her being gone without it hurting too much. I wouldn't mind an end to the daily battles."

"She loves you. She just doesn't know how to show it."

"Neither of us is very good at that, always wanting to have the last word. But damn it, I'm her mother, so I'm allowed. To top all, she's never right. If she were right, that would be one thing. But she won't admit to any mistakes. She'll argue herself blue in the face, rather than consider she might be wrong."

"Sounds familiar." Bernie gave her a knowing smile.

Aileen shook her head. "She's far worse than I ever was."

"They say each generation gets taller—maybe they get more argumentative too." Bernie got up and looked out the window.

"Expecting someone?" Aileen asked.

"I thought Kate might be back in time for tea."

Kate again. Kate. Kate. Kate. Aileen was a grown woman, but she felt as if she were in primary school, competing for the role of best friend. This was their time—hers and Bernie's—just the two of them. "I'm sure she's fine."

"Do you think so? The lanes are narrow." Bernie's face was dappled with shadows from the play of sunlight on the lace curtains.

"We travel them all the time, and nothing's ever happened to us," Aileen pointed out.

"But it could." Bernie sat down at the table again, poised on the edge of the seat in case Kate appeared.

"Yes, but it won't." Aileen knew what this was about. *She's not her*, she wanted to say. *She's not Saoirse.*

Bernie gave her a long, sharp-eyed look, as if she knew what Aileen was thinking. "Your tea's getting cold." She topped off the cup, steam rising in a narrow column between them.

Aileen didn't dare say more.

Chapter 9

Dirty Laundry & Contraception

Aileen couldn't open Rosheen's door, thwarted by a blockade of clothes on the other side. She'd put a moratorium on new purchases until she could at least hoover the rug. Not that Rosheen listened to anything she said. She'd tried threats; she'd tried humor. "You definitely have a disorder," she said, half-joking, but Rosheen hadn't laughed at the pun.

Aileen pushed again. There were so many obstacles these days when it came to dealing with Rosheen. Perhaps she should get a battering ram? She could give up, set the clothes outside the door, but then the mess would begin to take over the rest of the house, and she couldn't allow that to happen; it must be contained. She glanced at her watch. It was nearly time for the lace society meeting that evening at Bernie's house. She just needed to complete this last chore—and a chore it surely was.

One more shove, and the door finally yielded. Aileen stumbled into the room, hopping over a pile of jumpers and boots, laundry basket balanced precariously on her hip. The things she had to go through just to put away some clothing. She stared at the wreckage within and shook her head. It was worse than usual. She snatched a scrap of notebook paper and pen off Rosheen's desk and scrawled a single word: "Clean!" so that Rosheen would know what was what. It was meant to be informational, that note, not a reproach, not entirely.

Now, where to put it? There weren't many choices. The vanity was out, with its open pots of eye shadow, liner, and lip gloss, depressions where her daughter's fingers had dipped into the war paint (she wore too much, in Aileen's opinion). Ditto the desk, with its cairns of half-completed homework and seldom-opened books. Too late to earn high marks now.

She'd try the dresser. She set the pile there carefully, as if she were playing Rosheen's favorite childhood game, Jenga, taking care not to upset the balance. Aileen thought she'd completed the maneuver successfully, but the moment she turned her back, the pile slid to the floor. She swore under her breath, thought of leaving it there, one mound among many, but to do so was to admit defeat. She was as inclined to neatness as Rosheen to disarray, yet another way in which they seemed the opposite of each other, no matter that people said Rosheen looked just like her when she was young. (Rosheen didn't take it as a compliment. Aileen wasn't sure she did, either.) The same high spirits too. Aileen wondered how they could see the resemblance, given her daughter's make-up and tattoos and piercings.

She studied the lines of poetry (most of it illegible) Rosheen had written on the walls, along with pictures of rock bands and glittery stars, trying to gain insight into her daughter's mind.

"It's the history according to me," Rosheen had said.

Aileen didn't think Rosheen had lived long enough to have much of a history—the most recent entries to the volume of her life being one colossal muck-up after another.

There had been better times. Happy memories tucked in photo albums with scuffed edges and fading pictures in the bookshelf downstairs, where sometimes, late at night after the rest of the family was asleep, Aileen pored over the snapshots of those joyful moments—the day Rosheen first rode a bicycle, or celebrated her first birthday (she'd shampooed her hair with frosting), or modeled her costume for the *feis*, where she won first prize at the age of four.

Aileen sighed over the drifts of garments littering the bedroom. This is what her daughter wore now. Not the neat skirts and shirts of her St. Agnes uniform. Rosheen said she was finished with school. She was smart enough to continue. Or she would have been, if she'd bothered to apply herself. She'd gotten good marks until the year she turned fourteen. It went to hell after that. Aileen nagged and cajoled and threatened. Nothing did any good.

Rosheen had apparently acquired more thongs over the past week. "I love my cabana boy," announced the crotch of one pair. Lovely. Aileen didn't know how she could stand to wear them—they were uncomfortable, creeping up the bum, whatever Rosheen claimed about their eliminating knicker lines. A zebra-print bra hung from the doorknob. Her daughter had the lingerie of a stripper.

She refolded the jeans, shirts, and underwear, one by one, taking solace in the meditative process of smoothing and tucking, as if Rosheen were somewhere in each strap and sleeve. Aileen could care for her in this small way, though her daughter might see it differently, the precisely arranged garments standing out

among the rest as an accusation. *These are neat. You are not.* Or
maybe she wouldn't notice, the laundered items swallowed by the
nest of sheets (the girl never made her bed) and cast-off clothing.
Aileen suspected she probably ended up doing twice as much
laundry as necessary, because Rosheen couldn't tell which were
clean and dirty and chucked them all into the hamper.

A foil packet glinted on the floor. The cold medicine Aileen
had gotten for her at the druggists in Kinnabegs, probably. She
picked it up, intending to set it on the vanity where Rosheen might
have half a chance of finding it.

Wait: It wasn't cold medicine at all. It was a package of birth
control pills. Aileen supposed she shouldn't have been surprised,
and yet she was. The pills were another indication of how far
Rosheen had moved away from her. She couldn't have gotten them
in the village—or anywhere nearby for that matter. Where *had*
she gotten them? Galway? Who was she having sex with? That
lout Ronnie? She hoped not!

Just then Rosheen walked into the room, headphones clamped
as usual over her ears. For a split second, her eyes widened with
fear when she saw Aileen holding the pills, then she reverted to
her habitually sullen expression. "Why are you in my things?"
She snatched the packet away.

"I was trying to put your clothes away, and everything came
tumbling down," Aileen said. "Where did you get these?"

Rosheen didn't reply.

"Answer me." Aileen felt her irritation rising. "Unless you
want to get grounded for a month of Sundays."

"Does that mean I don't have to go to mass?"

"Don't be smart."

"Isn't that what you've wanted me to be?" Rosheen stared at
her, defiant.

"You know what I mean. I could call Reena's mother. Perhaps she'd have the answer for me."

"You wouldn't dare."

"Oh, wouldn't I?" Aileen moved toward the door, in the direction of the phone, downstairs in the hall. "Watch me."

"Fine. A clinic. Satisfied?"

"No place around here." Aileen wasn't done yet.

"Yeah. We had to drive for them."

"You didn't have permission."

"It's not like you'd have granted it—or I have to ask. This is private. It doesn't involve you."

"I'm your mother."

"Give the woman a prize," Rosheen said, adding, "You might be my mother, but you're not me."

"Thank God for that. I do, however, have certain rights and responsibilities. You wouldn't understand that. You're too young."

"I'm not a child anymore."

"If your father, if Father Byrne—"

"What do they have to do with it? It's my body. It's not like they have to worry about getting pregnant. I'm not going to rely on the rhythm method or whatever it's called, fat lot of good it's done you."

"That's enough."

"Well, it's true. I've seen the look on your face. The fear. Don't tell me you didn't think about it yourself."

"It's against the Church. There are values, choices. You shouldn't be doing these things. You shouldn't—"

"I'm sixteen," Rosheen said. "I can't stay a virgin forever. Did you save yourself for one guy?"

Aileen didn't answer.

"See. My point exactly."

"You don't know anything about me."

"Why don't you tell me, then?"

"Some things are private."

"Exactly. You should be glad I'm taking care of myself. You should too. Then you wouldn't have a scare every month."

"Yes, you're sixteen. Sixteen, Rosheen—and while you're under this roof—"

"Well, I might not be much longer," she interrupted. "I might just fecking leave."

"Watch your language."

"Why don't you watch what's going on around you? You're only forty-eight, and you're already old."

Aileen resisted the urge to slap her. "You're yelling so much you're drowning yourself out."

"What's that supposed to mean?"

"It means you can't even hear yourself anymore. If you could, you wouldn't say these things, you wouldn't—"

Rosheen cut her off again. She was forever cutting her off, not allowing Aileen to finish a sentence. "No, you're the one who can't hear me. You don't get it, do you?"

"That's not what I meant—"

"All you do is sit there making lace every night, looking at me over the top of your glasses."

"That's such utter shite."

"Now who needs to watch their language?"

"Don't you take that tone with me. I'm a human being, damn it. Being your mother doesn't make me less of one," Aileen said. "Or have you somehow overlooked that fact?"

"Doesn't it? You act like being my mother puts you in line for sainthood. A martyr to the cause."

"That's not true, and you know it."

"All I know is that I have to get out of here."

"Rosheen."

"How many times do I have to tell you? My name is Jane." She stomped out of the room, down the steps.

"No, it isn't!" Aileen yelled after her. "It's Rosheen. And if you were going to change your name, you could have at least picked something more interesting!"

The only response was the slam of the front door. Aileen wilted against the wall, beneath the crucifix of the long-suffering Jesus, nails in his hands and his feet, and closed her eyes, the fight gone out of her. Aileen hardly recognized this girl with her lips curled back, speaking with such vehemence that spit flew through the air between them. Her throat hurt from shouting, shouting so loud, she wondered if the whole neighborhood had heard them. Sound carried easily over the hills. It had been quite a row. One of their best. At least they could excel at something, she thought bitterly.

The silence settled around her, pressing in on all sides. She sobbed, crossing her arms over her chest. Loud, heaving sobs, part frustration, part sadness. The children could reduce her to tears more quickly than anyone except her husband.

This wasn't the person she meant to be.

She'd told herself she was going to keep her temper, that she would say the right and wise thing, the phrase that would penetrate the churlish attitude Rosheen carried before her like a shield, a new coat of arms, that consisted, not like the family crest of a hawk on the wing, from the days the Flanagans had been warriors, full of power and promise, but of blades and beer bottles and pills. Tolerance and patience had been one of Aileen's Lenten intentions, but she'd broken it more than once, and now Easter had passed without progress. Maybe that meant she was going to hell with the other mothers who'd failed their maternal duties.

The tears started again. She sounded like a child. She wanted her own mother, with whom she'd fought, yes, when she was a teenager, especially when she was sneaking out to see Rourke. (Oh, yes, her mother did watch, did come out of her room and try to offer guidance, sometimes. Though it was too late by then, and there was nothing she could do but hold her tongue over the worst things and not say *I told you so*.) Her mother was dead now. Heart disease. Five years ago.

Aileen wondered if she had it too. She felt pains sometimes, by her left breast, as if she were being stabbed by little knives. Rourke said it was heartburn. She wasn't so sure. One of these days, she thought the frustration of being Rosheen's mother might kill her—the blood pumping in her skull would trigger an aneurysm, and she'd fall down dead in her rose-patterned apron, there on the kitchen floor.

How to reach Rosheen? How to let her go? The question kept Aileen awake at night, her mind spinning like the toys the children used to love, purchased on a seaside holiday on the Dingle Peninsula. There had to be some separation, it was necessary, natural, and yet couldn't it be more gentle than this brutal wrenching that felt as if her heart was being torn in two? Her family had no idea how Aileen felt or who she was. Did it even occur to them to wonder? Did they care? To them, she was the cook, the nagger, the worrier, the chauffeur, the nurse, the laundress, the accountant. They didn't realize she'd been at the top of her class, a champion camogie player. That she lived and breathed and felt just like them. That they were a part of her and she of them. Always. Always.

She took a ragged breath, quieter now. She was grateful that no one else had been home to witness the screaming match. Rourke was off, making deliveries—there were benefits to him being on the road so much. And her youngest, twelve-year-old Sile—who didn't mind the spelling of her name and would, if she'd been home, have given Aileen the hug she desperately needed—was staying the night at a friend's house in the next village.

Aileen was alone in that house in which she'd raised five children. How would it feel when they were gone? What would she do? "You're nearly free," her friends said. Though at the rate things were going, she could be a grandmother soon, if one of the boys settled down, or if, heaven forbid, Rosheen continued in this reckless manner. (The pills weren't 100 percent, were they? Nothing was.) No, Aileen wouldn't think about it. She would pray. She supposed the saints rolled their eyes at her too, from their seats in heaven—*not her again*. She imagined their floor in God's highrise: the Department of Saints, a door just for her: Desperate Mothers & Whiners Division.

There was a part of her that wanted to strangle Rosheen—oh, that sneer, that eye roll, she had the gestures of disdain, of disregard for parental guidance, down cold—that could imagine, even anticipate, her departure. Without the rebellions and arguments, her leaving would have been too hard to contemplate. But there was another side that yearned to hold the girl in her arms and sing Irish lullabies and rock her to sleep. *Oho oho oho mo leanbh / Oho mo leanbh is codail go foill / Oho, oho oho mo leanbh / Mo stoirin ina leaba ina chodladh gan bron*. It didn't seem that long ago that Rosheen was a baby, crying for hours, yes, raging against the world even then, but in the end consoled, face pressed into Aileen's neck, surrendering at last to sleep.

The years had passed quickly: Rosheen sitting on her lap, reading *The Tales of the Brothers Grimm*; Rosheen singing carols in the school choir—her face, her voice, those of an angel—wings on her back, a glittered halo over her head; Rosheen shrieking with glee, riding her bike down the lane, finding her balance for the first time.

Rosheen hadn't really left, not for good. She couldn't have meant it. How could she live on her own?

Aileen pulled the bedroom door closed behind her, as if sealing off the scene of a crime. The walls of the house seemed at once flimsy, paper-thin—not strong enough to support the life she and Rourke had tried to build within—and confining. She put on a jumper, picked up her basket of lace, the tea cakes she'd made for the potluck in a tin, and went outside. She gazed up the road, in the direction she thought Rosheen might have gone. There was no sign of her. She must have run, hard and fast. She'd always been good at running, even now, a camogie champion like her mother, though she didn't compete anymore. There was so much she'd given up on. The shadows gathered, evening coming on; her daughter was lost to them, blending into the landscape, into wherever it was she was going. Away from home. Away from her.

Chapter 10

The Lace Society

When Kate came in the door that evening, the gathering was already in progress. Five women huddled around the table, drinking ale and working lace, each with a cushion on her lap, a web of delicate threads anchored to bobbins and pins to keep the pieces in place.

"There you are," Bernie greeted her. "Come and sit down." She pulled a plate from the oven and set it at the place next to Colleen. "We've already had the potluck, but I kept some food warm for you. Colleen brought her husband's smoked salmon. It's such a treat."

"You haven't had smoked salmon until you've had Finn's," Oona chimed in.

Colleen patted the chair next to her. Her silvery hair and calm expression gave her an aura of wisdom. "Yes, have a seat," she said, her eyes sparkling. "You might learn something."

"I'm sure you're right—though I suspect lace making is even more difficult than it looks," Kate said.

"Like life, one might say." Oona tucked a strand of dyed red hair behind her ear and studied a stitch sequence that had been giving her trouble.

Colleen said she could always spot Oona in a crowd. Their husbands were both fishermen. The two women had bonded as young wives on the rain-lashed docks, waiting for the boats to come in. The men were getting too old to test the waves often now, though Colleen's husband, Finn, had gone out again late last week, because they needed the money. He was due back any day.

Kate sampled the fish. "This is incredible!" she exclaimed, polishing it off in a few bites. "I didn't realize how hungry I was."

"It's all that fresh air. There's more. Here, let me take your plate," Bernie offered.

"Oh, no, thank you. I've already had too much." Kate wiped her hands with a napkin.

"And too much contact with our Irish earth, by the look of it." Aileen gestured at Kate's mud- and grass-stained skirt, her voice sharp as a pinch. She knew how to find the tender spots.

"I hit a rut when I was delivering the papers." Kate brushed at the grime, but her efforts were fruitless—it was ground in deep.

"You seem to have a tendency toward falling. Didn't you lose your footing on the cliffs the other day?" Aileen asked.

"Yes. The terrain here can be challenging," Kate said, her tone light, but her eyes narrowing.

"A little dirt never hurt anyone. Don't pay it any mind," Bernie said, taking her place at the table again after setting the dish in the sink. "I'm sure the stains will wash out fine."

Aileen shot Bernie a look.

Bernie didn't meet her gaze. She picked up her lace and continued to work on her pattern.

"Greegan's Face, was it?" Moira, Aileen's younger sister, said. The relationship between the sisters was apparent in the slim-fingered hands, the high cheekbones, the phrasing of speech, though they would have said they looked nothing alike, citing Moira's wild dark curls, peppered gray at the temples, Aileen's pin-straight hair, which framed more severe features. "It had to have been. Lucky you made it down all right. You could break your neck out there."

"That's what I thought when I was in the middle of it, but then when I reached the bottom, it didn't look so intimidating after all," Kate said.

"That's the deception of it," Moira replied. "Even the rocks can play tricks on you around here."

"So now you're saying we have enchanted stones, do we?" said Aileen, a bite to her teasing.

"I'm just saying that things aren't always as they seem."

"You've got that right." She cast a look in Kate's direction again.

Kate frowned at her. She'd had enough suspicion cast on her for one day. First the priest. Now Aileen.

"I keep thinking someone should organize climbing excursions in the area," Oona interjected. "What with so many people mad for adventure travel these days."

"It's not grand enough for that, is it? And who would lead them—you?" Aileen said.

"Lord, Ailey, there's no need to be so disagreeable. No, of course I wouldn't lead them," Oona said. "I'm just saying it might be a business opportunity, if anyone had the inclination."

"Look around you," Aileen gestured toward the window. "Last time I checked, we're weren't much for business in Glenmara."

"Some people's perspectives are narrower than others'," Oona pointed out. "Some of us are barely getting by. We could use some fresh ideas. We had another call from the bank this afternoon."

"We did too," Colleen echoed. "I don't know how much longer we can put them off. That's why Finn's at sea again. He wouldn't go out in the boat anymore but for the money. My son says we should give up and live with him. But I don't want to start over in another place, and neither does Finn. Glenmara is our home."

"Is the village really struggling so much?" Kate asked. "It seemed prosperous enough when I came into town the other day."

"That's because it was market day. Haven't you noticed how quiet it's been since then?" Aileen said.

"At least Rourke has a job," Oona said, speaking of Aileen's husband.

"It's not as if his being employed makes much difference. The company still hasn't given him a raise."

"One door closes, another opens," Bernie ventured, ever the optimist. "We'll find a way. We always do—"

"Yes, but when, and to where?" Aileen reached for the lace she'd dropped in her lap. "Platitudes don't put bread on the table, do they?"

"Not with that type of attitude. We've weathered many storms, surely we can make it through this. It's only a squall," Oona said, taking up another strand. "That's what my grand-da used to say."

"Exactly. Shall we get started, then?" Colleen handed Kate a hook and thread. "Crochet lace is easier to learn, so we'll begin with that. See," she said, "it goes like this." The hook whipped up and down, slowly at first, then faster. "We won't bother with frames or pillows just yet. We use those mostly for bobbin lace or appliqué, and we don't want to complicate matters too much for you in the beginning."

Kate mimicked Colleen's movements, but the thread tangled almost immediately. "Do you have a book I can study?"

"A book? Heavens, no. We learned from our grandmothers, and they from theirs. It's a skill handed down, you see, from the days the wealthy Irish ladies brought the methods home from Europe and opened the lace schools, to help the people during the Famine, our ancestors too, making the lace to keep themselves alive," Colleen said. "You learn from watching and doing. Don't worry about making mistakes. You can always start over again."

"Lace made by hand comes from the soul, my gran always said," Oona added. "Machine laces can't touch them in terms of quality."

"What type do you do?" Kate asked.

"What type don't we do? There's flat needlepoint lace, raised needlepoint lace, embroidery on net, either with darning or chain-stitch; cut cambric or linen work used for guipure and appliqué laces; drawn thread work, such as Italian cut point; pillow lace, which is something like the Devonshire style; Mountmellick embroidery and Carrickmacross, and of course the more basic crochet," Colleen explained. "I like needle lace the best—it's our specialty, you know, the most delicate—though the appliqué sort is lovely too, especially for pillows. You can make trims or insets or complete garments of lace, though we usually go in for the embellishments. People like things they can use."

"Meaning linens—you know, tablecloths and towels and such," Bernie said. "We used to make baptism gowns and communion dresses, but the demand has gone down. Not enough young people staying in the villages to buy them."

Kate watched as Colleen's hands flew, looping, twisting, and braiding the threads together. The women seemed to appreciate her keen interest and focus. No one had cared so much about their craft before.

"What are you making?" Aileen asked, breaking the spell. "That won't work for any trim. It's a waste of good thread."

"I know," Colleen said. "I'm demonstrating the technique. I can undo it if I want to, can't I, when I'm done?"

Kate took the hook again, tried to follow the steps Colleen showed her. The thread snarled right away. "And here I thought my fingers were nimble from sewing," she said in frustration.

"It's a different craft," Aileen said. "One doesn't necessarily translate to the other."

"But it can't hurt," Bernie said, adding, "I didn't know you sewed, Kate. What do you make?"

"I used to make clothes," Kate said. She held up a knot of thread that resembled a tattered spiderweb. "This can't be right."

"That's the idea." Colleen guided her hands. "Drop those threads to make an opening, then braid these together to bind the ends. There. See? The pattern is emerging. Now you have the petals of a flower."

Kate ran her fingers over the design, feeling each twist and knot.

"It's just a matter of knowing which thread to pull," Moira said.

Kate laughed at herself. "I feel so clumsy."

"Everyone does at first. You need to find your rhythm, that's all," Bernie said.

"My gran used to say the hook moves like a chicken, pecking grain," Oona said.

"Mine said it was an agreeable husband," Colleen said.

"Your pious mother? She did not!" Oona exclaimed.

Kate and the others burst into giggles.

"An agreeable husband? Is there such a thing?" Aileen said.

"Ask Bernie," Moira said. "Hers was the marriage everyone envied."

"Maybe not having children is the key," Aileen said.

The group fell silent. Even Kate sensed that Aileen had said the wrong thing.

"That wasn't what John and I wanted." Bernie picked up another thread, her voice soft. "It's just what happened."

The other women gave Aileen admonishing looks.

"I didn't mean—" Aileen said, realizing she'd gone too far.

"It's all right." Bernie took a spool of thread from her basket.

Kate wondered if Bernie ever got angry with anyone. She seemed so even-tempered, so willing to forgive.

"Drop, drop. Hook, hook, throw," Oona said, getting back to work.

"You sound like a boxing coach," Colleen said. "You're not still watching the WWF on satellite, are you?"

"I never!"

"It's just theater, though some of the men aren't in bad shape." Aileen was clearly making an effort to be more agreeable.

Moira raised her eyebrows. "Really?"

"That's what I heard. From the boys."

"The boys, eh?"

"You having an affair?" Colleen teased.

"I wish," Aileen said, her voice bantering now, but hinting at dissatisfaction. "I was referring to my sons, actually. They're the ones who watch it on satellite at their flat in Galway."

"Of course you were," Colleen said.

"Lord, look at the time," Moira said, glancing at the clock. "I've got to get home. Cillian will be wondering where I am."

"But we've only just begun Kate's lessons," Bernie protested.

"Let's meet again tomorrow. We can start in the afternoon. We'll have our own lace-making marathon, won't we?" Colleen said, and the others agreed, though Aileen seemed less enthusiastic. "Bernie, why don't you keep tutoring Kate tonight after we leave? She'll have the hang of it in no time."

Once the women were gone, Bernie took a sewing kit from the closet at the top of the stairs. She set the woven basket decorated with straw flowers in front of Kate.

"I had one like this when I was a little girl." Kate fingered a red daisy. Her mother had given it to her when she was first learning needlework.

"Did you?"

"My mother taught me to sew."

"I meant to teach my daughter," Bernie said. "There were many things I bought in the beginning, before I realized John and I wouldn't have children. I gave most of them away, but I saved this for some reason. I don't know why. It's good to finally put it to use."

Fergus wagged his tail.

"No, Fergus," Bernie said. "What would you do with hooks and needles and thread? You'd be all paws. You'd probably poke yourself in the nose, and then where would we be?"

He whined.

"But you can watch."

She turned to Kate. "Now, then. You have a flower, yes?" Bernie indicated the lace fragment she'd made under Colleen's supervision. "You need to decide what you want to do with it. Would you like to make a field of flowers for a larger piece, or use a single bloom as an embellishment, say for a collar or a cuff?"

"So we'd use it for an insert or overlay?" Kate asked.

"You could. That's what we do, attaching the lace to existing pieces. Or you could get more ambitious and make fabric of the lace itself, say for a scarf. You look like more of a scarf person to me. Collars and cuffs are too old-fashioned for you. We're kind of stuck in a time warp here, you know. Maybe you'll open our minds a little, show us something new."

"It's me who has a lot to learn." Kate frowned as she dropped a stitch.

"Like Colleen said, mistakes aren't necessarily a problem," Bernie told her. "Sometimes they lead you in a different direction. Who says you always need to follow the rules? Breaking the pattern can be the very best thing, even though it can be scary at first."

"That's kind of you to say."

"Not kind. True."

They worked until the fire burned low, their eyes grew heavy, and Kate began to understand the process. She'd always been a quick learner, especially when it came to needlework. Her meadow of lace flowers wasn't perfect—it had pulls and ripples, didn't lie flat—and yet it was pretty in its way, and she began to see the possibilities. "I might be getting the hang of this," she said.

Bernie smiled. "I've never seen someone take to lace making as quickly as you."

"I have good teachers," Kate said.

They left the work there on the table, for the women to see when they returned the next day: pieces so delicate, so fragile, a single breath might carry them away.

Chapter 11

Kate's Idea

The next afternoon, as the lace society worked on trimmings and inserts for the linens they planned to sell at the market, Aileen took up where she left off the previous night, seeking someone on whom to vent her frustrations—finally settling, as she often did, on her sister. Rain pelted the windows, echoing Aileen's sharp-voiced observations, both starting quietly, threatening to come down hard. It was warm in the cottage, the fire sparking every now and then in the hearth, fog lacing the edges of the windows. A cozy gathering to be sure, and yet there was an underlying tension, thanks to Aileen.

Aileen took off her jumper, muttering something about hot flashes again. Oona fanned herself with a piece of paper. The teapot on the stove built up steam and whistled, Bernie hurrying to serve tea.

"It's like a sauna in here today," Aileen said.

"I'm sorry," Bernie said. "The turf must be burning faster than usual. I'll open a window."

"Better do it on the south side, so the rain doesn't blow in," Colleen said. "What a storm."

It had been coming down all morning. The women's raincoats and boots were by the door: Aileen's olive green, as if she were going off to war; Moira's threadbare brown, a cast-off from her sister; Oona's red polka dots; Bernie's practical black; and Colleen's patent navy, a towel on the floor below to catch the drips.

Bernie moved around the table, pouring cups of orange pekoe.

"You don't have to wait on us like we're customers, Bee," Aileen said. "We're perfectly capable of serving ourselves."

"Oh, you know me, always playing the hostess."

"And a fine one too," Oona said.

Kate blew on her tea, sipping too soon and burning the tip of her tongue. She set it down to give it time to cool, taking up her lace again. There was still so much to learn.

Aileen unwound another length of thread with an impatient flick of her wrist. "How are things at home?" She asked Moira.

No one had said anything about the fresh bruise on Moira's cheek. They'd learned these problems couldn't be confronted head-on. Only Moira could complain about her relationship. Care had to be taken about joining in, lest she become defensive, retracting the drawbridge, fortifying her marriage, she and Cillian against the world, struggles concealed behind the gates.

"Grand, grand," Moira answered too quickly.

"Cillian find a job yet?" Aileen knew she shouldn't bring it up, not in her state of mind, but she couldn't help herself. They had two older brothers, one who ran a popular Irish pub in Boston, the Wolfe & Whistle, the other a lawyer in Dublin, high-powered, on his second marriage, who'd left village life far behind, and a sister, a professional home organizer in London, who specialized in cleaning up other people's messes. Moira was the bonus baby, Aileen a teenager when she arrived, tending her as if she were her own because their mother was in too dark a place to raise her. It was a hard habit to break, that caring, that need to protect, to control.

"Not since you asked last time," Moira replied, her tone sharper, as it often was whenever anyone, especially Aileen, inquired too closely into her domestic situation. "He's still looking," she went on, taking pains to soften her delivery. "His back is bad. He can't do the work he used to."

"Not that he ever did," Aileen said under her breath.

"What did you say?" Moira frowned. She was only thirty-two years old, but worries were taking their toll: she already had deep furrows between her brows and threads of gray in her hair. So many children to raise, her husband too.

"A shame he took that skid—losing his footing," Bernie said, ever the peacemaker. She'd never had sisters, never been embroiled in the jealousies, the arguments, the resentments. "Sure to damage one's backbone."

"If he ever had any in the first place," Aileen said.

Bernie shook her head.

Kate listened, the talk moving too rapidly for her to comment, even if she were inclined, words darting and swooping like an agitated flock of swallows. She felt comfortable with everyone— except Aileen, who might as well have had a yellow sign around her neck reading "Approach with Caution."

At least she wasn't in Aileen's sights that evening. Moira was— and she wasn't about to put up with her sister's interference.

Moira's husband was often the topic of conversation at these gatherings, particularly when Moira wasn't present. The women thought he drank too much and worked too little. Things had looked fine enough when they married twelve years ago, with a child on the way, another following every year or two after, though the warning signs were there from the very beginning.

Moira had left the children at home with her eldest, Sorcha, in charge that evening. Cillian was probably there as well, in his usual spot in front of the telly, a beer in hand, unless he'd absconded to the pub again—not the convivial one in town, no, the Cell Block, to the south, so named because it was once a jail, and now the place where the hard drinkers in the region congregated to brag and brawl, Cillian among them. Hardly the picture of the helpful househusband.

"What's that on your cheek?" Aileen said, unable to hold back any longer.

"I ran into the door." Moira stabbed herself in the finger with a pin, swore under her breath, took up the hook again, working faster this time.

"You sure it wasn't a fist?" Aileen said.

Bernie rolled her eyes. *Here we go.* She'd done her best.

"At least my husband pays attention to me," Moira said.

"You call that attention?" Aileen asked. "I have another word for it. The one you don't want to hear."

"Can we please not have an argument?" Colleen said. "I'm getting a headache, and we still have a lot of work to do."

"Someone has to say something." Aileen brandished her hook as if it were a sword of justice.

"Even if it's wrong?" Moira asked.

"It's hard to create beautiful lace when there's so much negativity in the room," Colleen said.

"Yes. What must Kate be thinking of us, carrying on like this?" Oona agreed, giving their guest an apologetic smile.

"It's all right, really," Kate said.

"She's like one of the family. Isn't that what you said?" Aileen glared at Bernie.

Everyone fell silent, the only sound the tick of the clock on the wall above the cross made of bog oak and the tap of a lacecap hydrangea branch against the window pane.

"What's going on, Ailey?" Bernie asked finally. If anyone could ask the question, it was her. "You've been acting strange lately."

"Have I?" Her lips thinned.

"I saw Rosheen at the crossroads on my way over tonight," Colleen ventured, taking another stitch. Colleen had gotten there later than the rest. She'd been talking to her daughter, Maeve, on the phone. Long distance, it was, from the UK.

"So she's still in town, is she? Hitching a ride again, I suppose." Aileen shrugged as if it didn't matter, though clearly it did. "She does what she wants, that one. Damned what I say."

Colleen had had her share of trials raising children—her strong-willed daughter Maeve among them. Maeve, who lived in London now, working in the fashion industry. Oh, the battles they used to have. "I'm sure she'll come back."

"You're surer than I am, then." Tears welled up in Aileen's eyes. She swiped at them with her hands, seemingly furious for letting weakness—yes, she saw tears shed before others as weakness, would rather turn them into anger, into a force to be reckoned with—get the best of her. "I'm sorry. I swore I wasn't going to cry. It's just that she— That I—"

"Nothing like a teenager to make you feel like a bitch, a nag, and an old woman, all at once," Colleen said.

"She has so many piercings, she's like a connect-a-dot puzzle." Aileen laughed and sniffled at the same time.

"She has a belly ring now, doesn't she?" Moira asked. "I always wanted one of those—or a tattoo."

"At least she has the midriff for it. Mine's like a fallen soufflé." Bernie poked at her midsection in dismay.

"I think they call those a muffin top now," Oona said. "At least that's what my daughter tells me."

"That makes me feel so much better."

"Rosheen's got one of those leopard bras too," Moira said. "I saw the strap when I was down at the shops a few days ago."

"Brilliant," Aileen sighed. "Now everyone knows my daughter has the underwear of a prostitute."

"I wouldn't mind a leopard bra myself," Colleen said.

"Those are quite popular now," Kate ventured now that the conversation had shifted to fashion again.

"Go on . . ." Oona giggled.

"Anything other than industrial-strength bras and granny pants," Colleen continued. "If I've lived this long, I ought to have the right to wear some pretty knickers."

"Exactly," Kate agreed.

Aileen set her work down. "Look at us, working away at tea towels, collars, and cuffs. No one needs them anymore, if they ever did. They don't make us any money. They aren't sexy."

"Tea towels have never been sexy," Moira said.

"I don't know about that. John used to do a little dance for me, trying to get me away from washing the dishes . . . ," Bernie said.

The others whistled and laughed.

Bernie blushed. "Well, he did."

"Too bad he wasn't a professional," Colleen said. "Then we could have hired him for my birthday party."

"He only did it for me. And now, of course, he—" Bernie broke off.

Colleen patted her arm.

"Towels and collars and cuffs and runners are all we know how to make," Aileen said, more quietly now.

"You could make the lace into something new," Kate said, an idea taking shape in her mind. Her hands fluttered with excitement. "I made some sketches—"

"What good are a bunch of drawings going to do us?" Aileen asked, a note of challenge in her voice.

"Everything starts with a design," Kate insisted, sure of her plan. If Aileen would only let her explain—

"Of one sort or another." Aileen gave her a piercing look.

Kate pressed her lips together. She didn't want to stoop to Aileen's level, though it was hard. Stitch 'n' bitch indeed.

"What are they designs for?" Colleen interjected.

"Lingerie," Kate said, more determined now. "I've been thinking: you could incorporate the lace, creating overlays or inserts for the garments you already have, or make new ones, crafted entirely of lace—"

They stared at her in surprise.

"What a waste of good lace, and anyway, what would people say? What would the priest say?" Aileen broke the silence.

"I can't believe people worry about such things in the twenty-first century," Kate said, though even at home in the States, there were those who did—Extreme Catholics, she and her friend Ella called them. "Besides, I doubt Father Byrne has much experience in the matter, unless he's keeping a few secrets under his cassock."

The women, except Aileen, laughed, talking at once:

"Yes."

"Why not?"

"We'll make the most gorgeous bras and knickers the world has ever seen."

"So instead of tatted lace, it's tit for tat, is it," Oona said.

Aileen glared at them. "You must be joking."

"No, she isn't. It's brilliant, isn't it?" Bernie said. "We can make ourselves feel beautiful again. That's what you said, Kate, remember, when I brought my things in from the clothesline that day?"

"Yes," Kate said, as all of them save Aileen nodded. "Yes, we can."

Kate laid the scissors, needle, and thread on the table in Bernie's kitchen. She'd deconstructed many a garment, but had never undertaken anything like this. She could tell Aileen was waiting for her to fail. Some people were like that, expecting the worst at every turn. Kate wouldn't let Aileen stop her. She took stock of the materials. They'd need more supplies—bands of elastic, hooks and eyes, straps—but those could be ordered easily enough. For the moment, they would remove portions of the existing material, add inserts and overlays. They'd make do with what they had.

She felt the weight of the tools in her hands, the place where the skin rubbed, blisters formed, as they had when she'd first learned to sew. The craft had been part of her life from the very start, when Lu hung the golden thimble over the bassinet, letting her baby daughter bat at it while she worked. Lu sewed for pleasure until Kate's father left them when she was eight years old, and then she sewed for money. Before she worked those late nights, she sat with Kate, beginning with a needle and thread. She showed her how to snip the ends, lick the tips to bind the fibers, slip them through the eye, knot the strand firmly. Kate studied embroidery, made pillowcases and pictures of flowers and cats and dogs, her fingers sore at first from needle pricks. Later she advanced to hems, and finally, when she was older, the machine itself, her mother's arms encircling her as she told Kate what she needed to do. Lu never raised her voice, even when Kate snarled the bobbin and misthreaded the machine. *It's all right. Let's try again.*

Kate had heard her mother's voice when she sat at the machine later, after her death three months ago, part of the melodic hum that intensified as the needle raced frantically to the edge of the fabric. She'd run it so hard in those first days after the funeral that the needle snapped in two—the before and the after. She focused all her energies on finishing her debut line in time for the spring shows, sewing in a fury that verged on desperation, barely sleeping or eating, Ethan spending more time away from the apartment to escape the noise. "I never see you," he said. "When will you be done?" In the end, he was done—with her.

But she didn't know that then—she was too busy reworking the concept, trying to get it right, until she gave up and hung the garments on the racks, ready for model fittings, the Seattle rains falling that March outside the studio. A ragged faerie-in-a-dustbin look, faerie punk, Kate called it, struggling to find a marketing hook, but in the end the pieces were only a poor imitation of the latest runway darling. She thought that was what Jules wanted. But it wasn't, not at all. What had she been thinking? Why hadn't she been true to her vision, stuck with the 1950s silhouette she loved? She was sure it wouldn't have happened if her mother hadn't gotten sick. Kate showed her everything. It was part of her creative process. Her mother seemed to realize this, did not generally offer advice, let Kate talk, understanding she was thinking things through, but her mother had fallen ill that winter, and everything changed.

Kate didn't know anything was wrong at first. Her mother

didn't tell her until it got bad, the cancer winning, the cellular occupation firmly entrenched.

"You should have told me," Kate said when she finally confronted Lu about her "little appointments" as they ate dinner one night, one of the last in the home Kate grew up in.

"It wouldn't have changed anything." Lu's sewing lay on the sideboard. She was working on an elaborate design of a peacock in the art deco style. Lu didn't know if the cancer would allow her to finish it, but she kept on, stitching the texture of each feather, the tips crowned with watchful eyes. She bit off threads with her teeth, because she couldn't find her snips. Kate meant to bring her another pair. Her mother had been misplacing things lately. "It's chemo-brain," she said. The drugs took away more than the cancer. They robbed her of her hair, her thoughts. It wasn't like her, this forgetfulness. Lu had always been so organized, spools of thread lined up in the sewing box, glowing like gems: peridot, amethyst, aquamarine, garnet, ebony, cerise, jade, cobalt.

Kate wondered what else would fade from memory, if she too would be lost, her mother unable to recognize her in the end. If everything in that room, the table and chairs, the Murano pendant lamps, the bamboo shades, the sewing basket itself, would become artifacts of her mother's past, forgotten, sold.

"I didn't want to worry you."

Kate felt betrayed and frightened. She had the sense that her mother was tucking her in bed as she had when Kate was a child, kissing her cheek, turning off the light, closing the door—except now, for the last time. Kate wasn't ready for her to go. She didn't know if she'd ever be ready.

"I wanted to protect you," Lu said.

"By lying?"

"I didn't lie. I just didn't tell you everything."

"Isn't omission the same thing?" What else hadn't she told her? About this? About other things?

Lu toyed with her steak, lifting the edge of the filet with the tines of her fork as if something were hidden underneath. (She'd given up the vegan diet the previous year, saying she needed more iron.) The salad, a bitter radicchio and butter lettuce, lay in a crumpled heap next to slices of Comice pear. She had no appetite, but went through the motions of someone who had once enjoyed eating, traveling the world with her palate—Persia, Tunisia, Ethiopia, France, Italy, Thailand. "No, it isn't. Not always."

"But—" A flock of crows alighted on the maples outside the window, the trees' branches stripped clean, the birds black shapes against ashen clouds.

"We can't tell each other everything." Lu held up her hand, warding Kate off. She'd never done that before; she didn't have the energy to pursue the matter further. "I thought it was for the best."

Kate cradled the thimble in her hands, remembering her mother, remembering William's words as he returned the lost notion to her. "Give it time," he'd said.

Was the time, finally, right? Kate hoped so. She told herself she was ready to take up the needle again. Or as ready as she'd ever be. She had a purpose now, a true reason to stay: she would help the lace makers of Glenmara. She felt a surge of excitement, followed by trepidation at the prospect of the challenge she'd taken on, the specter of past failures and Aileen's doubts still on her mind.

Her arms were bare. She worked better without sleeves, which had a tendency to get in the way. She tapped her fingers to the ticking of the clock, anticipating the beginning of the dance, when scissors and needle and thread would transform the pieces into something new. The women had gone home for their lingerie, Colleen for her sewing machine; they might need an extra for the finishing work, for strengthening attachments and making reinforcements. The garments must not fall apart. They must be made to last.

Bernie had accompanied Colleen, leaving Kate on her own. What have I gotten myself into? she thought. The minutes seemed to stretch into hours, her uncertainty growing with each passing second. She took deep breaths to still her shaking hands. *There's no pressure. No pressure at all.* There were no deadlines, no critics— well, other than Aileen. It was all in fun, wasn't it? *Don't overthink.* Each woman, each garment, would dictate the design.

Soon, she heard the lace makers coming up the walk, the clatter of heels, the chatter of voices. Someone bumped against the door, calling, "We're back!" Kate let them in. Colleen brought up the rear, lugging her sewing case behind her, Bernie trying to help.

"Lord, this thing feels like it weighs ten stone!" Colleen gasped. Kate and Bernie helped her lift the machine onto the table. "We might have to make a lace back brace for me."

"I don't know why we're cutting up perfectly good knickers and bras," Aileen complained.

Kate didn't listen. She heard her mother's voice in her ear: *You can always start over. All it takes is a new thread.*

The women had brought their best lingerie, as uninspired as the everyday pieces but unworn, wrapped in tissue. They proffered the pieces as shyly as the schoolgirls they'd once been, all those years ago. When Kate laid the pieces before her, considering each in turn, a design suggested itself, as if emerging from the women's skin, their very selves. Yes, she knew what they would do: for Bernie, who went first, there would be a garden of wild roses to accentuate her lovely complexion; for Colleen, seashells—

descended, as she was, according to family legend, from the sel-
kies and merrows that swam below the cliffs, full-figured and
otherworldly. For Aileen, deco—sharp lines and geometrics, each
locked inside the next, optical illusions, tension and razzmatazz,
blue, gray, black, like her eyes and hair and moods, and a tassel
in the very middle, because she wouldn't expect it, needed it. For
Oona, golden threads to match her bright personality; Moira, the
green of the land, to help her feel more grounded, sure.

The lace makers held their breath as Kate opened a seam in
Bernie's garments, where the first insert would go, the stitches
pulling away, taking everything apart, before putting it back
together again.

Chapter 12

Father Byrne on Patrol

Every evening the women worked, long into the night. The priest caught wind of their meetings, having overheard the local gossip. He walked the fields, binoculars in hand, in the guise of a naturalist, determined to discover the truth with his own eyes, watching them come and go from Bernie's cottage, straining to see what they carried, what they intended, with little success.

Priests had walked the roads for years, keeping watch over their flocks. Father Byrne remembered when he was a young man on first assignment, accompanying Father Keene as he patrolled the lanes, flushing lovers from bushes, beating the boys with a stout stick till the blood ran, taking the girls aside, slapping them across the face, hard, as they clutched their clothes to their breasts, the priest's eyes darting down before he hit harder, thrashing the sin from them, from himself. Young people weren't meant to consort, to touch, not even to hold hands. No one spoke of sex.

The point was procreation, in the marital bed. No pleasure taken, only Christian duty fulfilled. Nothing was innocent in the eyes of the Church, not a glance, not a smile. Sin was everywhere, in the mating of the beasts in the stockyards, the cats yowling on the heath, the birds at their nests. Humans must overcome their animal nature, be pure in flesh and soul. Father Keene gave Father Byrne a stick too, told him to go after the boy fleeing through the hedgerows, strike him down, strike a blow for God. Father Byrne hit a tree instead, told the boy to scream for effect. He'd been too young then, too soft. He'd learned, learned that there were people who must be stopped.

People like Kate Robinson. Who hadn't left as expected, who'd stayed to assist the women with the lace. What help did they need? They knew the traditional patterns already. What could she possibly have to show them? It couldn't be good. He'd been complacent, he saw that now, assumed his congregants were safe in their little hamlet of Glenmara—that those with the wrong sort of ideas kept to the cities where they belonged. The flowering of Ireland, the Dublin papers called it, immigrants flooding into the country, the young Irish too, filling the suburbs, bolstering the GNP. Not there. Not in Glenmara. Glenmara was too remote, too lacking in opportunity. An embodiment of the pure soul of Ireland. Or so he thought.

"Out for a stroll, Father?" Oona's father, Denny, asked on his evening constitutional. He paused to catch his breath, winced at the ache in his knees, but it was clear he was most interested in discovering what the priest was up to.

"Bird-watching."

Denny nodded. "Any luck?"

"Luck?"

"With the birds? Mating, aren't they, at this time of year?"

"Yes." The priest grimaced.

"Happy hunting, then." Denny limped away, whistling to himself, intending to warn Oona. But she'd already gone by the time he got home, and the news would have to wait.

Yes, each night the women worked, their husbands supportive of the venture, except Moira's. Cillian called every few minutes some evenings, eventually demanding she come home. "He just wants to see how I'm doing," she said, making excuses for him. "It's because he cares."

"All he cares about is being the biggest control freak in western Ireland," Aileen declared, setting off yet another round of sniping between the sisters. She and Moira wouldn't let it devolve into a full row—they saved those for when they were alone, outside their houses, after a family gathering, the tensions having built all afternoon, or perhaps longer, days, weeks, years, depending upon the subject and mood. They hoarded the hurts and transgressions, let them spill out after everyone was gone and it was just the two of them.

Not now, in Bernie's kitchen. This was only a warm-up act, during which they would peck at each other, peck and peck and peck.

"Well, he's my control freak." Moira jabbed at the cutwork with a needle, the knuckles of her left hand whitening as she clutched the lace pillow.

"Congratulations. They should give you a prize," Aileen replied, teeth clenched around a pin. "You know, it's curious how you'll stand up to me, but you won't to him. I mean, you've clearly got the ability to argue—"

"You have no idea how I handle things," Moira retorted. "You aren't there, are you? Inside my home at night with my family."

"Doesn't take a genius to figure it out."

"You want me to strangle you with that bra?"

Kate and the others looked from one sister to the other as if watching a tennis match before Colleen stepped in: "Ladies."

They paused for a moment, giving Oona an opportunity to change the course of the conversation. "The men wonder what we're up to, don't they?" she said. "They're not used to having us out so many nights. It's usually them, off to the pubs, isn't it, leaving us home alone. Padraig asked if I'm having an affair. Said he was joking, but he half meant it. 'At my age? And in my condition?' I asked."

"They can't believe there's anything we might need to do that doesn't involve a man," Colleen said.

"Mine just falls asleep on the couch, snoring. You can hear him all the way out to the gate. I have a hard enough time sleeping without that racket," Aileen said. "The Change is driving me mad. It's robbing me of my hair and sleep."

"It will pass. You'll see," Colleen said.

"Not soon enough," Aileen replied. "I've tried everything: soy, fish oil. I thought they were supposed to help."

"Depends on how low your estrogen levels are," Moira said.

"Thanks for the advice, Fertile-Myrtle."

"I read it in a magazine."

"The *Economist*, no doubt."

"Don't get highbrow on me. You're no better than the rest of us. I've seen you scanning the headlines of the tabloids and the women's magazines in the shops when you think no one is looking."

"There's nothing else to read when the lines are long."

"As if they ever get long around here."

"There's word of a golf resort going in on the coast," Oona said.

"Where would they put the ninth hole? In the sea?"

"I don't know. It's just what I heard."

"There's always the rumors, aren't there? The things that might save us—or drive us to an earlier grave."

"I wouldn't mind. Might make for more jobs. Maybe my son would move back here then."

"Have so many moved away?" Kate asked.

"Yes, but people have lived in Glenmara since the beginning of time—remember the arrowheads my da found on one of his walks?" Oona said. "Prehistoric, they were. Our ancestors made it through the Famine, the Rebellions, and God knows what else. We must have inherited at least some of their strength. We'll be fine. I have to believe we'll be fine."

"At least we'll have the prettiest knickers in the county," Bernie said. "That ought to count for something."

Just past 7:00 p.m., there was a knock at the door. "Do you think it's Mrs. Flynn?" Oona asked. "I told her to stop by."

"The poor woman works too hard, what with housekeeping for Father Byrne and taking care of her mother," Aileen said.

"And a new grandbaby too," Bernie added. "Have you seen the pictures? What a darling she is. Mallory, they named her."

"I'll let her in." Colleen rose from her chair and disappeared into the front hall.

"Oh," they heard her exclaim seconds later, in a voice louder than she usually used. "What a surprise to see you, Father Byrne. To what do we owe the pleasure of your visit?"

"Just making the rounds, Mrs. McGreevy. Is everyone here then?"

The women exchanged glances of alarm. Bernie pulled out a straw picnic basket, into which they tossed the bras and panties on which they'd been working, then shoved it under the table at her feet. They set to work on the old trims.

"Yes," Colleen said. "It's our usual lace society meeting." Since he didn't move from the stoop, she felt compelled to admit him. "Would you like to come in and say hello?"

"Certainly. I like to keep up on the doings of my congregation. Perhaps you could make a new communion cloth? Mrs. Flynn wasn't able to get the red wine stain out. I'm afraid the altar boy spilled a drop or two. Accidents happen, but we can't have soiled linens at God's table, can we?"

"I daresay not."

A few steps, and he was in the room, his eyes taking in every detail. "Hard at work, I see."

"Indeed, Father, indeed," Bernie replied.

"And what are you making this evening?" His eyes met Kate's.

She looked down, intent on her sample. She didn't want to do anything to attract his attention, but felt his scrutiny just the same.

"The usual trims for towels and hankies, Father," Bernie said.

He peered over Aileen's shoulder. "This is a new design, isn't it? I haven't seen one like it before."

Aileen didn't meet the others' eyes. They were sure she'd give them away. "It's spring, Father. Flowers are a spring design," was all she said.

"Would you like a cup of tea, Father?" Bernie asked, trying to divert him—and perhaps hoping he'd decline.

"No, thank you." He took a final turn around the table. "Just stopping in for a moment to wish you a good evening. God's grace be with you." He bowed his head, hands clasped before him.

"God's grace," they murmured as he left the room.

They didn't breathe easily until they heard the crunch of his footsteps growing faint on the gravel path, and it was only then they crossed themselves in relief.

"What was that about?" Kate asked.

"A surprise visit from our local theological authority," Oona said, adding, "That was a close one, wasn't it?"

"I'll have to say ten Hail Marys for lying," Aileen said.

"Don't you dare make a confession to Father Byrne. Keep it between yourself and God," Colleen said. "Besides, you didn't lie. You just didn't tell him everything. There's no harm in that."

"Isn't there? If he knew what we're doing, he'd think we were going to hell in a handbasket," Aileen said.

"Or a G-string," Kate said, making the others giggle. "Does his opinion matter so much?"

"Of course it does. We take our religion seriously here," Aileen said with a superior look.

"Some of us too seriously," Oona said.

Aileen glared at her.

"So you think he suspects?" Bernie asked.

"I don't know," Colleen said. "But it's not as if we're committing a sin. All we're doing is making lace."

"Are we?" Oona wondered.

The lace was different. They weren't just telling themselves that, were they, so filled with hope? They ran their fingers over the threads, which shone as if enchanted. They weren't imagining it. No, something special was happening in Bernie's kitchen, something special indeed.

Chapter 13

Imaginary Breasts

By that Friday, it was Oona's turn. She didn't seem enthused about going next.

"Did you bring the bra?" Colleen asked her. "You said you would."

"Yes, thanks to your incessant nagging, I did, not that there's any point," Oona replied. She'd been subdued all night. She'd been lively when the spotlight was on the others, but withdrew as it moved toward her. "My chest isn't worth notice anyway."

"Don't be ridiculous," Aileen said. "Of course it is."

"Ah, yes, my imaginary breasts," Oona said. "Padraig won't even touch me, you know."

"Are you sure?" Bernie asked.

"What do you mean, am I sure? I live with the man, don't I? Have done for nearly forty years."

"What she means is: is it because you won't let him?" Colleen asked.

"I feel like I'm being interrogated. Can't you see this is an exercise in futility? That I don't want to talk about it right now?"

"Then when are you going to talk about it?" Colleen persisted. "Don't you think it's time?"

"You don't know anything about it. None of you do." Oona shrank back in her chair like a cornered animal.

"Our sister had it, you know," Aileen said. "I keep wondering if the sea being poisoned by that oil spill years ago had something to do with it."

"Who knows?" Colleen said. "There are no definite answers. One moment you're fine. The next you're not."

"But it's gone now, isn't it?" Moira asked.

"So it seems," Oona said. "Along with some other crucial things."

"Is there anything I can do?" Kate asked.

Oona didn't reply.

Kate didn't press, sensing the delicacy of the matter.

"Aren't you going to tell her?" Colleen touched Oona's arm.

"So I have to come out and say it, do I? Make everything crystal clear? A public service announcement about my illness? Sometimes I swear I could slap you, Colleen McGreevy."

"That's what friends are for, dear."

"I'm sorry. I don't mean to seem— I've always been positive, kept my problems to myself. That's how I am. How I get along." She turned to Kate. "But now they want me to tell you, and since I've been called out like this, I guess I have to."

"I'd like to help you, if I can. It's your turn, that's all. You don't have to take it if you don't want to," Kate said.

"But I do, I do. It's just that I'm afraid." Oona fell silent.

The women wondered if they'd done the right thing, pushing her that way.

"No, it's all right. It really is," Oona continued. "You can probably guess already. We talk too much about some things, not enough about others. That's the way with women, isn't it? Me more than any of us. . . ." She paused. "I had cancer. I lost my breasts. That's why there's no point in making me anything but knickers. There's nothing to hold up anymore. I'm flat as the Australian Outback."

Colleen squeezed her hand.

"Let me see the lingerie," Kate said gently, thinking of her mother, how thin her body had become, like a child's, the contours and curves wasted away. There hadn't been anything Kate could do for her in the end other than hold her hand—but she could help Oona in this one small way. "I'm sure that there's something we can do to make you feel beautiful again," she told her.

Oona didn't reply. She pulled the bra from her bag, balled it up in her hands, and quickly passed it to Kate.

"No wonder you don't want to wear this." Kate held it up. "It's the ugliest thing I've ever seen."

"Terrible, isn't it?" Oona sighed with a sad smile. "A right old booby prize."

They laughed, perhaps a bit harder than necessary.

"The saleswoman could have done better than this—she should have," Kate said with a shake of her head.

"Maybe she would have if I'd stayed longer, but I wanted to get out of there as fast as I could," Oona said. "I thought nothing would be worse than going to the wig shop. I was wrong. At least the wig was temporary. My hair grew back. But I can't grow new breasts. Not real ones, anyway."

"Padraig loves you. Anyone can see that," Bernie said.

"I'm afraid I'll scare him." Oona stood in front of the mirror, traced the lines on her chest, no more mounds of flesh, no nipples. Padraig had loved her breasts. The Alps, he called them, for their size and majesty, even after the children and the nursing and the passage of time made them droop. She hadn't realized she was grieving for her breasts—the denial, the anger, the sadness. She hadn't reached the point of acceptance. She didn't know when she would. There were worse things, of course. So many worse things. And yet—

She'd gone to Dublin for the procedure. Her son knew a doctor in there, David Corcoran, the best in his field. But the scars remained. Some days, Oona thought they were the great rivers of the world. The Yangtze, the Danube, the Nile. Others, the wise visages of elderly women, with wrinkled eyes and mouths. The woman she was becoming with each passing day. She didn't tell anyone, fearing they'd send her in for a psych consult, though, truth be told, there were days when she thought she'd lost her mind too. "Padraig wants to help," she said. "I don't know what to tell him. I just want things to be as they were before."

"You're more than your breasts," Colleen said.

"In my head, I know that," Oona replied. "But it's so strange and ugly. There's no getting around that. It takes getting used to. Even for me. But there are some good things: I've always wanted curly hair, and look at it now. After the chemo, it grew back in ringlets. I can squeeze through smaller spaces, wear the clothes they make for those stick-thin models, though I'm too old for the styles now." She had a slender figure, it was true.

"You've always had grand legs," Bernie said.

"So I think, in time, everything will be okay," Oona said. "I have to get accustomed to it, is all. We both have to get accustomed to it. At first, it was as if when the doctor took my breasts away, he took something else as well. Suddenly, there was the possibility that things would change between Padraig and me, that that loss would reveal what had slipped away from us over the years. How far we'd drifted from each other. I don't know what he's thinking now. He's such a quiet man." Tears came to her eyes. "I can't believe I'm crying about this. I thought I was done with the crying. Isn't it funny, how undergarments call things up in you?"

"They lie close to the skin," Colleen said. "They're called intimates for a reason."

"You deserve better. We can do so much better than this," Bernie said, looking to Kate for confirmation.

Kate nodded and squeezed Oona's hand.

"So you think you could," Oona's voice broke. "So you think you could make me something lovely?"

"I know we can, and we will." Kate took out her measuring tape.

Later, the members of the lace society sat back and admired their handwork. "They're too pretty to keep to ourselves," Bernie said. "Maybe we should make more and sell them in town at the Saturday market. There might be some money in it."

"No one came last time, remember?" Aileen said.

"Kate did," Bernie said.

"She's just one person, isn't she?"

Kate shot a glance at Aileen. What an unhappy woman she seemed to be.

"Kate's worth ten people—and we weren't selling these, were we?" Bernie insisted.

"The lace is gorgeous," Colleen agreed. "Surely other women will think so too. We'll get extra supplies. It won't take any time.

There's the sewing shop in Kinnabegs. They should have everything we need."

"We can make samples, take orders," Oona said. "That's what the professionals do, don't they?"

"Isn't anyone listening to me?" Aileen tried to break in, but they paid no attention. "*No one came last time.*"

"I'll send another release," Bernie said. "Stir up interest."

"For all the good the last one did," Aileen said. "A waste of time and paper. Why don't you just—"

"Let's try the Internet. Send a—what do you call it?—an e-mail blast."

"Sounds like a terrorist act."

"We could take pictures of the pieces. Kate has a digital camera."

"You planning on modeling them?"

"I just might!"

"One problem: no one has Internet around here."

"Sullivan Dean has a computer. He takes it into the bar in Kinnabegs, doesn't he? They have Wi-Fi there for the tourists. We could ask him."

Kate had met several of the villagers, but he wasn't among them. Perhaps he lived on the outskirts of town.

"Fine idea. Thank God he moved back to Glenmara. Staying at the old family home, he is."

"Shame about what happened in London. Devastating for him."

Colleen crossed herself. "He didn't tell you, did he?"

"No, he never speaks of it, except once at the pub, when he got drunk and the Guinness loosened his tongue. Couldn't bear being in England any longer. Let his partner buy him out and moved here. Been making pottery ever since."

"Not much of a way to make a living."

"He's got plenty of money. Set for life, I hear."

"But not happiness."

"No."

"You'd never know to look at him. He looks right enough."

"Don't they all?"

Kate wondered what had happened to him but didn't feel it was her place to ask.

"Remember Eamon Greene? He was never the same after that bombing in the North. Caught on the border. Just up to work on that construction job for his cousin. Bad business."

"Eamon's still in that home, isn't he? Near Galway."

"His poor mother. She moved there, to be near him."

"He was going to be married, wasn't he?"

"Yes. The girl left him. But who could blame her? He wasn't the same. Looked right enough on the surface, but broken inside. Doesn't speak a word."

They fell silent for a moment.

"Do you really think people will buy the lace?" Moira asked.

"There's only one way to find out," Colleen said.

"What if the pieces don't sell?" Aileen asked.

"No matter." Bernie shrugged. "All the more for us. Besides, we're only going to make a few samples, aren't we?"

"What do you want to call yourselves?" Kate asked.

"Call ourselves? We're the lace society. And you're one of us now," Bernie replied.

"I mean for a business name."

"Are we in business?" Aileen asked. "With a few pairs of knickers to our name?"

"You could be," Kate said. If nothing else, the lace could

give the women some extra income, help make ends truly meet. "People love things that are unique and handmade, especially these days."

"We need something catchy," Colleen mused.

"Catchy," they echoed.

"Sweet Nothings?" Oona said.

"Bare Necessities?" Moira offered.

"I think those have been used," Kate said.

"What about Sheer Delights?" Bernie suggested.

They considered. "That's good. Yes, that might do. Sheer Delights."

"How about a slogan?" Colleen said. "We need some sort of a catchphrase, don't we?"

"A slogan?" Aileen said. "Are we running for office?"

"No, but we're trying to get people's attention," Colleen replied.

"You're right. Marketing is everything. That's what my son says," Oona said.

"And he knows a thing or two about that. Top of his class at Trinity."

"You'll be taken care of in your old age, that's for sure."

"Except I haven't heard from him in weeks. He's getting on with his life. Out in the great wide world, far from here."

"He won't forget you. Give him time."

"He has to, at least for a while. They all do. Otherwise they'd be with us forever, wouldn't they, and where would they be then?" She wound a piece of thread around her finger. "What about that slogan?"

"I know: Lingerie for Every Body," Bernie said.

"Brilliant, that is."

"The priest will say we're going to hell," Aileen pointed out.

"What difference will one more sin make?" Oona said. "I'm still mad about the way he spoke to me after my surgery. 'God works in mysterious ways.' Easy for him to say. I closed my eyes and pretended to fall asleep, hands clenched under the blankets, so I wouldn't reach up and slap him."

"What commandment are we breaking exactly?" Moira asked.

"Thou shalt not expose thy underwear?" Kate said.

They laughed, Colleen adding, "If we want to pull ourselves up by our bra straps, what business is it of Father Byrne?"

When Oona got home that night, her father was already upstairs in bed, asleep. (He was an early riser, couldn't stay awake past 9:00 p.m.) The accordion sat on the chair by the back door. She shook her head in exasperation. He'd been playing for the chickens again. She'd told him to stop, that he was frightening the birds, putting them off laying, but he wouldn't listen.

"They like to dance," he said. "Why deny them a little fun? The wrens and the larks and the rooks sit on the line too, coming from miles around to listen."

"Sure," she said, "you'll have a gold record on the avian music charts. Before you know it, they'll be starting a fan club. What will they call you: Fowl Man?"

"I have a gift."

"For driving me crazy," she said, adding, "Don't come crying to me if there aren't any eggs for breakfast."

"Not me who's bothering the hens. It's the Cluricans, isn't it, sneaking in in the middle of the night, stealing the eggs."

"Don't blame it on the leprechauns, Da. They won't take it kindly."

"Know them better than you, don't I? You don't believe in anything anymore, my girl."

Didn't she? Had the years and the cancer changed her, made her cynical and hard?

She'd reinforced the henhouses, because a fox had gotten in the previous week. Perhaps the fox had a taste for accordion music as well as chicken. She took a quick glance to make sure all was well before going inside. Her husband, Padraig, sat by the fire, reading the *Irish Times*. Jars of last year's honey gleamed on the kitchen shelves. This summer, he'd bottle the next batches. "Gaelic gold," he called it. He spent hours among his bees whenever he could, a space-suited figure moving among the white boxes, dispensing smoke like incense from a censer, the bees his choir, buzzing, buzzing. That he could make something so sweet gave her hope and made her sad too. They'd been mad for each other once, before the children, before the tide of years rose between them. She still glimpsed the young man he'd once been in the lope of his walk; he'd always been rangy, loose-limbed, even now, with the arthritis setting in; even now, in the jut of his chin, the wildness of his hair, gone silver; in his voice, so deep she felt it near her breastbone when he spoke to her in the soft tones she loved so well. It was easy to forget these things as life rushed by, forget how much she'd loved him in the beginning, loved him still, if she only paused long enough to think about it, to page through the old anniversary cards she'd kept in the corner desk, years of greeting-card sentiments and the addition of a few personal words that still brought tears to her eyes when she read them, because he was such a reserved man: "You are the most precious thing in the world to me, you are my pearl of the sea."

She didn't halloo like she usually did when she came in the

door. She entered quietly. She wanted him to know something was different. That she was different.

He glanced up, his eyes, his blue eyes, gorgeous still, regarding her over the banner at the top of the paper, the day's headlines trumpeting an oil spill in the North Sea, a march in Belfast, another bombing in the Middle East, battles and strife, but not there, not in that room. Not if she could help it.

The shyness, the fear, would stop her if she let them. She had to be brave, see it through.

"What's the worst thing that could happen?" Colleen had asked her.

Oona hadn't answered, but she thought, That he will close himself off from me, as I've closed myself off from him. That when I reach out, he won't take my hand.

She carried her clothes in a canvas bag, the same one she took to the market, a scattering of dried parsley at the bottom. She'd worn the new bra and knickers home from the lace society meeting under her balmacaan coat. That was all. She shivered, not so much from cold as from anticipation. She'd never done anything like that before, not since she skinny-dipped in the bay on a dare as a girl when she had beauty and youth on her side, when she had her breasts. She hadn't known Padraig then. She met him shortly thereafter, at a dance, when she was sixteen, him staring at her across the room with those blue, blue eyes, everything else receding into the background. He was all she could see, all she wanted.

She'd gotten pregnant on their honeymoon, their first, a girl, now living in Galway with three children of her own. Six babies she and Padraig had, gone now. Padraig had been away fishing much of the time. He didn't go now, but the money was running low and he might have to, like Colleen's husband, Finn, still at sea,

Colleen beside herself with worry. Padraig had almost gone with him. Next time he might, even though they were both too old for such business. Padraig preferred being with his bees. If only more people knew about the honey and the lace, he might not have to consider sailing again.

Oona had spent years of praying to Saint Christopher for his safe return, years watching for the hull of his boat to round the cape and steam toward the shingle beach where she waited, a thermos of coffee and a tin of biscuits clutched in her gloved hands. She didn't want to do that anymore, didn't want to risk losing him.

She could tell from his face that he thought something was wrong, that she'd had word from the doctor the cancer had returned. He'd been with her through it all—the surgery, the chemotherapy, holding her hand, his face set with the same calm, penetrating expression with which he watched the horizon, reading the weather for what would come.

A drop of honey glistened on his lip. He liked to lick the spoon after putting a drop or two in his tea.

She crossed the sitting room where they'd spent so many hours of their lives, with the children, then just the two of them, this room with its accumulation of belongings, the braided rug, brass fire tools, framed pictures on the console where their youngest son, Paul, once cut open his head and had to be taken to hospital, the stacks of history books and novels, spindled tables and lamps, candlesticks dripping with old wax.

"What is it?" he whispered.

She wiped the drop of honey from his lip and sucked on her finger. "This," she said.

She took the paper from him, folded it neatly in two places and set it on the hassock, then opened her coat. "And this."

She stood before him, threads of lace shining, golden as the honey he'd made, the first time she'd undressed for him, let him see her in the light, in so very long.

"Oh, love." He pulled her toward him, pressing his face against her chest. "Love."

Chapter 14

Sullivan Deane

Bernie had been awake since 5:00 a.m., thinking. Kate needed another reason to stay in Glenmara. The lace was a start, a thread tying her to the community, but she could snap it any moment and walk away, up the road down which she'd come. Had it only been days she'd been in the village? It seemed as if Kate had been with them longer, with Bernie longer.

Bernie looked for clues each day as she straightened the guest room—she didn't snoop, no, of course not, that wouldn't have been right, but she looked for hints in the arrangement of things: the rumpled sheets at the foot of the bed (restless sleeper, something on her mind, nightmares? About what?), the markers in the novels (thank goodness she wasn't one of those people who turned down corners; Bernie couldn't abide that)—the girl had gone for Edna O'Brien's latest novel, no great surprise, and the William Trevor collection. Hmm, interesting. As Bernie emptied the wastebin, a crumpled scrap of paper tumbled out, a single letter on the lined page: *E*.

A lover perhaps? Had it gone wrong?

The girl needed someone new, Bernie decided, not necessarily a permanent attachment, but to take her mind off whatever it was, whoever it was, that haunted her from across the sea. Not that there were many candidates in Glenmara. Most of the men were middle-aged and married or elderly and widowed, not for the likes of Kate.

Bernie stared at the ceiling. The light fixture looked like an angel from one angle, a devil from the other, her eyes playing tricks on her. *Hmm.* Sullivan Deane. Sullivan Deane might do. He'd suffered a loss of his own, could use the company too (though he probably found enough in the neighboring villages, he wouldn't have met anyone like Kate). How could she get them together? She'd already had Kate deliver the week's *Gaelic Voice*. She could hardly put out a special edition. Wait. There was something one of the women had said the night before about Sullivan Deane. What was it again? Yes: Sullivan Deane's laptop computer. She'd send Kate to see about it. So much could be accomplished with a little thought. She lay in bed as the sky brightened in the east, the sun rising through a break in the clouds, light spreading into the room. She let it envelop her in the possibilities before turning back the covers and hopping out of bed, one foot into a slipper, then the other, her robe next, a magician putting on her cloak. She'd make scones. The British occupation had its good points, scones being first among them. She loved scones and clotted cream and homemade strawberry jam. That's what she'd serve that morning. And bangers and eggs. Juice too. Orange? Americans liked orange juice; everyone knew that. She lit the stove. What first? A handful of fresh flowers for the vase on the table. The peonies were in bloom, early this year. She walked out into the dew. A squadron of swallows circled her in tight loops. Pure joy, it was, joy. A sign that anything could happen. She was sure of that now.

"I'd do it myself, but I've got to run these down to the printer. I'm behind this week—and I never miss a deadline. So you'll be doing me a favor, you see, asking Sullivan about the computer."

"I'd be happy to help," Kate said. "As you said, the *Gaelic Voice* must be heard."

"Yes!" Bernie waved a proof of the next newsletter for emphasis. The latest crime headlines ran across the top:

Man calls Garda, says neighbor's bull is remodeling his house. Garda asks if he's putting in a new kitchen. No, he says, the bull is taking it down.

Woman calls Garda, says neighbor won't stop gardening in the nude. Garda asks if he's good-looking. No, she says, he has a potbelly and skinny legs. Well, Garda says, the weather's changing and he'll have to put on a raincoat on the morrow. That should improve the view.

Fergus sat by Bernie, whining for a scone. Bernie shook her head. "I'm sorry. You know the vet said they're bad for your health. You have to eat your senior dog food now."

Fergus sighed and shambled over to his bowl, giving her a backward glance filled with reproach.

"He dreams of burgers and scones," she told Kate. "My husband spoiled him something awful." Her gaze settled on his picture on the mantel, a brief yearning in her eyes, before she looked away again. "Take the car if you want," she added. "Can be tricky to start, though."

"The bike's fine. I like the exercise," Kate said. "Where does Sullivan Deane live?"

"Take the west road out of town, then left at the blue farm. It's a stone house. He spent summers there with his grandparents when he was growing up. Holidays too. Been in the family for generations. Only place of any size around here that didn't get taken over by the English. The Deanes were fighters. Always were, always will be."

"He's not going to shoot me, is he?" Kate laughed.

"No, that was long ago." Bernie winked. "You'll be safe enough."

When Kate arrived at the house, she was almost relieved there wasn't a car in the drive, no answer when she knocked on the door. She'd sensed a setup in Bernie's proposal. The last thing she needed was a romantic entanglement. She peered in the front window, saw a fiddle, an upright piano, an unlit fireplace. In a detached outbuilding, she glimpsed lines of pots, dripping with glaze the colors of the surrounding landscape—blues and lavenders, grays and pearls, greens and umbers—he must have made the bowl she liked at Bernie's cottage. And in the corner, a sculpture: the curve of a woman's torso and breast. Kate had never seen anything so beautiful.

"You're not a burglar, are you?" Niall Maloney cycled up behind her.

She hadn't heard him coming. His chain was well oiled, and he'd ridden straight over the turf, the wheel leaving a thin trail in the grass. She pressed a hand to her chest. "You shouldn't sneak up on people like that."

"My daughter lives up the road—though it seems I'm not the only one doing the sneaking," he teased. The straw basket mounted on the handlebars held a bag of meat pies, the grease seeping into the paper, the smell of warm, fresh-baked pastry and beef making her hungry again. Sometimes her mother had made pasties when Kate was growing up, using her Butte Irish grandmother's recipe.

"Here," Niall said, insisting when she shook her head. "Have one." He handed her a small turnover, more of an appetizer, really.

She took a bite, somewhat disappointed. Lu's pies had been bigger, made the way her grandmother made them, crammed with potatoes—potatoes being all her ancestors could afford; the meat came later, when they were done with the mines and secured jobs aboveground at the power company, her grandfather working his way up from the mailroom, her mother the first to go to college, the mines still and silent now.

A wind came up off the sea, bent the grass and lupines to earth, let them go—on and on it went, the pressure, the release.

"What are you doing here?" Niall asked. "After some pottery for a souvenir?"

"I'm looking for Sullivan Deane."

"The girls are always looking for Sullivan." His eyes sparkled. "Lucky man."

"It's not like that—"

"It isn't? And here I was hoping for a bit of gossip."

"Sorry to disappoint you, but Bernie asked me to find him," she explained with a good-natured smile. "She said he has a computer."

"What's she need that for?"

"A project for the lace society."

"Entering the modern age, is she?"

"Something like that."

"My grandson knows computers. Works for a software company in Dublin. I don't understand a thing he says when he starts going on and on about cyberspace. Might as well be speaking Greek. But he's made a go of it. Took me for a ride in his fancy car last time he visited. Christmas it was. The young ones don't come home often enough—which makes your being here even more of a novelty," he said, adding, "How do you like our little village?"

"It's a lovely place."

"It is, isn't it? I've lived here my whole life. Wouldn't want to be anywhere else. It's important to have a place to call home. A place where people know you." He scratched his chin. A scruff of silvery beard had started to grow. "You're from Seattle, aren't you? Were your people Irish?"

"Some of them."

"No wonder you seem so at home here."

"It's hard not to be. Everyone has been so welcoming." Well, almost everyone; she thought of Aileen and Father Byrne. "Do you know where Sullivan is?"

"I think he went to the market in Kinnabegs. It's his day to sell the pottery."

"Is it far?"

"It's a thirty-minute cycle from here. One of the towns scattered along the coast, bigger than ours, gets more tourists, though not much," he said. "Some of the best scenery in the area."

She thanked him and set off again. Even if she didn't find Sullivan Deane, she'd see more of the countryside. She supposed the place looked much as it had for centuries, an occasional standing stone breaking the low rolling hills, monuments to forgotten gods, a horse among the buttercupped fields, whinnying for a handout as she went by. She hummed to herself, her voice blending with the wind, the spinning of the wheels, and headed for the sea.

Kate skirted the bay with its flotilla of boats, painted green and blue and red, some advertising trips to the convent ruins offshore. A man sang in Gaelic as he mended his nets, a cap over his frizzled hair, his skin the texture of dried fruit. Another sold cockles by the bucket. Market stalls crowded the square beyond, where vendors displayed teas, preserves, and the usual linens—though none as fine as the lace society's work. Kate searched for Sullivan Deane's awning. Yes, there it was, by a stand selling local cheeses flavored with chives, rosemary, and pepper. He wasn't at the table, only a blond, curvaceous girl—Kate had never seen anyone with such a small waist—who seemed to attract more attention than the goods themselves.

"You looking for Sullivan?" she asked Kate with an assessing look that suggested she knew him well. "You've just missed him. He went to the pub. He sometimes stops there before going home." A slyness in her smile hinted Kate wasn't the first woman to seek him.

"I'm not—," Kate began to explain, then thought better of it. What did it matter if the whole countryside thought she was chasing after Sullivan Deane? That wasn't her purpose.

As she turned away, she glimpsed a van parked behind the stand—the same van that had nearly run her off the road days before. The van driven by the man from the cliffs. Wouldn't that just figure? He must be Sullivan Deane. She had mixed feelings about encountering him again, equal amounts anticipation and annoyance. But all she had to do was use his computer. How difficult could that be?

She rattled down the cobbled lane in the direction the girl indicated and parked the bike outside a pub called the Hungry Gull. Someone had had the foresight to print the name in English for the benefit of the tourists. She smoothed her hair before going inside. There were five patrons in the bar at that hour. The one nearest the door looked up as she walked in.

It was him. He wore black leather sneakers, jeans, and a fisherman's sweater, a vaguely bohemian look that managed to be both put together and unstudied; his hair somewhat shaggy, a scruff on five-o'clock shadow on his chin. "Down off the mountain, are you?" he asked.

She'd half expected to see him, and yet she found herself having to catch her breath before speaking, and not because she'd been pedaling uphill. "So it would seem," she said, adding, in reference to his nearly running her down in the lane a few days before, "though the hazards of the road are just as dangerous."

He leaned back in his chair and grinned. "Scared you, did I?"

"I'd describe the experience differently."

"As?"

"As: You nearly killed me."

"The roads seem narrower than they are. There was plenty of room for both of us." He shrugged.

"They do, do they? Easy for you to say from the comfort of a driver's seat."

"Looking for someone?" he asked.

"Yes, as a matter of fact, I am. Do you happen to know Sullivan Deane?" she asked with a knowing smirk.

"You're looking at him. What can I do for you?"

"I need to borrow your lap—," she began, stumbling over the words. He had such a brilliant smile—and that dimple next to his mouth—

"My lap? That sounds interesting."

"No, your top—" She was completely flustered now.

"Do I get to wear yours?" he asked.

Why wouldn't he let her complete a sentence? She was perfectly capable of expressing herself eloquently. "What I was trying to say was—" She broke off again, expecting another quip.

"Yes?" He tried not to laugh.

"That I need to borrow your computer."

"And here you got me all excited," he said. "You American girls are rather fresh."

"I wouldn't have bothered you, but Bernie sent me. She said you had the only computer in Glenmara."

"No hookup, though. Good you caught me here. Fine thing, their setting up Wi-Fi." He offered her his chair, brushing her arm as he passed. She barely reached his shoulder. "For the tourists. Like you."

"I'm not a tourist. I'm a traveler. There's a difference." She felt the warm spot he'd left behind when she sat down. She scooted to the edge of the seat and uploaded the pictures from her camera.

"Here, a traveler means a gypsy," he said, "though you don't look much like a gypsy to me."

She could have been. She could have stayed with William, traveled the coast. "I'm on a trip, that's all."

"And what's your destination? Surely not Glenmara?"

"Why not?"

"It's not exactly a metropolis."

"I've had enough of cities for a while. It seems you have too."

"Yes." He didn't say anything more.

She suspected his reticence might have something to do with the tragedy the lace makers had alluded to, but didn't press.

"Do you have a name?" he asked, changing the subject. "Or are you like one of those characters in an existential novel?"

"It's Kate."

"As in *The Taming of the Shrew*?"

"As in Katharine Hepburn."

"You're not sending pornography, are you?" He leaned over her shoulder. "I could get in trouble for that."

"It's a business proposition."

"I'm sure it is."

"A new line for the lace society."

"I see. Stirring things up, are you?"

"Just trying to help. Would you mind?" She couldn't work with him standing over her like that.

"Sorry. Didn't mean to distract you." He went to talk to the barman, glancing in her direction occasionally. She looked away whenever their eyes met, stole another peek when his back was turned.

She tried to focus on the task at hand. After all, she had things to do. She sent pictures of the lingerie to the various tourist boards. She thought about sending some to Ella, who'd wanted another update. "You have to let me know how you're doing. Promise me that, Kate, or I swear to God I'm not letting you get on that plane in the first place," she'd said as she saw Kate off at Sea-Tac Airport. But then she decided against it. Better to wait until she was sure where this was going first.

She logged into her Hotmail account. Not much in her in-box but advertisements offering to enlarge her nonexistent penis and, of course, another message from Ella: "It's been raining here for days. We might as well be in Ireland!" Kate's pulse quickened, as it always did when she checked the column of new mail lately, anticipating a message from Ethan that never came. She'd gone over the scenario in her mind, considering whether she'd want to hear from him—they'd broken up and reconciled before. Or did she just need to have the last word, to be the one to reject him, once and for all? If he did try to make contact, it would be by instant message, she supposed, sent on the impulse, the cursor flashing. That would be what he was reduced to—a miniature blinking rectangle, a door too small for her to walk through.

"Kate?"

"What?" She looked up. Sullivan had been saying her name. She quickly closed the screen, hands shaking.

"Is everything okay?"

"Fine," she lied.

He raised an eyebrow but didn't pursue the matter. "At least let me buy you an ale," he said. "I owe you one after teasing you so mercilessly."

"You don't owe me anything, and besides, to be honest, I don't like ale very much."

"Are you sure you're Irish?" He slid a glass across the table. "Why don't you give it another try? Maybe you'll change your mind. Besides, I could use the company, and I'm guessing you could too."

How soon did she know she was going to sleep with him? Maybe from the beginning. She hadn't meant to that day, but he was irresistible, presented her with the possibility of forgetfulness in another's touch. He took the bicycle by the handlebars, intending to give her a ride to Bernie's house in his van.

"I can manage, really." She took hold of the seat. She wasn't exactly drunk but had had enough—one glass was all it took, she had so little tolerance—to make the prospect of riding to Glenmara challenging if not impossible . . . and that of being with him more appealing.

"Are you kidding?" He laughed. "You can't walk a straight line, much less cycle one."

They engaged in a playful tug-of-war over the bicycle and the direction they were taking. She let him win.

He stood on the running board and lifted the bike up with one easy movement, fastening it into the rack atop the van, which also had slots for kayaks and surfboards. "There," he said. "All set."

The van smelled of clay and paint, the air moist and close. She felt the springs through the seats, but they didn't bother her. Nothing bothered her. She was warm and relaxed. She hadn't felt this way in weeks, maybe ever. He turned on the radio, hummed along to a song by the Frames. Kate hadn't heard that particular tune before. A melody that would play in her head over and over in the next few days, reminding her of him, of that night.

He rolled down the windows, the wind in their hair as they sped along the lane. He drove with both hands on the wheel. She wondered if he'd always done that, or if an event in his past had made him more careful.

She touched him first, needing something from him, a temporary oblivion; perhaps that was what made her put a hand on his thigh. He might have asked her if she was sure, stopping the car along a deserted road. She didn't remember if she replied or if she just let her lips meet his in answer. At first she was aware of the boxes of fragile vessels around them, the vases and bowls and plates he'd made, the few that remained unsold that day, the gannets shrieking in triumph as they dove for fish in the sea below, the wind buffeting the car, another change coming. Fair weather could only last so long. But at that moment, there was only him, with his breath on her cheek, his hand on her breast, his brown, brown eyes. Him.

Chapter 15

Held So Close

Kate kissed Sullivan again, unable to pull away, neither of them willing to say good night. His lips were perfect, neither too full nor too thin, softer than she'd expected. A light mist fell from a band of clouds overhead, stopping and starting, dripping from the blackthorn trees in a rhythmic patter. Kate didn't mind the cold or the wet. She didn't feel anything but Sullivan's arms around her. The shower would pass within moments—there, it already had, the clouds moving off to rain in another place—the memory of the squall contained in the puddles that reflected shadows and stars, Kate and Sullivan too, standing there in the lane below Bernie's cottage.

"I'll be away for a day or so, selling, upcoast, but there's a *craic* on Friday," he said, still holding her close as they lingered by the van, which he'd parked just outside Bernie's gate, the bicycle resting against the wall. "You'll be there, won't you? Say yes."

"Well—"

"There will be dancing." He rocked her gently, side to side. "A girl like you must love to dance."

"A girl like me?"

"With such fine, strong legs."

"Now who's being fresh?"

"We're past that now, aren't we?"

Yes, she supposed they were. She'd only been with him a few hours, and yet it seemed longer in the best way. It must have been past midnight by then. A crescent of moon shone down on them, ribbons of cloud trailing across the sky, and the breeze stirring the trees and carrying the scent of primrose and lily of the valley.

"Come home with me," he said.

"I can't," she replied, though she wanted to. "Not tonight." She took a step toward the house, as she knew she must, because Bernie was waiting, because a part of her sensed that this was too much too soon, that she needed to slow things down. They had days ahead of them, didn't they? Days and days to get to know one another better. She wasn't going anywhere anytime soon. She liked Glenmara. She could stay for a while, learn about the lace, about him.

"Please." He held onto her hand.

"I have to go." She laughed. The light was on in Bernie's front room. Her hostess was still awake.

He gave her hand a squeeze before releasing her at last. "Friday, then. Don't forget."

When Kate opened the door, Fergus woofed a greeting as she hung her coat on the peg in the hall and went into the sitting room. Bernie looked up from her chair by the fire, reading glasses perched on the end of her nose, a book open on her lap. The turf glowed in the hearth, burning low.

"I'm sorry I'm late," Kate said. "I should have called. I didn't mean to keep you up—"

"Not at all," Bernie said. "I'm glad you were having fun. With Sullivan, were you?"

"I don't know where the time went."

"It passes quickly, doesn't it, when you're with the right person." Bernie gestured to a teapot on the side table. "I was getting ready to have a bit of warm almond milk. Helps me sleep better. Would you like some?"

Kate took the cup Bernie offered. She tucked her hair behind her ears and blew on the milk to cool it, realizing, with a twinge of embarrassment, that she had a smudge of clay from the van on her cheek. She quickly wiped it away, hoping Bernie hadn't noticed. "He asked me if I was going to the *craic* Friday night," she said.

"Oh, yes, you must. We'll all be there for the music and dancing. Sullivan is part of the band. He learned to fiddle from his grandfather during the summers he spent in Glenmara. He's a fine musician," Bernie said, adding, "A fine man too. They're getting harder to find these days."

"Yes, they are," Kate agreed.

"John was one of them," Bernie said, her voice softer. "I remember the day I saw him for the first time, across a field not far from here. The cowslips were in bloom. He'd moved to the area to take a teaching position at the school in Kinnabegs. He was out walking that evening—he loved to walk.

"I'd been seeing a young man I'd met at one of the dances near Tarryton," she continued. "Thought I was serious about him, but then I saw John and everything stopped. I wouldn't call it love at first sight. No, more like a sense of recognition that passed between us, as if we'd been looking for each other, but we didn't know it until that moment."

"The first time I saw Sullivan, I was clinging to a rock wall." Kate laughed.

"You saw him that day you went out walking?" Bernie's eyes brightened with interest.

"I did—and I certainly caught my breath—whether from the sight of him or the fear of falling, it's hard to say."

"You never said anything—"

Kate shrugged. "The lace meeting was in progress when I came in. I got so caught up learning the stitches and talking with everyone that I must have forgotten to mention it. And besides, I thought I'd never see him again."

"And yet you did."

"Yes, I did." She shook her head.

"What is it?"

"I was just thinking how funny life is. Seems like the more you want something, the more it eludes you. Then, when you least expect it, there it is."

"One of life's lessons, isn't it? At least, I've found it to be true," Bernie replied, adding, "Sounds as if you like our Sullivan Deane."

She gave Bernie a conspiratorial little smile. "I like him very much indeed."

Later, after Kate went upstairs, Bernie brushed her hair, gazing out the bedroom window, the moon's eyes covered with a strip of muslin cloud. Was it playing blind man's bluff or a part in a masquerade? She smiled to herself. She'd always had an active imagination. Things looked different at night. The eye could play tricks, turning hawthorn trees into giants, currant bushes into trolls, thistles into faeries. Oh, the frights she'd given herself as a child.

She'd draped the lace lingerie over the back of the chair, threads gleaming in the half-light. Such a lovely rose pattern it was. Somehow, Kate had known it was the perfect one for her. The girl certainly had insight. Bernie was surprised she hadn't been more successful with fashion design in the States, but destiny had a number of tricks up her sleeve, didn't she, both joyful and tragic? Perhaps Kate's coming to Glenmara was such a gift. It was as if she belonged there. Bernie hoped she felt that way too.

She fingered the lace. Sumptuous blooms, they were, the petals full, beckoning, in shades of pink and red, a tracery of green, here and there, for the leaves. The flowers nearly covered the entire set, except for the band and straps and elastic. Perhaps she'd make a nightgown with the same pattern too, worked along the yoke, smocking at the waist. She'd fill the drawer with beautiful things by the time she was done.

If only John were there to see.

A bank of mist moved in from the sea, spilling into the valley, one tendril touching the edge of the garden. She felt the coolness of it but didn't close the window. She kept it open, a small slip of an opening, near the sill. She wanted to feel the air on her cheek, the nearness of him, her husband, who had fallen on that patch of earth, just there, past the back gate. Fergus had run back to the house to get her that evening, and she'd known right away something was wrong, though not how bad it would be: John, prone on the ground, his cap and glasses askew, the bouquet of wildflowers—lupine, daisies, a spray of ferns—he'd intended to give her scattered on the grass. She'd said his name, over and over, as if he was only asleep, and she had only to wake him. *John, John.* Put her head to his chest, his lips, listening for his heart, his breath, but he was still. She'd never known he could be that still.

Later that night, Bernie lay in bed, staring at the ceiling. She missed him. She felt as if she were a puzzle, an essential piece lost, leaving her incomplete. It was worse at this time of night, when there were no distractions and her mind spun with endless thoughts—of not having enough money to live on, of being alone. She took deep breaths to calm herself, but the tears came anyway. Not a torrent, just a few, sliding down her cheeks and wetting the pillow.

A gust billowed the curtains. Fergus, who had been snoring at the foot of the bed, raised his head and whimpered, gazing toward the window.

"What is it, boy?" she whispered. Did he smell a fox or rabbit in the garden? They'd never had prowlers, though she'd taken the precaution of locking the doors before going to bed just in case, now that she was a woman living alone, heeding Aileen's advice.

Or was it only the wind? "Is someone there?" she called.

No reply. Not that a burglar would announce himself, would he? *Hello, don't mind me. I'm just here to steal the silver.*

Silence. No one there but her.

Another gust. Perhaps a front was moving in. They'd had some fierce storms that spring. Whatever the source, she'd had enough. She got up to close the sash, shivering. Heavens, why was it so cold?—too cold for this time of year. Strange. She could see her breath in the room. She'd have to pile more blankets on the bed. She headed for the closet to get another quilt, muttering to herself—

And then she felt him behind her.

John?

She couldn't see him. She didn't have to. He was in the center of the room. Fergus sensed it too, wagging his tail, before he trotted out into the hall, as if he'd received a command from his master, the one John used to give when he and Bernie wanted to be alone.

"Do you want to see the lace?" She didn't ask him why he hadn't appeared to her before, glad to have him there again at last, if only for a moment. She knew it couldn't be long.

She put the lace on for him, slowly, there in the pool of moonlight. "Stay with me for just a little while, will you?" She lay down on the bed, felt him holding her, until she drifted off into the realm of dreams.

Chapter 16

Craic

The pub was packed with people two nights later, babies crying, children laughing and complaining, lifting their cups in honor of Saint Brendan, cheeks reddening, words slurring as the evening wore on.

Here's to Saint Blenna.

Here's to Saint Blender.

Here's to Saint Brenda.

What, did he have a sex change?

Didn't have those back then.

If God could change loaves into fishes, he could certainly—

Once called the Lion's Head, the bar had been in the Greene family for generations. Decades before, the painter hired to make a new sign botched the job, having sampled too much ale before taking up the brush, the result being that the bar's namesake looked more like a rabid canine than a regal ruler of the animal kingdom. Despite his initial dismay, the head of the Greene family at that time embraced the error, rechristening the pub the Mad Dog—and so it had been ever since.

The place was all wood and tarnished brass, its patrons inclined toward camaraderie or scheming, depending upon which corner they occupied. Plaques and pictures covered the walls, including shots of winners of the annual fishing derby (Colleen's and Oona's husbands had won several), the coracle races, a yellowed *Irish Times* article about Gaelic villages with a brief mention of Glenmara highlighted, and another about Shamrock Fields, a portion of the ever-enterprising-but-ultimately-unsuccessful Declan Moore's holdings, once hyped as a tourist attraction for the excess of four-leaf clovers allegedly found among the grass—until the cows ate them one spring. "That's my retirement, you stupid cow!" he cried. His wife was mad at him for a week. She thought he was talking about her. All that was left now were a few framed, pressed shamrocks scattered about town, in the bar, and above the mantel in Declan's house, botanical samples brittle with age, their value purely sentimental, though some people claimed they brought them luck.

The peanut shells and beer spills of the previous day's dart tournament had been cleared away. The *craic* was one of the highlights of the Saint Brendan's Festival, and Richie Greene, the bar owner, took special pride in his establishment. Kate sat with Bernie and Aileen at a table near the door. Sullivan Deane smiled from across the room, where he was with the band, playing a tune. Oona was nearby with her husband, Padraig; Colleen had stayed home, waiting for Finn's boat to come in.

Mrs. Flynn, Father Byrne's housekeeper, wore her leopard-print jacket for the occasion. She stopped by the table on her way to join Oona, who she'd known since grade school. "Have you heard?" she said. "The priest has been asking questions."

"What's he on about this time? Is it the tithing again?" Bernie asked. "I think I'm up to date."

"No. It's the lace. He hasn't spoken to me about it directly, but I have a feeling he's going to."

"Does he want a pair of knickers?" Kate asked in mock innocence.

Mrs. Flynn chuckled. "That would be a sight to see, wouldn't it? No, he's up to something. Got that light in his eyes, he does. Don't know exactly what it means, but I thought you'd want to know," she said, adding, "He's not a bad man. Just rather limited."

"He can't help himself. He's a man of the cloth, steeped in the old ways," Bernie said. "He came by to check on us the other night."

"Yes, he mentioned it, but I had the sense he wasn't completely satisfied with what he saw, that he'd be keeping watch."

"He's always keeping watch," Bernie replied.

"Perhaps he should have been a spy," Kate said.

"Agent double-oh seven, eh?" Mrs. Flynn laughed. "But then he'd have all the women—wouldn't that get him into trouble—"

"You shouldn't poke fun at him. He's our priest," Aileen said.

"True enough," Bernie agreed, "though why is the lace any concern of his? We're not harming anyone, are we? Some might say we're sewing by the grace of God."

"Oh, you'd get his cassock in a bunch if he heard that!" Mrs. Flynn said.

"He's not here, is he?" Bernie cast a look around the bar.

"Lord, no. Doesn't touch a drop of the drink. Hard enough for him to sip from the communion cup—and only because it's the blood of Christ. Maybe his da was a drinker. Who knows? He never talks about his past." She patted Bernie's shoulder before moving away. "I'll let you know if I hear anything."

"Hey, ladies." Moira's voice rang with false cheer, alerting them to Cillian's presence right behind her.

"Moi, I'm glad you made it." Aileen hailed her. "Sit here."

Cillian gave the women a curt nod, a hand firmly on Moira's elbow, and whispered something in her ear.

"Thanks, Ailey, but there's no room," Moira replied, barely pausing before Cillian steered her away. "I'll catch up with you later . . ."

"No room indeed," Aileen muttered after they settled at a table on the opposite side of the pub, "at least not for the likes of Cillian."

"There weren't enough seats, Ailey," Bernie pointed out. "She no doubt thought it was easier—"

"We could have pulled up another chair, could have squeezed in," Aileen insisted. "We've done it before."

"But would you really want to sit at the same table as him? Remember what happened last time? Moira was probably trying to avoid another scene."

Aileen pressed her lips together and didn't say more, studying the various messages others had written on the table in pen, hinting at varying levels of maturity and inebriation: *Piss off. The fighting Gaels rule. Rosheen's a good shag.* "Look at that. The shame of it." Aileen licked her finger and smeared it away. "Probably that lout Ronnie wrote it. He doesn't even have a good Gaelic name. Ronald. He sounds like an accountant, when the only numbers he cares about relate to drugs."

"Are you sure? I mean—" Kate ventured.

"Yes, dearie, we have addicts here too. It's not all green fields and bright smiles in Ireland," she retorted.

"I'm aware of that. I had my pack stolen by one in Dublin—"

"Not Rosheen, though," Aileen continued as if Kate hadn't spoken. "I'd know if she were into drugs. It's bad enough she runs with that crowd. I keep telling her she's going to get hurt."

"So she's still seeing Ronnie, then?" Bernie asked, biting into a chip. "I thought you'd forbidden it."

"I have to be careful what I say. I don't have proof of his wrongdoing, and I definitely don't want to do anything to make the prospect of him more appealing to her than it already is. She has a bad-boy complex." Aileen picked at her nails. She'd been at it with a vengeance from the look of them.

"Has she called yet?" Bernie asked.

"Maybe there's a message at home. I'm trying not to think about it. I've already lost too much sleep over that girl. She's of age; she can do what she likes."

"Do you really think so? My mother always said—," Kate began.

"What does your mother have to do with my Rosheen, with me? Is she here with us now?"

"No." Kate toyed with the thimble around her neck.

"Do I really think that?" Aileen continued. "Of course not, but that's what I tell myself, so I don't go mad. You wouldn't know. You don't have kids."

Kate didn't reply, crossing her arms over her chest and glaring at Aileen.

"Last time I checked, one didn't have to have children to have a conversation," Bernie said.

"Depends upon what comments one makes." Aileen's face

tightened, clearly annoyed that Bernie seemed to be taking sides.

"Guess I'd better watch what I say too," Bernie said. "Childless women, take heed."

"I didn't mean you—"

"I think we should make our guest feel welcome. Ireland is supposed to be the land of smiles," Bernie said.

"Only on the face of things," Aileen said.

"What?"

"Oh, never mind. Let's have another round of Guinness," she said with forced cheer. "It's getting hot in here. Or is it just the flashes?"

"Flashes of what? Brilliance?" Bernie was eager to bring some much-needed humor into the proceedings.

"I wish."

"Isn't that Sullivan Deane over there with Declan's band? Haven't seen him out in awhile." Bernie made another effort to steer them to a lighter topic.

"Well, it is a special occasion," Aileen said. "No one misses the Saint Brendan's *craic*."

"Or maybe he thought a certain person would be here." Bernie nudged Kate.

"Gotten to know him, have you?" Aileen raised an eyebrow.

Kate tried to shrug it off. "He has a computer, remember? Bernie asked me to talk to him about it. For the lace."

"That and more, from what I hear."

Kate tapped her foot under the table. What the hell was Aileen's problem?

Richie, the barman, pounded the countertop, sparing them a confrontation. "Time for the dancing!"

"What's going on?" Kate asked.

"It's the step-dancing competition," Bernie replied. "Been big here long before that Riverdance business in the States. You know it?"

"I took lessons when I was a little girl."

"That's grand. You'll have to enter, then. Oona, did you hear?" she called over to the next table. "She dances!"

"Get her up there!"

Kate was tempted to slip out the door. It was close at hand, the knob gleaming. *This way.* But Bernie was too quick for her. She didn't understand that the last place Kate wanted to be was on a stage in front of everyone. "I haven't danced competitively in years," Kate demurred. "I don't remember the steps . . ." Which wasn't entirely true. She'd danced that March, but it was on the spur of the moment—and things were different then.

"They'll come back to you," Bernie said. "Once you know them, they're a part of you, that's what my gran used to say."

"Are you dancing?" Kate asked.

"Me? Heavens no," Bernie said. "I've got a bad knee. Threw it out last year and learned my lesson. Aileen's the only one of us who does anymore."

"Aileen?" she echoed.

Aileen smiled, eyes glinting, letting Kate know she was looking forward to this. "Nothing like a little friendly competition, eh?"

"Besides, you're young, Kate," Bernie continued. "There's nothing holding you back."

"No, really—"

Bernie didn't listen. She went ahead and wrote Kate's name on the list. Kate was about to erase it, but Bernie passed the sheet forward to the caller, and then the band struck up another tune, and it was too late. The dancing had begun. Everyone began singing at the top of their lungs. Kate didn't know the song, but she managed to join in the chorus. The first groups of dancers stomped on the bar as the band played, Sullivan Deane bowing a fiddle. Her breath caught, his eyes pulling her in, as if there was no space between them.

"Kate," Bernie said a short time later. "Kate, they're calling your name. It's your turn to dance."

"Oh, I—"

Everyone was pounding on the tables. There was no way she could get out of it. She felt a rush of adrenaline, equal parts fear and excitement. The last time she'd danced was at Kell's, an Irish pub in Seattle, during the Saint Patrick's Day celebrations. Ethan had dared her. She'd had too much to drink, said yes, she'd dance, for him, for her mother's memory. People clapped in time with her feet. "That's my girlfriend," Ethan shouted. "Isn't she incredible?"

She guessed not incredible enough. What did The Model do? Burlesque? She wouldn't put it past her.

That night at the Mad Dog in Glenmara, the dancers went in pairs. Four women and men had already gone, their scores written on the board above the bar. One man had been disqualified for falling. (His friends caught him, though one sprained his finger in the process.)

"And in this corner, we have Aileen Flanagan, the local favorite, defending her title," Richie said as if he were announcing the contenders in a boxing match. "How many years in a row has it been? I've lost track."

Aileen laughed. "So have I, or I'm trying to!" She could be charming when she wanted to be.

Kate headed for the bar. Her legs shook. Nerves. Sullivan

Deane caught her by the elbow and helped her up. He gave her a smile of encouragement before joining the band once again. "Good luck."

Kate had a feeling she'd need it.

Aileen gave Kate a superior smile, as if she knew what it took to win—and she'd no doubt stood on that very spot many times before. She unleashed a flurry of steps right away, hardly waiting for the starting bell. Kate stood there, frozen, until Bernie called her name, and the spell—it had only been a matter of seconds, but felt longer—was broken and her legs released from momentary paralysis, her mind from the fear of taking the first step.

"Your feet know the way," her mother had said when she'd nearly panicked before a *feis* years before. "Let them guide you."

Kate matched Aileen step for step in two-four time, dancing the "Downfall of Paris," one of the old jigs she probably thought Kate wouldn't know, but Kate's teacher had been from Ireland. She knew them all.

"Draw!" Richie called.

They danced again. And again. And again. "The Planxy Drury," "The Blackthorn Stick" in six-eight time, "Yougal Harbour" in four-four. Kate couldn't feel her legs anymore. They moved with a will of their own, like those of the girl in *The Red Shoes*.

Neither woman would stop dancing, constantly challenging the other with flourishes. No one could say exactly how long the duel lasted. What a spectacle it was: their legs flashing, heels stomping. The bar would bear the marks of that night for years to come. The cheering rose and fell in waves.

Kate remembered her mother applauding at the first *feis* she won, how she put the trophy on the mantel where everyone could see. The cup shone there on the day of her mother's going-away party. Lu had worn wings, like an angel, white and feathered. She wouldn't want to miss a party in her honor. "I want to celebrate with you while I'm alive, not after I'm dead," she said. And they'd danced long into the night—everyone from the theater, the college, the co-op, her book group—dancing her to heaven. Lu was too weak to join in, but she sat in the red velvet chair by the fire, clapping her hands, flames in her eyes.

Kate found the cup, later, still shining—her mother must have polished it before she went into the hospital for the last time. It almost felt as if Lu were with her, in that lone Irish village, cheering with the crowd, willing her to win, holding that gleaming cup aloft, a reminder of what she could achieve.

Aileen felt victory slipping away. She'd thought about scratching. Despite her bravado, her hips weren't what they used to be. Nothing was what it used to be. And yet when she saw that the girl planned to take the stage, she knew she couldn't back down. The prize had always gone to a Gaelic speaker. To her several years running. It would again.

"That's a girl!" Richie cheered. She'd dated him in school before the business with Rourke—who wasn't there that night, because he had to work. He worked hard, did his duty, supporting the family, supporting her. Richie never married. He still had his freedom. He asked her to meet him once, not directly but in a roundabout way, or at least that was what she thought, and she'd almost gone to him, last year, but she'd sat in the chair by the fire and watched the minutes tick by, the opportunity slipping away. They'd never talked about it. They'd let it go. And it was all right, because she'd made her life with Rourke, loved Rourke, yes, though it frightened her, the thought of the children going and the two of them alone together for the first time in years, ever, really, because the first baby had come so soon, as they often did.

She had a stitch in her side. Her knee ached. She'd never experienced such pain, thought her leg might give out entirely, but her determination had always seen her through. It would again. She heard her gran's voice in her head, counting the steps. Hours and hours she'd practiced to be the best. And she was. For years. No one could touch her. She felt the music in her bones. The cheering, the stamping, the clapping. Oh, the energy of that room. It filled her, as it always had.

And then it stopped. Just like that. Her ankle collapsed. She tumbled into the crowd, and as she fell, it seemed as if she were watching someone else. That couldn't be her.

But it was.

She cried out, more from the pain of losing—of losing to *her*— than the twist itself. The villagers passed her to the corner by the door as if she were a sack of flour, their eyes on Kate, hailing her triumph. You would have thought the girl had won the World Cup, for all the commotion. Bernie, her best friend, part of it too. She barely stopped to ask Aileen if she were all right before pressing forward with the throng. Aileen plugged her ears. They were ringing, the decibel level deafening. Brilliant. She'd suffer hearing loss along with everything else. Her knee and ankle throbbed, her body felt bruised. Her joints couldn't take it anymore. Youth was defeating her at every turn, first Rosheen, now this.

Where was Rosheen, anyway? She'd attended the *craic* every year before. Had even danced herself. She was talented. She could have beaten the girl if she'd been there. If she'd—

But things had changed, hadn't they?

Still, Aileen had hoped that her daughter would walk through that door, take the first step toward reconciliation. Aileen was there alone, no family to support her. She hadn't asked them to. She didn't let them know how important it was to her. She hadn't realized it was, until then.

"Let's see the ankle." Bernie had procured a bucket of ice from the bar.

Aileen stuck her leg up on a chair. "It hurts."

"Doesn't look too bad. You'll live to dance another day."

"Not if she has anything to do with it. She did that on purpose. A dirty move, it was." She shot a poisonous glance in Kate's direction, but Kate was surrounded by admirers and wasn't paying attention.

"What are you talking about?"

"That flip kick. It knocked me off balance."

"Ailey, she wasn't anywhere near you. You lost your balance because you turned to look. You never turn to look, remember? You concentrate on your own dance. That's one of the first things we learned in class. Why do you keep comparing yourself to Kate?"

"It was a competition, wasn't it? A competition I've won every year up to now," she said. "And there you were, suggesting she put her name on the list when you knew how important it was to me."

"I wanted her to feel like part of the community," Bernie said. "She's a lost soul. Can't you see that? She doesn't have anyone but us."

"Looks like she's got plenty now, including my prize and my friends." Aileen gestured toward the bar.

"You're not being a very good sport."

"Why should I be? Do you know what I've been through lately? Oh, wait. Maybe you don't, since you haven't paid any attention to what I've been saying over the past few days. If you had, you'd have realized that this was the last thing I needed," she said. "The very last thing."

Bernie paused for a moment. "If it makes any difference, I didn't realize what a talented dancer she is."

"You don't realize a lot of things."

"That's enough, Ailey," she warned. "Your temper's getting the best of you."

"You've been taking her side ever since she got here. You're my oldest friend, and you don't give a damn about me anymore."

"Yes, you're my oldest friend, Ailey, and you always will be, but you're forgetting that there's plenty of room in our lives for other people. Just because I've welcomed Kate into my life doesn't mean I'm shutting you out."

Aileen stared at the wall. She couldn't look at Bernie. If she did, she was afraid she'd cry. She heard Bernie sigh and join the others. Aileen could have followed. She could have walked on the ankle. It was no more than a bruise, really. It would heal. What kept her from the rest of them was another kind of hurt. She watched as they placed the crown—gold paper, easily torn, but still—on the girl's head.

This was her village, her dance. Why had Kate taken everything away so easily? It wasn't fair.

What does fairness have to do with anything? Her mother's voice. Words from her youth, when she came to understand, quite literally, the black places in which a woman could find herself.

When the commotion died down, Sullivan Deane escorted Kate to her seat—or rather the seat next to him. Bernie grinned from across the room, as if that was what she had in mind all along. The other musicians went to the front of the bar to play a ballad.

Sullivan stayed with Kate, his fiddle resting on the table, two strings sprung.

Kate's face felt flushed from dancing, and the victory too. She'd gotten the best of Aileen, if only for the moment. "You play hard," she said to Sullivan.

"I do."

"*Player* means something different in the States," she told him with a knowing smile.

"Does it?"

"It means someone who strings along several women."

"And which meaning do you ascribe to me?"

"I haven't decided yet."

"Maybe in time, I'll help you reach a favorable conclusion," he said, adding, "I didn't know you could dance like that."

"There's a lot you don't know about me." She smelled the wool of his sweater, the sea in his hair.

"Ah, she has an air of mystery this evening."

"The same could be said for you." She tapped her foot beneath the table, adrenaline still flowing—or maybe it was the nearness of him—wondering if they'd leave together again that night. No, not wondering, knowing. Knowing what she wanted.

"Could it?" He looked away, lifting his hand to greet a friend across the room as if to cover his sudden unease, but she noticed it just the same, touched his arm. He met her gaze then, his eyes the same warm brown as ever, making her wonder if she'd imagined it. "Is that why you're studying me so carefully?" he asked.

"Just looking," she teased. The banter flowed easily between them again, without a second thought.

"There's too much going on in that head of yours to ever just look."

"I'm really not that interesting," she said, enjoying playing the coquette for once.

"I think you're very interesting indeed." He wound a strand of her hair around his finger.

"It's the dancing."

"Yes, the dancing." There was that endearing dimple near his mouth again. "You know, you're technically supposed to wear something shorter."

"Why, so you could see my legs?"

"Or up your skirt."

She nudged him with her elbow, though she wasn't in the least offended.

"Not that I haven't before." He pulled her chair closer. Their legs touched, hip to knee. "Perhaps I should speak to the barman about having you disqualified."

"So you'd take my paper crown?" she protested. "The one I worked so hard for?"

"Maybe you'd have to dance again."

"You'd like that, wouldn't you?"

"Or you could wear the crown later."

"Later?" she asked, but it wasn't a question as much as an agreement. Everything aligned, their words, their movements, as can happen early on, when nothing is at stake. They hadn't gotten to know each other well enough for matters to get complicated. For now, they were just two people in a bar, two people who liked what they saw, and when the band struck up another tune, he joined them, and it seemed as if he sang only to her.

Chapter 17

Singing to the Sea

Colleen supposed she should have grown accustomed to the waiting. She'd done enough of it during the years of their marriage, but by six o'clock, she couldn't stand being at home any longer: the tick of the clock reminding her of how late Finn was; the drip of the faucet hinting at leaks, in plumbing, in boats that could sink; the wind rising, a gust blowing over a chair he'd leaned against the railing before he left, stronger at sea, where the waves were tall, engulfing.

She'd argued with Finn before he departed, telling him not to go, that the boat was barely seaworthy. In the early days, its brass had gleamed, its wood too, the grain so complex it flowed through the timbers like elegant script. She'd helped him refinish the vessel. The state of her hands was terrible from the solvents afterward, even though she'd worn gloves, but it was worth it in the end, yet another thing they'd accomplished together. The boat was pure magic then. He'd named it for her, both of them his loves. The *Fair Colleen*.

They didn't fight often, but when they did it was fierce—the raised voices, flashing eyes. They became strangers to each other, transformed by the fury. He'd turned his back on her, slammed the door. She didn't go after him. She banged pots, called him names. She didn't mean any of it. It was the anger talking, spending itself.

Maybe she should have opened the door, called to him, and yet it would have been too soon. He would have been too angry to listen. Only now could she think of what she should have said: that she was sorry for calling him crazy, the boat a piece of shite.

She didn't want to be right. Not this time.

She bustled around the kitchen, baked a rhubarb pie, his favorite. Cleaned the house, top to bottom, even hoovering the curtains with the attachment, for something to do. The place hadn't been so neat in weeks. Every time she turned off the machine, waiting for the motor to go quiet, she hoped to hear the sound of his step on the porch, his laugh, feel his arms around her again.

But he wasn't there.

The hands on the clock moved to the hour, the half hour, the chime making its report. She had to get out of there. She walked down to the bay, past the budding hedges of eglantine, the wild, apple-scented roses he'd picked for her when they'd first gone walking in the lanes, so in love, so young, together every moment that summer, before the fall fishing season, their first, learning to be without each other for days at a time.

She'd never gotten used to the separations, to standing on the docks, as she was now, looking for signs of him, the horizon empty but for roiling clouds, darkness falling. She listened to the ping of lines on masts, the groan of wood, the bones of everything bleached, exposed. The lanes and marina were deserted at that hour. Everyone celebrating at the *craic* or at home, eating dinner, watching the telly, arguing, making love, whatever they did to pass the evening. Everyone except her.

Where are you?

He said she was his figurehead, that he could always see her when he rounded the bend and entered the bay. No different from that first day long ago, her brown hair gleaming in the sun, gone silver now. Her face lined, but as beautiful to him as ever. His constant, she was.

Is.

Nothing was past tense, not yet. She wouldn't allow herself to entertain the possibility.

She wore a knit hat, gloves, a wool coat, a cardi underneath, jeans, boots for warmth. She was out in the elements. The only person as the light bled from the sky and night came on. And she wore the lace her friends had made for her, lace the colors of the ocean, with sea fans and mermaids—if he could only see it—lace that made her feel she could dive into the sea and swim to him, bring him home.

Where are you?

He was due hours ago, hours and hours. Another boat had gone out to search for him, no word yet. They didn't know where he'd gone. He never filed a plan, said he'd go where the fish took him, changing the route every time, sailing by instinct. She wished they'd send a helicopter, but it was too soon, and besides, the machine in the nearest village was grounded. Too much wind. No one could raise him on the radio. No surprise. He'd been having trouble with the instruments lately, insisted on fixing the problem himself, didn't listen when she told him to take it to the repair shop in Kinnabegs, stubborn as always.

She stared at the sea. There was a time when she sang to the waves, and they to her. Her grandmother said the women on her father's side of the family had seawater in their veins, thanks to a selkie who'd come ashore and married her great-great-grand-father, before returning to the depths. Colleen had felt the connection when she was young. As a girl, she could swim mile after mile in any season.

"You'll catch the hypothermia," the old women said. They didn't know what she was capable of.

She hadn't tried in years, but she must now. For him.

She sang to the wind, the waves, like a madwoman, not caring who heard, convinced the land, the sea, could be made to understand the yearnings of the human soul.

She closed her eyes, not daring to open them, to see the emptiness. Time bent. She was in a place without watches, without clocks, without measured chronology.

She hadn't sung to the sea since she was a girl. She'd done it often then, felt the pull, as if she were one with the tides, the power and strangeness of it, telling no one, lest they think her mad. No one taught her. She discovered the gift on her own. Had lost it somewhere along the way.

She had to believe again.

Was it too late?

What if the sea wouldn't listen?

Her heart, her blood, pulsed with the beat of the waves on the shore, her breath with the sigh of the wind. She threw her arms wide, sailing over the water, toward his boat.

Follow me home. Follow me.

Finn.

The feeling left her as quickly as it had come.

No.

The sea spat and rumbled; it wasn't in the habit of granting wishes. The doubt was rising again, her mother's voice after her father drowned one crisp October day, no clouds, no wind, the sea hungry all the same; it would take people on fair days as well as foul: *You can't bargain with the sea. It always exacts a price. He's gone, child. He's gone.*

And then she heard it: the sound of the horn, hailing her from the mouth of the bay. He was there, no more than a speck at first, rounding the cape where the currents were treacherous, the waves clawing each other to spume, her heart catching at the buck and pitch of the stern, but he held firm as he always did, guiding the vessel through the worst of the trouble. He sailed past the buoys and neared the shore, the moon shining on the water, making a path on which she might walk without sinking, or so it seemed, lighting his way home, lighting his way back to her. She ran down the gangway, feet clattering on the boards, scarf flying, and she jumped, yes, jumped that small distance between the dock and the boat and threw herself into his arms as if she were a girl again.

"What's all this, then?" he asked.

She couldn't speak. She took him down to the narrow bed where he slept on the nights at sea, and she lay with him there, his sea witch, as the fish tossed in the hold below, scales shining silver and green.

"I thought you were gone." She kissed his weathered cheek. He tasted of salt.

She closed her eyes in thanks. He didn't know how close they'd come to being separated from one another for good, the ocean taking him at last, collecting him, as she would a shell from the shore. She held him tighter as the water shifted beneath them, the currents teasing the boat. She would not let him go.

"This is new, isn't it?" He touched the lace. "You're a mermaid now for sure."

She buried her face in his neck.

"You missed me, did you?" He laughed. "Me, your crazy old man."

All they'd ever been, all they were now, all they would be, together, in that rocking vessel.

"More than you know," she murmured, running her fingers through his hair. "More than you'll ever know."

Chapter 18

Hail the Long-Lost Mariner

Balloons dangled from the gatepost at the foot of the drive, signs posted at intervals along the lane to mark the way to the McGreevys' cottage. The villagers came on foot and bicycle, a few by car, to celebrate Finn's return. Colleen had called the lace makers the day before, told them to spread the word. It was a last-minute gathering, a casual potluck that made up for its simplicity with good cheer and fine weather, the sky clear all day, for once.

"Sure, now it's fair, isn't it, now that I'm not at sea," Finn joked late that morning, kissing Colleen's cheek and pulling her toward him.

"Stop, I have to get things ready." She gave him a playful shove.

"We have time," he said. "All the time in the world." He waltzed her around the room.

"What has gotten into you?" She laughed, breaking away. "If

you have so much energy, why don't you help me blow up a few more balloons?"

"That's not quite what I had in mind . . ."

"Everyone will be here soon—"

And indeed, that afternoon, the house and garden overflowed with guests, Denny and Niall among them. The two men stationed themselves next to the makeshift bar near the back door, their faces red from the sun and, more to the point, the Guinness. How they loved their Guinness.

"To Finn," Denny said, raising his glass in a toast.

"Finn!" the others echoed. There was Niall, Oona, Padraig, Aileen, Rourke, Bernie, Kate, and the rest, even Father Byrne, reserved as ever.

"He didn't show up with communion wafers, did he?" Oona whispered to Colleen as they pulled the bread from the oven.

"No, berry muffins. Mrs. Flynn said he made them himself. They're rather good."

"Who knew he had a sweet side?"

"Don't let it fool you."

Denny and Niall's voices carried through the window. "Did you hear on the news that Guinness is considered an old man's drink now?" Denny asked.

"We know best, don't we?" Niall took a sip and smiled in satisfaction. "The wisdom of the elders—"

"Yes, but it's more serious than that: the sales are falling off for the first time. Can you believe it? I never thought I'd live to see the day. I mean, they're buying more Guinness in Nigeria than they are in Ireland, for feck's sake."

"Language, Da," Oona warned as she passed by with a tray of crudités and dip.

"Nigeria?" Niall looked puzzled. "I don't understand."

"The young Irishmen aren't drinking it the way they used to. Their commutes are too long; they don't have time to pop out to the pub with the boys for a pint anymore, and when they do, they like the lighter stuff. Designer ales. Sacrilegious, it is. The whole country is beginning to fall apart."

"Not here."

"Not yet. We should launch a campaign. I can see the T-shirts now: 'Save the Guinness' on one side, 'Don't Go to Ale' on the other."

"I'd wear one. Size XXL on account of my belly." Niall patted his stomach. "I'd walk up and down the center of town getting the word out."

"What are you two cooking up now?" Oona asked as she handed them each a bowl of beef stew and bread, so they wouldn't have to stand in line.

"We're having an important meeting about saving the Guinness," Denny told her.

"The Guinness won't be in danger as long as you two are around." She laughed.

Kate found herself next to Father Byrne in the buffet line, near the kettle of stew. *Stew*, another word for trouble, her grandmother used to say—at least with him nearby. "Good afternoon, Father Byrne," she said to be polite. She couldn't bring herself to refer to him in the shortened form. *Father.* It sounded too paternal, too familiar, especially when he looked at her with such accusing eyes.

"Good afternoon, Miss Robinson." He kept to the formal mode of address as well. Everyone else in the village called her Kate. Not him. "Still soaking up the local sights, are you?"

"Yes. There's a lot to see." She ladled stew onto her plate, dripping some over the side, fumbling to wipe it up, him watching her every move. At least she hadn't spilled it on her clothes—she'd worn a dress she'd found at a vintage shop in Dublin in honor of the occasion (and the possibility of seeing Sullivan—she hoped he could make it; he was leaving town that day, but said he'd try to stop by). Her heart was beating faster than usual thanks to the proximity of the priest, his cold eyes, his disapproving mouth. The last thing she wanted to do was engage in a conversation with him, and yet he'd drawn her into one, like a spider to its web, and she could see no way out.

Why was she so nervous around him? It wasn't as if she had anything to be afraid of, and yet to her frustration, he continued to intimidate her.

"I wouldn't have thought we had enough to keep you here. We have so few tourist attractions." He served himself some stew with a firm hand.

"It's a beautiful place—and the people have been so friendly." *Except for you.*

"They're trusting souls." He set a hard roll on the edge of his plate.

She served herself salad, keeping her movements slow and steady. "They've been very kind to me."

"The lace makers most of all. You've been studying with them quite extensively, I hear."

"They've been patient teachers." She poured herself a glass of lemonade, the ice tinkling, her hands shaking now. She hoped he didn't notice. She didn't want him to know how much he unnerved her. He'd probably consider it confirmation that she had something to hide.

"Surely, your apprenticeship must be almost complete."

"It's only beginning." She had no intention of leaving—certainly not on account of him. "There's much to learn."

"And they're learning from you as well, though it might not be all to the good. Some traditions shouldn't be tampered with."

"That's not what—," she protested, feeling as if she'd walked directly into a trap he'd laid for her.

"Kate, there you are," a familiar voice called out. She turned to see Sullivan Deane walking toward her. "I'm sorry I'm late."

"I didn't think you'd make it," she said, pressing his hand.

"Just making a brief appearance before I have to go out of town." He turned to greet Father Byrne, before leading Kate away.

She felt the priest's eyes on her back. "Thank God you showed up," she said as they strolled through the old orchard at the edge of the property, the fruit just beginning to form, larks flitting from branch to branch.

"It looked like you needed rescuing."

"Was it so obvious?"

"Only to someone who knows you well." He put an arm around her waist.

Across the lawn, Declan Moore's band struck up a tune, and the partygoers lined up for a reel, clapping and shouting, the oldest and the youngest, too, Father Byrne on the sidelines, watching from the shade of a beech tree, his arms folded across his chest.

"To Finn," they cheered. "Finn, home at last!"

"And to my fair Colleen," he said, kissing his wife in front of everyone, her cheeks pink with embarrassment, and pleasure too.

"Aren't you going to play?" Kate asked Sullivan.

Father Byrne continued to glower from his position beneath

the tree. She made a point of not looking in his direction. She refused to let him spoil the afternoon.

"Not today," he said. "I have better things to do."

He took her hand and led her onto the green to join the rest of the dancers, Father Byrne's eyes upon them as if he were counting every step.

Chapter 19

All Ye Sinners
Bow Your Heads and Pray

The bell sounded, a cry against the wind. The gulls circled, taking up the call. They liked to sit along the roofline, taunting him. God's creatures indeed. They thought they could get away with anything, begging, shitting. Didn't they know it was an important day? That he'd stayed up all night, writing the sermon, getting the words right, in the thrall of inspiration that could only have been divine. Yes, Father Byrne had weighed the evidence, and now he was convinced. He knew the girl would bring trouble from the moment he'd set eyes on her. He'd bided his time, waited for his chance, and now she'd given him a reason to drive her from the village: corrupting a decent, moral craft. Corrupting their simple way of life. The lace being made into lingerie. Lingerie. He could barely speak the word.

"Mrs. Flynn, have you heard about this?" he demanded over breakfast, unable to contain himself any longer.

"Heard what, Father?"

She knew perfectly well what he meant. "About the lace."

"The lace?"

"What they're doing with it."

"Doing?"

"Knickers!" He choked on his tea.

"Pretty, aren't they? I bought some for my daughter." She moved on to the furniture now, shaking her head, as if to say, *Bachelor living. Doesn't matter if it's a priest or a fisherman.* "Sent them off a couple of days ago."

"You did what?" He felt a vein pulse near his temple.

"Well, a girl can't very well go without knickers, can she?" She snapped the cloth out the window, releasing clouds of dust into the garden.

"It's not the sort of thing we do here. It's not part of God's plan."

"Did you have a vision about the knickers?" She paused, a hand on her hip. She wore a dark-colored shirtdress, cotton for ease of cleaning. It had a white collar and looked almost ecclesiastical. She saved her brighter things—the exuberant Liberty floral scarves and even, yes, the leopard jacket her daughter had bought for her sixtieth birthday, the one she didn't think he knew about—for other occasions, when she wouldn't get dirty or be under his eye.

"Yes," he said, even though nothing could have been further from the truth. "Yes. God said they must be stopped."

"The knickers? What did they do? Launch a coup in a lingerie drawer?" She didn't laugh. Didn't dare.

"No, the women. The women must be stopped from making them." He dropped his napkin, bent down to retrieve it.

"Careful—if you stoop too low, you might find it difficult to get up." She polished the brass lamps. She could put a shine on anything.

He frowned at her. She had a ready wit, that Mrs. Flynn. She smiled her benign little smile, adept at sidestepping arguments, setting things right. "That girl— That girl—," he sputtered.

"What if her coming here was part of God's plan?" Mrs. Flynn swept away a cobweb. She'd put an old T-shirt on the end of a broom—she found a second life for almost anything—and swiped it along the corners of the ceiling. "What if He sent her to us?"

"Impossible." Father Byrne ground his teeth on a piece of toast, blackened crumbs scattering over the plate like ashes. He preferred it burned just short of a crisp. "Impossible. The only solace I can take in the matter is that she'll be moving on soon."

"I don't think so. First, she stayed because she missed the bus. But now I think she likes it here."

"A ride could be arranged if she's lacking transportation."

Mrs. Flynn gave him a sharp look.

He raised his eyebrows at her. *What?*

"She's good for Bernie," Mrs. Flynn said. "She's had it hard, what with John passing on. And Oona too, with the cancer."

"Her faith has seen her through," he said, referring to Oona.

"That and chemo. It's a hard thing, losing your breasts, Father. It's not something a man can understand." She was a plain speaker, was Mrs. Flynn.

His face felt hot. He dabbed his forehead with his napkin, muttering, "I suppose not, though Bernie hardly needs the strain of a houseguest, does she? The presumption of that girl—"

"It was the other way 'round. Bernie invited her, Father. She'd been thinking about letting the room anyway—and she likes the company."

"Taking advantage," he continued as if she hadn't spoken. "Does she expect a mention in her will?"

"Will? Heavens, Father. Bernie's not going to die any time soon, and it's not as if she's an heiress."

"People are always taking advantage of widows, aren't they?" He thought of his own mother, scammed out of her retirement, in her late nineties now, living with one of his brothers in London, far from everything she knew.

"God will watch over her, Father. He will watch over them both. Besides, Bernie's doing fine."

"So she says." The members of his flock didn't know what was good for them. He would guide them back to the proper path. Only he knew the way.

"There are those among us who would undermine the community we have taken such care to build." Father Byrne paused for effect, his eyes seeking theirs for emphasis, but the parishioners were looking down at their laps or out the windows, marking time before they could take communion and escape. "Evil is at our door." He lowered his voice. He had their attention now. He was a warrior for God, leading them into battle. If only he had a sword, like the Archangel Gabriel. "We must drive out this contaminating influence before it is too late, before the innocence of our children, the morality of us all, is irreparably damaged."

Bernie had never seen the priest in such a state. At first she almost found it entertaining, then she began to worry.

Outside, the sun pierced the canopy of clouds for the first time that morning, shone through the stained glass windows and lit Father Byrne from above, his robes aglow, as if he were one of the anointed. His voice filled the church, built to a roar, reverberated against the ears of the congregants, the flickering candles, the Virgin Mary and Jesus himself, traveled out the windows— cracked open, because the church could become too warm during mass—where the sound caused even the wrens and sparrows to stop their chatter, a quiet falling over the hills, as if God let the priest control nature itself, so powerful was his message.

The church had stood for over a hundred years, rebuilt after the fires and the Famine, with a special shrine for lost souls near the entrance. The church stood for something.

So did Father Byrne. This was, apparently, the moment he'd been waiting for.

Bernie remembered what her grandmother had said years before, a saying passed down from the days of hunger and revolution when men came into the villages on horseback and set everything aflame. *There is none so dangerous as a righteous man.* She watched the priest, fascinated and wary. How far would he go?

"The only thing we should be sharing with the world is our faith," he boomed. He seemed larger than life, up on the altar, above them all, hands slicing the air.

"What's he talking about?" Kate whispered in her ear, alarmed.

Bernie shook her head, waiting for more. She wanted to see where this was going, though she had a feeling . . .

"Some of you have already opened the door, unwittingly, per- haps, but you have done it. You have started this thing, and it must be finished." His bloodshot eyes locked on Bernie and Kate.

There it was. The first salvo.

She blinked, sat taller. He'd singled her out. If she'd been less well liked, the villagers might have taken a certain satisfaction in her shame. As it was, they seemed to be as surprised as she was, waiting to see what would happen next.

Bernie stared straight ahead. She refused to be cowed by

Father Byrne and his misguided attempt at saving their souls. It was laughable, making a crusade of banishing their fledgling lingerie business—what, would he have women go braless? He clearly hadn't thought the thing through. Well, if he didn't know how determined she was, he was about to find out. She'd been a member of this parish her entire life, long before Father Byrne came on the scene, her ancestors and her husband resting in the cemetery outside, and yet her cheeks felt hot all the same with the humiliation of it, his condemning her like this in front of everyone, making her a sacrifice to the greater good. Oona and Colleen gave her nods of support. Pious Aileen faced straight forward. Just as well Moira stayed home, nursing Sorcha, who was ill.

She was too angry to take communion, the first time she'd ever refused it. She wouldn't give Father Byrne the satisfaction of turning her away at the railing; though he might not take things that far, she wasn't about to test his resolve. She waited until everyone was lined up, glad she'd taken a seat in the back, since she and Kate had been running late—the Mini wouldn't start, and they'd had to walk—then made her exit. She nodded for Kate to follow and walked up the aisle, past the candles glowing with a host of intentions, and out onto the green.

Oona and Colleen followed. Only Aileen remained inside, avoiding Bernie's gaze.

The group marched up the lane to the car park, resolute. "Let's get out of here," Oona said. "I'll give you a ride home."

"I should have shouted him down in front of everyone. Maybe I will yet." Colleen took a step toward the church.

Bernie put a hand on her arm. "It would only incite him."

"Is he always like this?" Kate asked, clearly bewildered.

"Never this bad. I gave him a look before I left. I think he got the message. He knows I won't sing in the choir until he stops this silliness." Colleen took a deep breath. "He makes me so mad. How dare he set himself above us? Judge us. Appointed by God indeed."

"He'll be sorry to lose you. He says you have the voice of a seraph," Oona said.

"He wouldn't be saying that if I'd said everything I'm thinking right now. If only I had more courage—"

"You've more courage than all of us put together. You always have," Bernie said. "But now isn't the time."

"Yes, I suppose you're right. Better to take the high road," Colleen conceded. "Besides, I like the view."

"I don't understand," Kate said. "Why is he so upset?"

"He's one of those people who needs a certain order to his life, to his community. He doesn't like anything new," Colleen explained. "He fears the modernization of Ireland, that it's happening too fast, that too much is being lost."

"There's some truth to that," Oona said.

"Yes. But his thinking is too narrow," Bernie said.

"That certainly seems to be the case," Kate said, fiddling with the zipper on her coat and stealing uneasy glances at the church, as if she thought the priest might charge down the steps any second.

"I mean, taking issue with the lace, really," Bernie continued. "And Kate too, especially when she's a guest in our village—"

Kate gave her a nervous smile.

"Good thing Padraig was sick today," Oona said. "Otherwise, there'd have been a right to-do."

"I'm glad I let Finn sleep in," Colleen said. "He doesn't think much of Father Byrne either, though he's probably too much of a Catholic to say anything. I used to think I was too. But I have my limits."

"The nuns did their job well, brainwashing us with visions

of hell. Sister Thomas Aquinas was so quick with the rod. I still remember how she rapped my knuckles for playing with a loose string on my jumper during mass and nearly broke my fingers," Oona said.

"She was awful, wasn't she?" Colleen agreed. "But they weren't all bad. Remember Sister Marie-Claire?"

"Yes, she was a sweetheart. Young and pretty and kind."

"Did you have a parochial education?" Colleen asked Kate.

"No, I went to public school."

"Probably better for you," she said, "more freedom. The Church can be so repressive, even now, though I hear things are easier in the States."

"There are conservatives there too, though nothing quite like this." She shook her head, eyes wide.

"No, nothing quite like this."

"Isn't Aileen coming with us?" Oona asked.

"Doesn't look like it," Bernie said.

"Guess she's too concerned about the state of her soul," Oona said.

"Maybe she didn't notice we left," Bernie said, giving her the benefit of the doubt.

"Oh, she noticed," Colleen said with a knowing look. "Maybe she's deciding whose side she's on."

"Her family's always been Catholic to the bone, haven't they?" Oona said. "They never leave the pews until the priest has said his final blessing."

"Priest, yes, but he's still a man, isn't he, with the potential for the shortsightedness and weaknesses men are capable of, strong though they might think themselves to be," Colleen said.

"You're not becoming a feminist, are you?" Oona asked. "That would be something."

"I am myself, a woman in this village," she said, "and believe me, that can be challenge enough."

"So it is," said Bernie.

"Not everyone agrees with him," Oona said. "The priest, I mean."

"The question is: Will they stand up to him?" Colleen asked.

"I don't know," Bernie said. "They're probably afraid of going to hell."

"I'm not sure I believe in hell," Kate said. "My mother used to say that it's something religious leaders made up to frighten us into obedience."

"I think I'd like your mother," Colleen said, adding, with a sly grin, "but don't let the good father hear you say that."

"Though it wouldn't hurt him to consider a different point of view for once," said Oona.

"Since when has he ever done that?" Colleen declared.

They stared at the church. They could still hear the priest's harangue, even from there, though they couldn't make out the words.

"No doubt we've given him something else to talk about," Bernie ventured.

"Always glad to do my part to contribute to the closing remarks," Colleen said.

"I don't ever remember him being on such a tear, not even during Vatican II."

The lace makers pulled their sensible woolen coats tight across their chests to protect themselves from the chill—and the force of Father Byrne's words, which continued to pelt them from a distance. No one else emerged from the church. The members of the lace society, save Aileen, were the only ones who'd walked out in protest.

"How did he find out about the knickers in the first place, I wonder?" Bernie asked. "Though Mrs. Flynn did warn us."

"My da said he's been snooping around too," Oona said. "I didn't pay it any mind. Remember the night he stopped by your house?"

"He didn't find anything."

"There are other means to spy. Perhaps he surfs the Internet," Colleen said with a look of mischief, turning to Kate. "You did post the photographs, didn't you?"

Kate nodded.

"But he's a priest," Bernie protested. "Surely, he wouldn't go into the bar in Kinnabegs and—"

"It's a wonder the Church hasn't gone bankrupt, what with the scandals and settlements," Colleen said.

"And yet we still go to mass," Oona said. "We still believe."

"It's not about the priests, is it?" Bernie said. "It's about having faith. The world would be a grim place indeed if we didn't put at least some belief in a higher power."

"We might be doing it without our local parish at this rate," Oona said. "Do you think he could get us excommunicated?"

"Over the lace?" Kate asked. "Rome couldn't possibly take him seriously."

"You never know who they'll decide to make an example of," Colleen said.

"Anyway, we'd better push off before he's done. I don't want to give him any more ammunition." Oona motioned them into the car.

"Wait a minute. Don't you need to give your da a ride home from mass?" Bernie asked.

"Oh, that's right." Oona put her keys back in her pocket. "Maybe he'll cut out after communion. He sometimes does."

"I feel like a criminal, skulking around like this," Bernie said.

"It's the Catholic guilt. They get us while we're young. It's like a cult," Oona said.

"Here he comes," Bernie said.

Denny emerged from the church, shaking his head as he stamped down the path. He had a deliberate way of walking, as if he were putting out a series of small fires. Oona thought he had hip problems and tried to convince him to consult a doctor, but he wouldn't go. He hadn't been in years, had an aversion to shots and pills and bad news. He'd worn his best suit that day. He believed in dressing up for church, didn't approve of the casual attitudes of the young, though he took a liberal view of theological matters and had witnessed the priest's slide—yes, he would call it a slide—into a particularly intractable form of conservatism. "The man's turning into a zealot," he said more than once. "He'll drive people away. "

"Here they are, the sinful girls of Glenmara," he said. "Is there room for me?"

"Up front," Oona said. "The rest of you will have to squeeze into the back."

"I don't mind walking," Kate offered.

"You don't have to do that," Oona said. "We can make room."

"It's all right. I could use the fresh air."

"Especially after what Father Byrne put you through in there. The nerve of him," Bernie said.

"Don't let him worry you, the old fool. Oh, I haven't had this much fun in years." Denny rubbed his hands together and chuckled. "Wish Niall had been there. Too bad his daughter invited him on that weekend holiday down the coast. Can't wait until he gets back tonight."

"Glad you're entertained, Da, but Father Byrne could make

things difficult for us." Oona motioned for him to get in the car, clearly eager to drive away from the priest and his sermons. "Glenmara's a small place."

"I didn't mean to cause you trouble," Kate said. "I had no idea putting lace on a pair of panties could be so controversial."

"Don't pay Father Byrne any mind. He's been looking for a way to impress Rome for years," Colleen said.

"Like Oona said, he could make things hard for you," Kate said.

Colleen squared her shoulders. "Let him try."

Chapter 20

Another Life

Once the women were gone and she'd walked down the lane, away from the church, the tears came, tears of anger and humiliation at what the priest had done. The public nature of the condemnation was more than Kate could bear. She didn't like feeling so helpless, wished she'd stood up in the church and called him on his hypocrisy. It was easier to think of the right words, the right plan, in retrospect. He'd caught them by surprise—her too—launching a sneak attack in their place of worship, a look of triumph on his face, there, on the altar, putting himself and his judgments above them all.

How dare he?

Oh, but he did.

The question was: What would happen now? To the lace makers? To her? To the lace itself?

Kate had managed to keep her emotions in check until she

was alone; she didn't think the women noticed anything amiss. Well, maybe Bernie did, but she hadn't said anything, seeming to sense that Kate needed time to herself. It would take her at least twenty minutes to reach Bernie's house. By then, she'd have herself under control. But for now, her tears smeared the landscape into an impressionist painting, colors and shapes blurring, sobs audible, blocking out all sound except that of her own voice.

She was so distracted, muttering and fuming, that she didn't notice the van pulling up beside her at first.

"Want a lift?" Sullivan called through the open window as the car idled.

She shook her head, not trusting herself to speak, her throat tight, the tears continuing to fall. She bit her lip and looked away, toward the wide, sloping fields.

He killed the engine, perhaps sensing that something was wrong. "What's the matter?"

"Father Byrne, he—," she began, her voice catching as she tried to explain.

He got out of the car and pulled her toward him. "Gave you a dressing-down at mass, did he?"

"Were you there?"

"No, but I could guess. He does that occasionally. Very old-school."

"That's one way of putting it." She rested her head against his chest. "He was so angry, so righteous—about the lace, and my being an outsider, and— Oh, I don't know. I think he hates me."

"No, he doesn't—"

"And he went after Bernie for taking me in," she continued. "And Colleen and Oona—"

"He'll come around. He can't condemn everyone. He'll lose the entire congregation." He took her by the hand. "Come on."

"Where are we going?"

"On Sullivan Deane's tour of the Glenmara hills, just the thing to take your mind off your troubles."

"But what about Bernie? I told her I'd be back—"

"We'll let her know on the way. She'll understand."

As Kate changed her clothes at Bernie's, her hostess insisted on packing them a picnic. Kate heard her talking with Sullivan in the kitchen while she pulled on the boots that had already seen her through so many miles and her fleece jacket and jeans; then she and Sullivan set off on their excursion.

"How do you feel about climbing a mountain?" he asked.

"You know my skills in that regard after seeing me on Greeghan's Face."

"I really didn't notice. I was too fixated on the view of your lovely ass."

"You really are insufferable." She gave him a playful slap on the arm.

"You know you love it. Besides," he continued, "the climb up Croagh Brigid isn't technical. There's a path to the top. It's a pilgrimage route."

"And what will we pray for?"

"That's entirely up to you."

The drive passed in no time at all, filled with interludes of conversation and companionable silence, the scenery more stunning than ever, all greens and golds, fields and cliffs, gentle hills giving way to the majesty of the peak itself, a veil of clouds at the summit. "Do you think it will clear?" she asked.

"The wind is coming from the west." He turned in the direction of the sea. "So it should."

She'd brought her rain jacket just in case, tucked in a day pack, a first aid kit and blanket and matches too. "I feel like such a Girl Scout."

"It's good to be prepared," he said. "The weather can change fast."

"I'm surprised there aren't more people here," she said as they set off on an unmarked trail.

"It's one of the lesser-known sites. We'll probably have it to ourselves." He went ahead, stepping easily over the rocks as she struggled to keep up.

"You don't have a problem with heights, do you?" he asked.

"Not usually," she said, keeping her eyes on the boot-beaten track. The drop was sharp in places. She paused, took a sip from her water bottle, and tied her jacket around her waist. The sun had indeed emerged—with a vengeance. Sweat was already dripping down her back. She was too breathless to talk. All she could do was try to keep up with him. He maintained a good pace. She concentrated on putting one foot in front of the other—and staying on the path.

When would they reach the top? Her stride shortened, so that she felt as if she were shuffling. And to think the devout made the trek on their knees. It was bad enough on two feet. The distance wasn't that far, due to the steepness of the pitch, but the incline made the hike challenging.

"We're almost there," he said. "Wait until you see the view."

"Provided I can still see straight," she muttered. But he didn't hear her, the breeze carrying away her words.

Then she crested the rise, and she knew exactly what he meant.

He took her hand. "Make a wish," he said.

And she did, though she didn't tell him what it was.

As they drove along the coast road that evening, a bank of mist hovered over the waves like smoke, forming shapes that shifted as the waves curled and broke. Kate thought she saw a woman and a horse among the spray, blinked, and they were gone. When she was a little girl, she and her mother would lie on the grass in the backyard and stare up at the sky. The clouds, which had been nothing but shapeless white blobs moments before, promising nothing but rain, transformed in the blink of an eye.

She wondered if Ireland would have been as her mother expected, what she would think of Sullivan. She felt the familiar ache below her breastbone, missing her still. She hadn't told Sullivan about her mother, or Ethan, or her struggling career.

"What are you thinking about?" he asked.

"Just curious about where we're off to now," she replied.

"You'll see," he said with an enigmatic smile.

The moon was full that night, the stars a glittering of celestial dust on the ink-black sky, a pale line of clouds to the north.

He slowed suddenly on a curve.

"Is something wrong?" she asked, thinking he must have seen an animal in the road.

"It's just a bad turn," he said. "It's worse at sunset, when it's a blind corner in every sense of the word. Good thing hardly anyone drives this way except the locals. We know it's treacherous."

They passed a highway memorial, and Sullivan made the sign of the cross. "The old Catholic habits die hard," he said, as if the gesture needed an explanation, "even if I don't put much stock in religion anymore."

"I know what you mean." She thought of her mother, of the string of unanswered prayers.

His hands on the wheel and shift were capable, strong. She liked the feeling of going somewhere, of being with him. The destination didn't matter as much as the journey, the two of them traveling together. He didn't turn on the radio, the only music the wind whistling through the open window and the bass note of the sea, rumbling below. The engine whined as they went higher, up the hairpin turns.

He stopped at a pullout at the top of the rise. They alighted from the car, and she rested her head against his chest, looking out at the dark seascape.

"I used to ride my bike up here when I was a boy," he said. "It made me feel as if I were standing on top of the world, the sea and the cliffs stretching on forever. It's as if you can see everything from here."

"Yes," she said. "It's magical. You know, it's funny, on the way up, I even thought I saw shapes in the waves."

"Such as?"

"Women and horses. Isn't that odd?"

He laughed. "My grandfather used to tell stories about how Cuculain drove his horses into the sea during battle; he said that sometimes you can see them cantering in the waves, the mermaids riding toward the cliffs, singing to lure men into the water."

"Has anyone claimed to have been enchanted?" She smiled.

"My friends and I went surfing there once and got pulled out in a riptide. We didn't think anything could harm us. We might have drowned if Colleen and Finn hadn't been out on their boat and come after us."

"And the horses? Did you see them?"

"No. One of my friends insisted he did, though we put it down to too much ale," he said. "But there's no getting around the fact that the waves made eerie sounds that day."

"Have you been surfing there since?"

"No."

"I'm glad to hear it," she said, "though I wonder, does that mean you believe the stories?"

"I enjoy the telling—and it's true that women can cast a spell on men."

"Oh, really?"

"One woman in particular." He guided her to the foot of a crumbled tower, little left but lichened stones, and yet it was enough to shelter them, wrapped in a felted wool blanket for warmth, as they moved in that palm of history, then lay still, breathing together, dreaming apart.

The dream again: Ekaterina waving good-bye from the tube entrance before vanishing into the underground, off to her job at the graphic arts firm. Sullivan had told her she didn't have to work anymore, that he could support them both, leaving her more time to paint. She wouldn't listen. She liked making her own way, as she'd done ever since she left home at the age of fifteen. She hadn't been back to Czechoslovakia since, wouldn't say why. *It doesn't matter anymore. It's all in the past.*

She wore a pale blue chiffon top, a pair of jeans, flats, because they were comfortable and she didn't need the height. She was thin and pale, otherworldly. That's what he thought the first time he saw her on the streets of Prague, two years ago. They'd been a couple ever since. They usually rode the train together, but he'd forgotten his mobile—she shook her head and laughed; he was always forgetting something. What would he do without her? He dashed back to the house to get it. He could make the trip in five minutes flat, but would probably have to catch the next train.

Five minutes flat. To the second. He knew by the hands of his watch. Such a small fraction of time, but enough for everything to change, for the streets to be in chaos, sirens wailing, people shouting, panicked. Some bleeding, others sooty, wandering, stunned.

He didn't understand at first, overheard cries, whispers, *terrorists, bombs,* tried to push through, but the police were already there and blocked the entrance, black smoke coming up behind them as if from the depths of hell.

"She's in there! I have to find her!"

They didn't move. They had their orders.

His emotions detached, like cars from a train. He played the scene back in his head, a slow rewinding of the day's events that had led them to that point, that place. First, breakfast in the nook overlooking the garden. The crunch of toast, the rustling of the newspaper. Neither of them talking much; they weren't morning people. She touched her foot to his, bare, warm. The glance at the clock, the realization that it was time to go, that they'd be late. The rush down the hall and out the door, running together, laughing. And then the forgotten phone.

He didn't know that in retrieving it, he'd lose her.

One bomb in one train: theirs. It wasn't supposed to happen again—not after the tube bombings a few years before. And yet it did.

He should have been with her. If not for his carelessness, he would have been. A fragment of charred gossamer floated past him. He chased after it, thinking it was a piece of her shirt, but it was only ash, carried away on a blast of wind.

For days, he heard the rumble of the trains. The doctor gave him pills to drive them away, but they found him in dreams, even now, in Ireland. Some people said that when you pressed your ear to the ground, you could hear the pounding of hooves, of the horses of the invaders, from years ago, soldiers on the march, that the earth held the memory of their passing, of spilled blood. And he heard them, he did, the trains, the Danes, the Vikings, Cromwell's men, the IRA, the Proddies, al-Qaeda, and Ekaterina's voice too, louder than the rest, calling him: *Sullivan, Sullivan.*

He opened his eyes to the tarred sky.

It wasn't her, and he had to face, once more, that she was gone. It was the other foreign girl, her name encompassed by the first: E*kate*rina.

Kate.

"What's the matter?" Kate asked, her voice filled with worry. He'd been lying facedown, he realized then, tearing at the grass. When she touched his shoulder, he jerked away. She dabbed at his cheek, blood on her sleeve. He hadn't realized he'd cut himself on a stone. "Sullivan?"

He shook his head. The dream was a figment of another life, one he'd tried to leave behind. "It was just a bad dream," he told her, because to speak of it would have made it real all over again.

Chapter 21

Of Bobbins and Pins

The next morning, Kate helped Bernie pin clothes on the line.
The weather was fickle, the sky edged with clouds. The women
seemed to stand in the only circle of light in the county, a place
where the sun had managed to break through, if only for a short
while. Kate's head felt heavy, not so much from the late night as
from her bewilderment over how distant Sullivan had seemed
when he dropped her off at Bernie's house. This was a side of him
she hadn't seen before, and she didn't know what to make of it.
"Do you think it's going to rain?" she asked.

"Hard to say." Bernie squinted at the sky. "The clouds seem to
be having a hard time making up their minds."

Kate fingered the faint stain on the cuff of her shirt, a
reminder of the unsettling scene on the cliffs; it wouldn't come
out, despite numerous rinsings in the sink, the mark a shadow
along the seam.

"At least that stain won't set," Bernie said, "not as it would have if we used a dryer." Bernie had told her she couldn't abide the machines. They ruined clothes, and since it was only her and John—and now, her alone—she had little use for them. "He cut his head, did he? Is he all right? How did it happen?"

Kate told her, adding, "He said he didn't need stitches."

."Even the smallest head wounds tend to bleed excessively." Bernie nodded. "Will he be by today?"

"I don't think so. He said he's busy. He was acting kind of strange when he dropped me off." She paused, then added, as if to convince herself, "But sleeping on the ground all night would make anyone irritable." She rubbed her back. "I know I'm feeling where some pebbles pressed on my spine this morning."

"You slept outside? In this weather?"

"He knew a place near the cliffs; there was some shelter, and he had a blanket in the van—"

"Kept you warm, did he?" Bernie teased.

"In a manner of speaking." Kate's smile faded as she touched the spot on her shirt again, the memory of trying to help him, help he didn't seem to want, returning. She pinned the garment on the line. The fabric stirred listlessly in the breeze. "He seemed to be having a bad dream. He wouldn't tell me what it was about."

Bernie didn't say anything, directing an inordinate amount of attention to the clothespins she was attaching to the line.

Kate touched her arm. "Do you know something?"

"I guess since everyone's aware of it, there's no harm in my saying . . ." She hesitated.

"Everyone except me."

"I'm sure he'd tell you, in time," she said.

"I hope so. I want him to feel that he can trust me—"

"You see, his girlfriend died in the London tube blast last year,"

Bernie said finally, "and I think he felt he should have been with her. That's why he moved back here. There's been the occasional woman since, but nobody he seemed to care for seriously—until you came along."

"How awful for him." Kate put her hand to her mouth. "He's never said anything—"

"He doesn't speak of it to anyone. He keeps it all inside."

That afternoon, Kate went cycling. She told herself she didn't have a fixed plan, no deliveries for Bernie that day, just sightseeing, to clear her head, but somehow she ended up near Sullivan's house, curiosity and desire drawing her there. To her disappointment, the van wasn't in the drive. Where had he gone? He hadn't told her what he was doing that day. She considered leaving a note, but what would she say? She stood there for a long time, unsure of what to do, waiting for some sign of him, the wind swirling around her, a few scattered drops of rain falling. She shivered. She hadn't dressed for the weather. She'd been too preoccupied. She sighed and glanced at her watch. It was time to go back. The lace makers were expecting her.

Fifteen minutes later, when she walked in the front door of Bernie's cottage, the lace makers were already gathered around the table, a pot of tea in a cozy in the center, a cup by each hand, a lace pillow on each lap. They were working on bobbined lace that afternoon, the threads woven with the complexity of snowflakes. The women were whispering among themselves.

"Why so much secrecy?" Kate asked as she joined them, trying to shrug off her mood.

"We have a surprise for you," Bernie said.

Aileen's chair was empty. Ever since the church incident, she'd kept her distance. Whenever Moira or Bernie called, she made excuses to hang up the phone. "She'll come 'round," was all Bernie had said. "She always does in the end."

Kate had to admit she didn't mind Aileen's absence. "A surprise?"

"You've graduated from the crochet to the bobbin method." Colleen handed her a lace pillow and a collection of pins and bobbins. "Now the real work begins."

"And here I thought you were giving me something soft to sit on."

"Not unless you want a bunch of pins in your arse." Moira laughed.

"Padraig sat on mine once. Never saw him get up in such a hurry," Oona said.

"Must have been why he was standing up so straight at mass that Sunday," Colleen said with a wink.

"I told him he could think of it as acupuncture," Oona replied, "but he didn't think it was funny."

"Ouch," Kate said, giggling with the rest.

"Cillian had a fit when he found a pin in the chair the other day," Moira said, eyes widening with the realization that they might take it the wrong way.

The women stopped to look at her. Cillian having a fit could be a dangerous thing.

"I didn't mean it literally," she said quickly.

"He'll be happy when he gets a look at your lace." Colleen pulled a bra and knickers from her bag. "I did the finishing work on these last night. They're ready for you to take home."

"Oh, thank you," Moira said, though she looked more pensive than pleased.

"You will wear them, won't you?" Oona asked.

Moira shoved the pieces into her bag and zipped it closed. "Of course I will."

Kate studied the bobbins the lace makers had given her. "These look old."

"They are," Bernie said. "We gave you one of each of ours. They were handed down through our families. Some are carved from bone, others wood."

"This one has a face on it, like a doll." Kate cradled the bobbins in her hands, aware of how precious they were. The women had given her part of their histories. She hoped she'd prove worthy of the gift.

"My da made me a set of those when I was young," Colleen said. "He thought they might cheer me up when I was getting frustrated learning the steps. He whittled in the evenings after the boats came in."

"Is he still alive?"

"Lord, no. He died a long time ago," Colleen said, her voice soft, before continuing, "Here, you set the pins this way." Her hands moved with swift assurance over the cushion as she set up the form. "Now, follow me."

Kate imitated Colleen's motions. "It's almost like meditation," she said of the focus required to execute the design. Even though she still felt shaky, there was a rhythmic quality to the endeavor that was deeply satisfying.

"That's it. You're getting the hang of it," Moira encouraged her.

"I don't know what I'd do if you weren't here, showing me the way."

"That's the beauty of it: there have always been others with us, helping us learn," Colleen said.

"So I'm the lace makers' apprentice, am I?"

"And we are to you, learning about garment design," Bernie said. "You're ready to take the next step, to enter the most challenging part of the lace and lace maker relationship."

"So we have relationship with our lace now? That sounds a bit kinky," Oona said, making them laugh again.

"But really, Bernie has a point: there's a give and take involved, the need to trust, open yourself up to the work," Colleen said.

"You're sounding rather philosophical this afternoon," Oona said.

"I have my moments."

Kate stretched a thread between one pin to the next, thinking of Sullivan, the distance between them another bridge to cross.

Chapter 22

A Hundred Little Bruises

At first, Moira thought Cillian wasn't home, that he'd gone off to the pub with his friends. She didn't mind it so much, his being away. The house was quieter then, no complaints, no roar of the telly—he tended to turn the volume up so loud the house shook, the voices in the box shouting at each other, giving her a headache, though she rarely complained.

Little fear of what he'd do for a while.

No, fear was the wrong word. She wasn't afraid of him, not always, rather she found it necessary to be attuned to his needs and moods. Life was easier that way, and it wasn't as if it was such a sacrifice, not really.

Moira had finally brought the lace home, the knickers and bra stitched with the green of the land, the green of her eyes. She'd left the lingerie behind each time before, uncertain about bringing it home, what he'd say.

"Why are you hesitating?" Oona asked. "Men like this sort of thing. You wouldn't believe what it's done for Padraig and me."

Moira hadn't even tried the pieces on until that afternoon. She didn't want to model them for the lace society. She was too shy.

"What about the fit?" Colleen had asked her.

"I'll bring them back if they need altering. I'm sure they'll be fine," Moira replied.

They all knew it wasn't the garments that needed fixing.

Now, in the bedroom, she slipped out of her clothes—the jeans and jumper Aileen had passed on to her. (Aileen gave her hand-me-downs, even though they were no longer children. Moira accepted them, grateful but resentful too that she should have to take charity, yet again, just to keep going.) She couldn't look at her naked self in the mirror yet. She'd never been comfortable in her body, not even when she was younger, didn't believe Cillian when he told her she was beautiful, suspecting that he was the only one who would think so.

What happened to your confidence? Aileen's words came back to her again.

Moira brought the hooks to the front to fasten them, as Aileen taught her to do years ago, when she kept trying to put on her training bra the hard way. A strap over one shoulder, then the other. Now she must turn and face her image. She closed her eyes at first, opened them to a squint. It was a small thing, but she felt different when she looked at her reflection, not a complete transformation, no, but a new perspective—one she could maintain as long as she kept the lights low so the bruises on her upper arms and legs were nearly invisible. The body she'd thought too thin, the face too haggard, looked softer, perhaps even hopeful. She touched the edge of the lace with shaking hands, considered the possibility that she could be stunning, strong, the type of woman who wouldn't settle for less, who Cillian could love without force, who could be attractive in her own right.

The children shouted outside where they were playing, reminding her of who she was, where she was. She took the pieces off quickly and got dressed, slipped the lingerie into her bag, the euphoria fading. She didn't know when she'd wear them, if she'd wear them. They were works of art, not meant for that body, that house, that life. She peered into the bag—the lace gleaming, gorgeous, a secret treasure—then closed it again. She might put them on for their anniversary. Cillian might like that.

She returned to the kitchen to start dinner. The children ran through the field behind the house, the grass uncut, a jungle. She'd need a scythe before going at it with the push mower. She'd gotten good at mowing in the dark. There weren't enough hours in the day.

She listened to the children's voices, musical as the notes of a pipe band: Rory, Riordan, Ronan, Sinead, and Sorcha. The babies she and Cillian had made together, Sorcha first, the reason they had gotten married. Moira had been home from college that summer—she'd been studying for her teaching certificate—dropped out soon after, but she didn't mind, she'd missed the coast, home, him.

Cillian had a boat then, a future. All that gone now. He complained of an old injury from his days as a rugger—another career that didn't pan out—worse now that he was older. He tried to hire on with other crews, but there weren't many venturing out anymore. He'd had a lead on a job to the north earlier in the month, but then a swarm of jellyfish decimated the salmon run. Not that he would have gotten the position anyway. He had a temper. He drank. He wasn't reliable. He had his good qualities, sure, but word had gotten around, as it always did in the end.

And so Moira tried to make ends meet, cleaning houses, cleaning anything for anyone that was dirty, bringing the children along when they weren't in school. Some people hired her because they needed the help, most because they felt sorry for her, because she had a husband who didn't provide for his family. It was as if he didn't know how. His mother had done everything for him while he was growing up, at least in a material sense. He'd been the only son in the family, a rugby star in school, catered to, adored. And then his father died when Cillian was seventeen, and his mother went off to Dublin and married a contractor, started a new life. They lived in the Algarve now, bought the grandchildren toys that broke within minutes or were too expensive to maintain, the scooters and bikes outside, a small junkyard, needing to be hauled away, fixed, something, the house too, the kitchen tap dripping, the fridge clunking, everything falling apart.

Moira put the soup on to simmer. Sorcha had dealt with the dishes, as Moira had asked her to do, but she'd forgotten the laundry. Moira thought about calling her in to finish the job, then changed her mind. The girl already did too much, saw too much. She was only twelve. She hardly ever went out and played with the younger ones, let herself be a child.

Moira hummed to herself, straightening cuffs and collars, crossing sleeves over chests, bending trousers at the knee, smoothing the worn cottons and knits and linens.

"What's this, then?" Cillian's voice was quiet in her ear. Where had he come from? He hadn't been on the couch when she walked in. Maybe he'd been in the garage, dabbling with another half-finished project, and heard her when she'd come up the drive, waited until she'd been lulled into complacency.

She felt the size of him behind her, filling the room—he was a big man, still built like the athlete he'd once been, though more flaccid now in the belly. He could move stealthily, as if he weighed nothing at all, when he wanted to. She froze, a creature seeking camouflage—a chameleon in Madagascar, an arctic fox in Alaska (The children had been studying them at school. "Will we go there someday, Mam? Will you take us?" the little ones asked. "Someday. Someday," she said)—finding none. Only walls so gray it seemed as if the ceiling would rain on them any minute, the weak-hinged cabinets, banged one too many times, the light fixture spitting and flickering above, the wiring all wrong, casting a long shadow behind them, him looming over her, the scene a page torn from one of Rory's comic books depicting a harrowing episode before the hero arrives.

"Just the lace," she said.

He dangled the lingerie in front of her face, straps looped like nooses, big enough to slip around her neck, tighten. "Who've you been tarting yourself up for?"

"No one. I told you. It's just the lace."

"Sure, sure it is."

Outside, the finches shook the hedgerow, quarreling over nigella seeds, last year's pods desiccated, shattering. Riordan shrieked from the field. He'd been found. He was it now. He counted: *One, two, three, four . . .*

"Cillian, please."

"What's this got to do with handkerchiefs and tea towels, I'd like to know?" She'd lost count of how many times he'd raised a hand to her. "What happens behind closed doors stays behind closed doors," he told her, and she agreed, because these were private matters, weren't they, misunderstandings. He'd hold her close. He'd be sorry. He didn't mean it. She knew that. It was only his temper. He'd always had a temper, especially when he'd been at the drink. He had a passionate nature; it came with the territory.

"I was going to surprise you." She tried to charm him. "I was going to wear them for you."

"A likely story." His face was expressionless, but behind the mask he seethed, his right hand balled into a fist, the other crushing the lace.

"We've each been taking a turn." If she could only explain—

"Whores, every last one of you." His voice pitched lower still, the violence in him building.

"It's not like that. If you'd only listen—"

He didn't, wouldn't. He wasn't a man easily persuaded of anything once his mind was made up. "Do you think I'm fecking stupid? Do you?" He didn't wait for an answer. He threw the lace across the room and was on her in seconds. She couldn't twist away. He held her firm. He could catch rabbits with his bare hands, her too. He squeezed her arms, skin oozing between his fingers like dough, rising, pale. Neither of them spoke. They were locked in a wordless place, filled with grunts and whimpers, feet sliding and scuffling on the floor. She mustn't fight him. She'd tried that once with near-disastrous results. All she had to do was survive the next few moments. She went limp, focused on her breath, *in, out, in, out,* thinking it would be over soon, but it went on longer than usual, on and on and on. She glimpsed the children as he dragged her past the window—back and forth she and Cillian went in their little dance—heard their laughter, their joy, out in the world, out there, as she finally hit the wall and crumpled to the floor, a heap of skin and bone.

"Get up." His shadow engulfed her. "Get up."

She couldn't move, arms and legs splayed as Sinead's rag doll, angles all wrong.

He stood over her, panting, shoulders squared, hands ready, bouncing lightly on his feet, still keyed up, and yet awareness began to dawn in those few seconds, the fear in his eyes growing at the realization of what he'd done. He turned and smashed his fist into the door frame, cracking the wood as he lumbered out of the house. She heard the car start, tear down out of the drive, wondered where he was going, if he was coming back.

He left her there against the wall for someone to find, later, as the lace lay tangled and dinner burned on the stove.

Her sister. Her baby sister.

Aileen could see it already: The swollen face. Misshapen lips. Broken arm. And worse, worse.

She knew this was coming. She knew.

A hundred little bruises scattered over the years, and now this.

Sorcha had called her on the phone, no sound at first, just breathing. Then: "Mam's not moving. She won't open her eyes."

"What's wrong?"

"He did it, Aunt Ailey. It was him. Da. I saw him through the window. I should have done something—"

"Is he still there?"

"I don't think so. I'm scared. She won't move. I think she might be dead. Is she dead? Is she—?"

"No. No, she isn't." She can't be. She can't. "I'll be right over. I won't let him hurt you—"

She'd nearly crashed the car, she drove so fast down the lane she'd traveled countless times before, tears streaming down her face, half blinding her. The minutes, the minutes, each one counted, each one passed— Couldn't the car go faster? She stomped on the accelerator, sped around a corner, up on two tires, then slammed back down, fishtailing, straight again, mud splattering the driver's window, puddles everywhere. She hit the steering wheel, bruising her palms, screaming. *You bastard. If she's dead, I'll kill you. I swear to God I'll kill you.*

Scenes flashed like jumbled snapshots, loose and torn, flying before her eyes, what had been, what was, what would be: the sun on the road where she'd walked Moira to school every day, practicing the Gaelic words for colors, so she wouldn't forget, would win the prize: *fionn, dubh, dearg, corcair, gorm, glas*; the buttercups Moira ate as a little girl, thinking they'd make her hair yellow; the night she'd burst through the door, telling them she was getting married, her face flushed, hair wild; there was no stopping Moira in those days, when she had a will of her own, such a strong will in some ways, such insecurity in others.

Aileen screeched into the driveway, gravel spewing from the tires. She fumbled with the car door. Her hands wouldn't work. She felt as if she didn't have any bones, but she had to *move.* Every second counted, every blessed second. She ran up the front walk, passing a single skate, scraggled daffodils; a bike lying on its side like a dead horse, wheel spinning slowly in the wind; the old nets, hanging on the side of the cottage, catching only dead leaves and spiderwebs since Cillian had sunk the boat he inherited from his father, too drunk to navigate the shoals that night three years ago—three years, and he hadn't gotten a steady job, Moira doing everything, he couldn't lift a finger, except to her. The welcome mat on the step, unreadable, worn down from the weather, the feet. The wreath Moira made for the front door from dried turf flowers and artemisia, weeping, scattering seeds Aileen crushed beneath her boots as she pushed her way into the silent kitchen, spattered red, the noise of the kids still playing outside, because Sorcha had kept them away. *Come out, come out, wherever you are . . .* The blood. Her face. Moira's face.

Aileen picked up the phone, called the Garda, then a neighbor to stay with the children, one of Moira's friends, Dee-dee, a nurse, who came running, who tried to help, but it was beyond her, beyond all of them, the brokenness.

"Where is he?" Sorcha tucked herself as far into a corner as she could get, samplers on the walls on either side, cross-stitched with sentiments of happy homes. "Is he gone? The phone rang right after. Do you think it was him, calling to see if she was all right? I was too scared to answer. You don't think he'll be angry, do you? He doesn't mean to lose his temper. Mam says he doesn't mean to—"

Aileen held Sorcha close and hushed her, told her everything would be fine, though she didn't know if it would.

The lace lay on the floor, the lace Aileen thought too fancy all along, coiled as a snake. She'd told the women, hadn't she? But her friends hadn't listened—and now . . . She nearly threw the knickers and bra away, but it wasn't her place. She tossed them into a drawer instead, slammed it shut.

Beaten over a bit of lace.

People had died for less.

Aileen trailed the ambulance to the hospital, took a seat by the bed as soon as the nurses let her, the hours flowing into each other, the hands on the clock moving too slowly. She spoke to Rourke on the mobile. He asked if she wanted him to come and sit with her.

"No," she said, "head straight home and stay with Sile. I'm okay."

He was just getting back into Glenmara after having been on the road. "I'm here if you need me."

Yes, he was. Even if it felt that they had drifted apart. He was still there. Her Rourke. She pressed a hand to her chest. She must not cry. Must not cry. She prayed to every saint in the book, regardless of their specialty. She needed them to come together, needed Moira to heal. She stared down at her boots, drab green Wellingtons, muddied as if she'd come in from weeding the garden, except there was a smear of her sister's blood on the toe.

She shouldn't have let Moira go back to the house. She should have offered to keep the lace. She should have known what Cillian would do.

None of them had. Maybe he hadn't even known himself, what he was capable of.

Moira was lucky, the doctors said, as 4:00 a.m. came and went and a garbage truck rumbled down the alley, taking away the waste. The damage wasn't as bad as it looked. She'd be able to walk. It could have been a different story. Aileen's hands shook then. She tucked them between her legs to make them stop, blinked away tears. The medical staff filed out of the room, continuing their rounds, the residents, the interns, the doctors, studying the sick, the broken, how best to mend them, send them home.

The hospital was all brick and mortar and lino and halls and cubicles and rooms and machines and tubes, cramped, claustrophobic, the statues flanking the front entrance chip-nosed, as if they'd been in a fight. Aileen didn't like hospitals, not since visiting her mother years ago. Her mother had been admitted for shock treatments; they left her looking stunned and betrayed, and young Aileen so frightened that she swore she'd never get sick enough to be put in that place.

And yet there she was, keeping watch over another relative: Moira. Aileen counted the dots on the ceiling, the tiles on the floor, the buttons on the monitors, watched the bubbles of liquid in the lines going in and out of her sister's body. "When will she wake up?" she asked the nurse.

No one could give a definite answer. "Time will tell," they said, as if time could speak.

She studied Moira's face for the slightest change, the rise and fall of her chest—she was breathing, at least there was that—the twitch of a lip, an eye, a hand. She took that hand, held it, as she had when Moira was a child and she guided her, reassured her, skipped down the road side by side, singing silly songs when no one was around to see, because Aileen was too old for such things by then, though in some ways she didn't want to be.

Aileen fell into a light sleep, waking with a jerk every time her head dropped to the side. She was exhausted, but she couldn't rest for long. The lights flickered. She and Moira were in a shadow world, a place of waiting and uncertainty, nothing clearly defined. It went on this way until the sun dragged itself over the horizon and brought light, or a version of it, back into the world.

"Ailey?" Moira murmured, finally coming around.

"Thank God you're awake," Aileen said.

"Have I been asleep?"

"In a manner of speaking." Aileen had to make her understand this time. She chose her words carefully, turning each phrase over in her mind first. She rarely spoke in such a measured way, and that alone seemed to get Moira's attention.

"Why am I in hospital?" Moira asked.

"Don't you recall?" Aileen wanted to know what she remembered, or what she chose to remember.

"It seems like a dream," Moira said, her voice faint.

"Dreams don't break bones."

Moira fixed her gaze on a corner of the room. "No, I don't suppose they do."

Aileen paused before continuing. "The police are looking for him now."

"Are they?"

"They haven't found him yet."

"He could be anywhere."

"Yes." Outside, in the parking lot, looking up at that very room. Or on a ferry, crossing the sea.

"Will you press charges this time?" Aileen asked. "For the children's sake."

"Did they see?"

"Only Sorcha."

A tear slid down Moira's cheek. "Is she all right?"

"I called Dee-dee. She's with them now. Sorcha's frightened. She needs to know she's safe," Aileen said, adding, "Will you do it?"

Moira shook her head. "There's no need. He's gone. He knows what he's done, and he's gone."

Aileen looked up at the ceiling, asking God for patience. What would it take for Moira to turn him in? "He's always come back before." And Moira had taken him in, saying things would be different, were different, the pattern repeating itself.

"Not this time. I saw it in his face. He went too far, and he knew it," Moira said, not meeting her eyes. One moment, she'd say she'd settled, that she'd made a mistake marrying him, the next, she contradicted herself, would hear no advice. He was her husband. It was her life. Hers. No one could tell her how to live it. "You don't understand. You weren't there."

Aileen saw a hint of regret pass over her face. "You won't take him back again, will you?" she asked, seizing what she thought was an opportunity. "Promise me you won't take him back."

"He isn't bad. He's just—" She and Cillian might separate, she'd said before, but she swore they'd never divorce. Never.

"I know, Moi. I do," Aileen said. "But he nearly killed you this time. If you could only see yourself—" She was tempted to put a mirror in front of Moira, forcing her to look at her bruised face, broken arm, but even then, could she be made to see things as they were? Aileen doubted it. "You can't keep defending him. Not after everything he's done."

Oh, but her sister could. She'd done it before. She'd made a vow. She'd make the marriage work if it took the last breath she had left in her body. She was, in some ways, the most Catholic of a very Catholic family, adhering to a strict form of the faith that cut to the bone. "We said 'till death do us part.' "

"That meant natural death, not one at his hands. You're beyond reach of any vow."

"Is that what the priest says?"

"Who cares?" Aileen snapped. "I'm so exhausted after sitting here all night, wondering if you'd wake up, if you'd walk again. Stay married to the bastard, for all I care. Just don't let him set foot in the house. Don't let him come anywhere near you. Your children need you. I need you. Alive." She buried her face in her hands. There. She'd said it, and now perhaps their relationship would be irreparably damaged along with everything else, but she had to speak, she couldn't not speak. Things had gone too far.

"Ailey," Moira said finally. "Listen to me: I won't. I won't let him come back. Not this time."

Aileen wanted to believe her, but she knew there were no guarantees, that he could beg and sweet talk, because he needed Moira, because he loved her, he did, even though it came out wrong. And Moira, yes, Moira, needed him too. "All over the damn lace," Aileen muttered, turning her attention to something she could influence. The anger and fear came in waves, had to go somewhere. "I knew no good would come of it. It's all because of Kate. This never would have happened if—"

"Yes, but don't you see? He'd still be there, wouldn't he, if this hadn't happened, if Kate hadn't come into our lives," Moira said. "It changes everything—for the better."

"How do you figure that? You could have died. You were lucky to come away with a concussion, a broken arm, and some cuts and bruises." Aileen shook her head. "I knew changing the lace like this would be our undoing. It has to stop. We have to stop."

"Ailey, no. It hasn't been your turn yet."

"Maybe there won't be any more turns."

"But you're the last ones. You and Kate. You're not thinking about what it's done for us."

"Put you in the hospital."

"Reminded us of who we are. Everything is laid bare with the lace, isn't it, like Colleen said," Moira told her. "You're tired, that's all. You need to go home and rest."

"It's not worth it," Aileen continued as if Moira hadn't spoken. "After what happened to you."

"I could have died, but I didn't," Moira said. "I'm still here, and so are you."

Chapter 23

Wear It Well

Aileen got home well past midnight. Sile and Rourke were asleep, Sile with an arm around her doll, Fi—she still loved her dolls and stuffed animals; the other children, except for her son Tom, who had his beloved Mr. Bear when he was small, hadn't had much use for them. But Sile, her baby, who was getting breasts and hips, who'd just had her first period at the age of twelve, clung to the remnants of childhood and was still willing, every now and then, to take her mother's hand.

Rourke must have stayed awake as long as he could, judging by the Dick Francis mystery open on his chest, waiting for Aileen to get home. He was sleeping on his back again, his natural position, to which he returned at every opportunity, catching a few blissful winks until she nudged him to roll over because he was snoring again. Despite the sharpness of Aileen's general disposition, she could be gentle, and she was gentle with her husband, because in spite of outward appearances—he was a large man—he was more sensitive, easily hurt, than people realized. She stood in the sliver of light from the hall, watching him. He slept on the right side, she on the left. He still had a fine profile. With his hands clasped over his chest, he looked like a sleeping king. All he needed was a crown and scepter.

Aileen didn't wake the one child who remained in the house, the husband who dreamed. When it was quiet like this, she felt her love for them keenly, touched the mementos on the bookcase, the pictures of her and Rourke at the seaside taken years ago, when he tossed her in the water, shrieking, then dove after her, held her so close it felt as if they were one person, skin to skin. Their faces were soft then, unlined, filled with wonder, at the start of it all. She sighed, thinking of how young they'd been, how quickly the years had passed, incidents, large and small, hurts and joys, passing, passing, until she reached this point, standing in her living room, remembering everything, as the moments continued to slip away, becoming part of the irretrievable past.

Her mind circled in on itself when she stayed up late like this. Too much had happened in the last twenty-four hours. It seemed like such a long time ago that Sorcha called, that Aileen tore down the road to Moira's house. She knew she should try to get some sleep, but her mind raced, one thought plowing into the next with relentless momentum. It was like being on a sinister carousel; she couldn't make it stop, couldn't get off. She looked in Rosheen's room, clean now, because Aileen had neatened it to cope with her absence, to avoid acknowledging the space devoid of her daughter's presence, the chaos that was Rosheen. It appeared her daughter had come home, briefly, when Aileen wasn't there, to retrieve a T-shirt and pair of jeans. Aileen wondered if she timed her visits, spying from the hedge to make sure she was out. The thought saddened her.

She kept thinking a dramatic event would force Rosheen to admit she needed her: that a friend would overdose, or Ronnie would cheat on her, or there would be an accident, and she would call Aileen, her voice shaking, tearful, *Mam, please, come get me*, Aileen crying too, coming to the rescue at last. Aileen could see it as if she were watching a film, she the star, the mother, who would do anything for her children.

But it wasn't a movie, was it? There was no phone call. Life didn't work like that. Not hers, anyway.

There was only that empty room with the fringed purse missing from the doorknob, letting her know Rosheen was moving farther away from her with each passing day, until she'd reach the point of no return. Aileen hoped it didn't come to that. But what could she do? She felt trapped inside herself, inside that life, clutching the snarled cord of their relationship, seemingly impossible to unravel.

Aileen sat by the window, arms locked across her chest, fingers pressing into her skin hard enough to leave marks. She gazed at the shelled drive, bits of broken cockle and periwinkle glowing dimly in the half-light, the winding lane, deserted now. A scythe of moon pierced a torn cloud. Wings fluttered in the dark, an owl or a bat most likely, though she let herself believe it was Rosheen somewhere nearby. The minutes crept by, Aileen sitting there, waiting, the futility finally too much for her, hands a-fidget in her lap. She had to do something.

And then she knew. She nearly laughed, wondering why she hadn't thought of it before. She went upstairs, the idea taking shape in her mind. She searched Rosheen's overstuffed drawers until she found what she was looking for: a plain sensible bra her daughter no longer wore, shoved in the back of the bureau, near some days-of-the-week knickers she wouldn't be caught dead in now.

Downstairs, at the kitchen table, Aileen took out her scissors and cut. She'd watched Kate lay the foundations; she knew what to do. She labored until morning, not in haste or fury but in concentrated precision, working the lace, the ribbons, until light, not from the buzzing bulb overhead, but the wide open sky, filled the room and revealed what she'd made. She held up her hands, those veined and roughened hands that had changed nappies and washed dishes and done laundry and slapped smart-mouthed faces and clenched in rage, hands that had made this one beautiful thing she hoped her daughter would like.

The finches in the hedgerow, where Rosheen had hidden as a little girl, sang as the sun rose, marking the beginning of another day. Aileen smiled to herself as she laid the bra on her daughter's bed, where she was sure to find it, the lace a cross and bones on the left breast. It was exquisite, that skull, true.

"I love you," she whispered. "Wear it well."

Chapter 24

Famine Ghosts

Sullivan had continued to be distant since the night by the tower. It was as if the walls of that place now stood between him and Kate, keeping them apart. He had to go out of town again, to a craft fair up the coast, he said, selling the pottery, conducting his business, and Kate told herself it was better that way. That perhaps a brief separation would give him the opportunity to realize he missed her, that it was time to talk.

Or would he reach the conclusion that he was better off on his own?

"We need to send out reminder e-mails to the tourist boards about the market," Bernie said that afternoon. "Why don't you drop by Sullivan's and ask to borrow the computer?"

"I don't think he's back yet." He'd promised he'd call as soon as he got in, yet there'd been no word.

"Niall saw the van parked in the drive."

"Oh." Kate tried to hide her surprise.

"So you'll go then?"

Kate hesitated, wondering how long he'd been back, when he planned to contact her. "Shouldn't I call first?"

"Heavens, you don't have to have a formal arrangement to visit your neighbors here, not like in the States," Bernie said. "You just pop over. Do you want to take the Mini?"

"No, the bicycle is fine. . . ." She paused. "But what if he doesn't want to see me?" At least Kate had a reason for visiting him, an excuse to offer if he seemed startled to find her on his doorstep, when really, she only wanted to see him, touch him, tell him about the incident with Moira and everything else. Perhaps he would finally confide in her, truly let her in.

"Of course he'll want to see you. A bad dream never kept a man from the woman he cares for."

The van was in the drive. A curl of smoke rose from the chimney, smelling of peat. Niall was right. Sullivan was home. Kate paused by the gate. Why was her heart beating so hard? She didn't have anything to be afraid of. She put a hand on the crumbled stone, steadying herself, feet on the pedals. She could change her mind. She could be on her way again, but she needed to see him and she had that one legitimate errand to complete, and . . . She hopped off the bicycle, headed for the door before she lost her nerve. His door. His house. Their separate worlds, joining with the thread of her presence, that knock on the door, the wood hard against her knuckles, no answer at first, so she rapped harder, harder still, wondering where he was, if he couldn't hear her, because he was in his studio—or because he didn't want to.

She saw movement behind the curtains, knocked again. She couldn't believe he might be trying to avoid her.

"All right, all right," he said, finally opening the door, his shirt dirty, eyes shadowed. He didn't greet her, didn't ask her in.

Already, she wished she hadn't come. "I'm sorry. I didn't realize— Is someone there?"

"No."

"Are you ill?"

"It isn't a good time, that's all."

"I just thought—"

"Thought what?"

"That you, that we might . . . I haven't seen you since . . ."

He rubbed his forehead, smudging charcoal on his skin. He'd been drawing, furiously, judging by the nub of a pencil in his hand. "You can't come by unannounced and expect me to drop everything—"

"I'm not," she insisted. "Bernie asked me to see about the computer, is all. She wants to send out some additional releases, and I thought you might be going to Kinnabegs again—"

"Not today. You can have the laptop if you want to take it into town yourself and dial up."

"We need to talk—"

"Look, I'm really tired, and I have some things on my mind. Let's not do this now."

"Do what now?"

"This."

"Sullivan, please. I know you want—"

"How do you know what I want? You hardly know me."

She'd never seen his eyes look so cold. "I know . . ." Her voice shook. She was on the verge of tears.

"Know what?"

She couldn't say, didn't want him to think she'd been talking about him behind his back, even if it was with the best of intentions.

"You just walk into my life one day, and you could just as easily walk right out of it," he said.

"If that's what you think, then it's you who doesn't know me at all." As she hurried up the path, she heard the door close behind her, and the tears came at last.

She pedaled hard down the lane. She wanted Sullivan to come after her, part of her yearning for the scene, the embrace, the reunion. She still couldn't believe how cold he'd been. She was stunned and saddened and—oh, she didn't know what she was, what she thought.

She heard a car, glanced behind her, couldn't see the driver. The vehicle was too far away, but at the rate it was hurtling down the road, it would be upon her in seconds. The roar filled her ears. Would Sullivan roll down the window? Would he call her name, beg her to stop? *Kate, please, wait. Kate, let me explain—*

But it wasn't Sullivan. It was Father Byrne, careening toward her in his Mini, its metal frame rattling like a saber. The exhaust pipe belched puffs of smoke. Kate hugged the wall, waved a hand in front of her face, choking. The car brushed her skirt as he passed, nearly pinning her against the stones. A short distance away, it lurched to a stop, as if the priest were hesitating. Or perhaps the shift was stuck—or he battled the urge to reverse and commit a darker deed. She wouldn't put it past him. In the end, he roared away, leaving her shaken and splattered with muck.

"I thought you were supposed to pray for people, not run them

off the road!" If he'd cut any closer, she could have lost a limb—
or her life. "You could have crushed me!"

Even over the rumble of the engine, he would have heard her,
for she screamed the words at him, screamed at the top of her
lungs. He glanced over his shoulder. She could have sworn he gave
her a small, icy smile, as if that was exactly what he intended.

Kate didn't know where she was going. It didn't matter as long
as she put distance between herself and that house and the priest
and everything else. Her grandmother said bad things happened
in threes. Well, this was three doubled, wasn't it—her mother's
death, her washed-up career, the breakup with Ethan, now the
priest, Moira, and Sullivan? She'd had enough. Enough. She rock-
eted along the lanes, over the greens, a blur of skin and hair and
cloth. *Stupid, stupid, stupid*. For letting herself care about Sullivan,
about the women, the lace, the priest's good opinion, any of it. She
didn't care what she hit or what hit her. All she could hear was the
gasp of her breath, the jangle of the chain.

She took a wrong turn, headed down a little-traveled track
that led to a rocky bay, which lay like an open wound between
the hills. She couldn't go any farther. The land wouldn't let her. It
stopped there, and so would she. She turned the wheel, intending
to return to the fork in the road, but her legs failed her. A moment
before, she'd been flying, but now, she couldn't move. She'd have
to rest, regain her strength. She put down the kickstand and sat
on a slab of limestone, slubbed with the skeletons of sea creatures.
The sense of history was strong there. She breathed it with the
salty air. It filled her, disturbed her, but she had to take it in. Boul-
ders lay prone on the heath, low walls all that remained of the
cottages, their thatch roofs lost to time and neglect. No one had

lived there since the Famine, this place with a name no one dared speak, a village no more.

The sea sighed against the shingled beach. She walked among the ruins, ran her fingers along the rough stones, as if she were reading braille. They would not reveal their secrets, not yet. She wandered down to the shore, threw stones in the water, watched them sink, then waded into the surf; the bay numbed her skin and she couldn't feel her feet and calves. Quartz, flint, chert, jasper. Pieces of things, once whole, part of this land, now broken, cast into the sea. She felt the stirrings of the old desolation.

No. She wouldn't let it come. She had mastered it. Or nearly so. The loss. Of Ethan. The clothing line. Maybe Sullivan now too.

Her mother most of all. If only she could hear her voice—

She was shaking now, the breeze tugging at her shirt, insistent. It blew through holes in the rocks, making hollow pipe music, notes a low, melancholy fugue.

And something else.

She couldn't move. The sound transfixed her, a sound so muted, she had to listen hard to hear it at first, listen, against her will.

A woman, crying.

She fell into a chasm that had opened between the past and the present, stumbled up the pebbled shore and into the remains of the village, her numbed limbs barely able to carry her, skin white, bloodless, as she stumbled into one abandoned croft after the next, searching for the source, finding none. She smelled smoke but there were no fires, heard weeping but there were no people, no one she could see, and yet they were there, all around her. She cut her hand, her knee, felt no pain, not yet—*keep going, keep going*— the stones unyielding, the wail unceasing, the sound her mother made as she lay dying.

"I'm coming," she cried. "I'm coming."

The wind settled then but for a moment, gathering itself for something greater, and in that breath of silence, the voice went quiet too. She spun in a circle. *Where are you? Please, tell me—*

But there was nothing, nothing except the distant screams of the gulls on the cliffs, the only sobs her own, night falling, the sky closing in like the walls of a dark, dark room.

Chapter 25

Lost and Found

Kate opened her eyes to a blackened sky. She sat up in confusion, finding herself in an exposed field, unsure of how much time had passed. Hours perhaps, the stars having shifted in the sky, as if the world were off kilter. She didn't know where she was, only she had to find her mother. She couldn't lose her again. She thought she heard a whimper, crawled toward the source. The crying, the crying. Unmarked graves at every turn. There hadn't been time for burials.

That crying. Her sobs mixed with the sound, as if they were one being, her skin colder still as she went deeper into that place, nothing to pull her back, and yet maybe this was where she was meant to be, this was her fate. She was so tired. She could just close her eyes and sleep.

A dog barked. She hardly registered the noise. She staggered forward, on her feet again, down a nameless road. The sky was bruised, stars flecks of bone. The wind keened in the grass. She heard the dog panting at her heels, paws scrabbling in the dirt. Another ghost? She didn't turn to look, had to focus on finding her mother, but the dog wouldn't leave, bumped its head against her hip, barked again. She pushed it away, but it stayed with her, wouldn't let her be lost to that place.

A car sputtered along behind them, headlights trained on her back. She stood in the middle of the lane, bewildered. She couldn't hear the crying anymore. "Where are you?"

A door slammed. Footsteps approached. A shape. A person, faceless in the shadows.

"Have you seen her? I have to find her." Kate fell to her knees, shivering. Blood on her hands, her legs.

"Find who?" Two hands on her arms, holding her at last. "Calm down, Kate. Tell me what's wrong. Jaysus, look at you—"

Kate. Yes, she had a name. She was there.

"Don't you recognize me? It's, Bernie, and Fergus too. We have to get you warm. You're chilled to the bone."

"I heard her," Kate said.

"Who?"

"My mother. She died last February, but she was there—"

She heard a sharp intake of breath.

"Where?" Bernie asked.

Kate waved her arm. "I don't know. She was crying. Now she isn't anymore, and I—" She couldn't stop shaking. "Oh, God, why is this happening?"

Bernie put an arm around Kate and led her to the car. "It's going to be all right. Let's get you home."

"The bicycle . . ." Kate remembered it distantly, as if in a dream. "It's somewhere, that way—"

"It doesn't matter," Bernie said. "We'll find it later."

As they drove eastward, Kate stared out the window, her face reflected in the glass, but she felt as if she wasn't there.

"I was so worried," Bernie said. "Sullivan's been looking for you. I told him you'd headed to his cottage—"

"Yes," she said. Sullivan. It seemed so long ago. "I got lost."

"Where were you?"

Kate tried to explain.

Bernie was quiet for a moment. "I know the place," she said. "No one goes there anymore."

"Why?"

"It's just a story." She kept her eyes on the road.

"Please, tell me. I need to know."

Bernie sighed. "It's the famine village I told you about when you first arrived. No one survived, cut down by illness or starvation. A girl had a baby toward the end, ailing herself. There was no one to take care of the child. When help finally arrived, it was too late, the babe was gone, the mother too. They couldn't bury them—the ground was too hard, and everyone too weak and fearful. People say their bones are still there. That they wail at night, searching for each other in the dark." She hesitated.

"What else?"

"I shouldn't mention it."

"I'll hear it from someone else, if not you."

"They say that only those who have suffered such a loss themselves can hear the ghosts cry."

Years ago, Bernie and John had prepared the room, a cradle, a crib, a mobile of bluebirds, a border of forget-me-nots along the walls, a changing table. When the pains started, she knew it was too early. She was baking a wild berry pie that morning. She was mad for the baking in those days, "nesting," John said, hugging her from behind. The sky was impossibly clear that morning. She was admiring it through the window when the contractions began. "It's starting."

"It's too early."

"I know."

"It's probably false labor."

"Yes."

They let themselves believe that as they drove to the hospital, miles away, the pains worsening. The midwife in the next village told them they had to go, that it was beyond her skill. John had never driven so fast.

Bare rooms. Drapes. Lino. Metal instruments. Serious faces. They put her in a gown, legs in stirrups. She had a corn on her toe. She didn't know why she noticed that. It was the last thing she remembered before she went under. All it took was a shot in her arm and she felt woozy, as if she were drowning. Voices came and went. John was there. They wanted him to go, but he wouldn't leave her.

"She mustn't see," a nurse said.

John tried to shield her. She never told him she'd glimpsed their child through the haze of drugs, perfectly formed. A girl, her skin the palest shade of blue. She let him think he'd protected her.

A girl, Saoirse, who would have been the same age as Kate, if she'd lived.

Bernie nearly called her Saoirse when she found Kate in the lane, as if she were losing her child all over again, Kate too distracted to notice. Bernie's lips formed the word. She thought she heard her baby girl cry at last, would have cried herself, the tears coming again, if Kate hadn't needed her.

"Sometimes I think there's too much history here," Bernie said as they sat in front of the fire later, holding mugs of tea with a shot of brandy. "That the land won't let us forget what pains us. It's not a bad thing, the remembering, it's an important part of who we are, the suffering that shapes us, that reminds us how strong we can be."

"I don't feel strong." Kate's teeth chattered as she talked and talked, the words spilling in a torrent.

"You are." Bernie watched her carefully, half wondering if she should have taken her to the hospital. "More than you know. I sensed that the moment I met you."

"I was a mess." Kate pulled the wool throw more tightly around her. Bernie had swaddled her in blankets as if she were a newborn child.

"No, you weren't. Though we wouldn't be very interesting without our messes, would we?" Bernie nudged a log that had tumbled toward the hearth into place with a poker.

Kate stared at the flames. "The voice sounded so real."

"The living are close to the dead there," Bernie replied. "It's one of the thin places, where the past and present touch."

"What was I supposed to learn? I was meant to learn something from it, wasn't I?"

Bernie didn't reply right away. "Perhaps to let yourself feel the pain, forgive yourself, as best you can, then try to let it go," she said finally. "That even though we lose the ones we've loved, they aren't gone from us forever, that they are with us, still, but in a different way." Saoirse, too. Bernie had thought the lanes were meant to run with children, with pitched battles and cycle races. And they did: other people's children. She embraced them, as if they belonged to her, part of the village, each and every one of them. It was only sometimes in the evenings that she felt an echo of what might have been, looking out on the quiet lane, the bare fields, the windows catching what light remained at the end of the day. "But I've wondered, if I went out there, if I would hear the crying."

"And did you?"

"Yes," Bernie said, adding, "The losses don't go away, not completely, but it doesn't hurt so much after a while."

The fire crackled, the clocked ticked. Fergus twitched in his sleep, exhausted after the search.

"Do you ever get lonely?" Kate asked.

"Now and then. I lead a full life—though I wouldn't mind having someone to show off my lacy drawers to some day."

"Perhaps you should try a personal ad." Kate managed a smile.

" 'Woman with fancy knickers seeks a bit of fun.' That would give Father Byrne new material, wouldn't it?"

"He nearly ran me off the road today," Kate told her. "It's clear he doesn't want me to stay. He might use what happened tonight against me. You won't tell anyone, will you?"

"Of course not."

The flames snapped in a volcanic burst of sparks before disappearing into the ashes below.

"Do you want me to call Sullivan?" Bernie asked. "He was glad to hear I'd found you."

"Was he?"

"I phoned him while you were in the shower. I said I was sure you'd like to see him, but he thought you might need to get some rest. He's a considerate sort of fellow—"

Kate didn't reply.

Bernie sensed she was holding something back. "What is it?"

She shook her head. "It's been an eventful day, that's all."

"I hope you're not thinking of leaving us," Bernie said. It couldn't have reached that point, could it? "You're just getting your bearings."

Fergus rested his head in Kate's lap. He had found her. He would not let her lose her way again.

"You have a home here, for as long as you like," Bernie said. "Besides, don't you want to know how it turns out? To finish what you started?"

Beginnings and ends. The knots that let the threads catch, the needles that made the stitches, each a step on the path she took, leading her to this place. "Yes," Kate said. "Yes, I do."

Chapter 26

The Things That Shape Us

To the casual observer, everything seemed the same: the sun rose over the far hills to the east, set beyond the sea, the roads traversed the hills in their set pattern, even the inhabitants went about their daily lives in the usual manner, and yet there was a hint of urgency in the air that morning as word began to spread: someone had dared to take a stand.

Have you seen it? They called each other on the phone, spoke in animated whispers in the lanes. *Yes, it's about time.*

Because the priest's sermon was having quite the opposite effect to what he intended: most thought him mad, didn't want to be associated with his narrow-minded ideas. They wanted to meet the new age in their own way, thank you very much, keeping the Gaelic and their traditions while still looking forward. He didn't speak for them. They'd been hoping someone would.

And then someone did.

Denny sat on the bench, his knee jigging as he waited for Niall to show up. He hadn't taken a chance like this in years, but what could he do after the priest had insulted his daughter and her friends, insulted them all with his misguided screed? He had to say something, didn't he? To defend the honor of his child—yes, still his child, after all these years—to defend the honor of Glenmara most of all.

Oona hadn't seen the paper yet when he'd left the cottage; Bernie came by with the copy after she'd gone out for her morning walk. But his daughter probably had by now. Would she be pleased, or would she be furious with him for kicking up a fuss, stoking the fires of the priest's wrath? Denny had known her for years, of course, his own child, yet he couldn't predict how she'd react. She'd always had a mind of her own.

"There you go, wearing your egg on your sleeve again," she'd say, over his tendency to drag his cuff through the yolk while reading the newspaper at breakfast—over his outspokenness, his passion. He knew there were times when she was growing up that she wished he could be as reserved as the other fathers, rather than embarrassing her with his antics, his schemes.

This too, perhaps. One of the biggest gambles to date.

And yet he was glad he'd done it. Yes, glad.

The *Gaelic Voice* lay on his lap, the headline running across the top, his column, "This Old Geezer," in the prime position. Bernie had given him top billing. "God bless you," she said, her voice trembling as she handed him the paper that morning. She must have stayed up all night judging by the shadows under her eyes.

Others might damn him. Father Byrne had his supporters.

It was early yet, the town barely stirring, too early for anyone to stop by the bench for a visit. No one expected him there at that time of the day. He usually didn't show up until mid-afternoon. People were in their cottages, having their coffee, *reading the paper.* Or they would be, soon. He'd called Niall right away, waking him from a sound slumber, asked for an emergency meeting.

"What have you done now?" Niall said over the phone, eager to be part of the mischief.

"No, it's not like that, you'll see," Denny replied.

Obviously, Niall hadn't gotten his copy yet. But he would. And then he'd understand.

Denny wanted to see his best friend now more than ever. He was sure of his convictions, there was no doubt about that, but he needed some moral support. A pinch, a dash, a soupçon, confirmation that he'd done the right thing. He plucked a spent dandelion from the base of the bench, blew, watched the seeds scatter, remembering how he'd played the game with Oona when she was a little girl. *Close your eyes and make a wish.* Sending hundreds of seeds into the air. She never tired of it. His grandchildren, great-grandchildren, either.

He'd lived all these years in this village, raising a family, outliving his wife and most of his friends. Here he was, on this bench. These things were real, they mattered. The heart of Glenmara mattered. His heart. Their heart.

He glanced at his watch again. What was taking Niall so long?

He didn't like having so much time to reflect. It wasn't his nature, and yet something had compelled him to write that column, to speak for everyone—

Yes, there he was: Niall at last, small at first, in the distance, a dot of a man growing larger, until Denny could hear the sound of his brogues on the lane, of his huffing breath. He had the paper tucked under his arm, and he was frowning, either from the seriousness of the situation or the physical exertion, Denny couldn't tell just yet.

"No bicycle this morning?" Denny asked.

"Had a flat. No patches left," Niall said, still breathless. "My daughter's buying replacements today, but I couldn't wait—not with this on the doorstep." He waved the paper at him.

"They delivered it early today," Denny said. "A special edition."

"Special indeed." His face, uncharacteristically, gave nothing away.

Denny couldn't take it any longer. "Well, for pity's sake, man, aren't you going to tell me what you think?"

Niall fixed him with a cold stare. "What I think—about your mouthing off to the priest in front of everyone, taking on the local representative of one of our major institutions? A few years ago, I might have said you were either very foolish or very brave."

"And now?"

"Fecking brilliant," he crowed, sitting down beside him.

Denny punched him in the arm. "You fecking play-actor."

"Good, wasn't I?" Niall gave him a gap-toothed grin. "Maybe I should try out for one of the theatrical productions in Kinnabegs, eh?"

"Then you'd really be insufferable."

"Maybe I'll get some dramatic practice in now." He began to read Denny's column aloud:

> This might surprise you, but you won't find any debates about the Manchester United, Chelsea, or Arsenal in today's column. I never thought I'd say this, die-hard

fan that I am, but there are more important matters that deserve your attention than the football standings.

A question has been raised about the limits of our tolerance, the state of our very souls.

Strong stuff, eh?

Are we talking about global warming, world hunger, the gas crisis (no, Niall, we're not referring about the state of your intestinal tract), or the wars raging beyond our borders?

Heavens, no. We're talking about The Great Knicker War.

It seems our esteemed local ecclesiastical authority has taken it upon himself to launch the assault (uniforms and ammo available at the sacristy door after this weekend's mass, no doubt).

Yes, it sounds like a comedy routine straight out of Monty Python, but it's not. It's dead serious.

But for entirely different reasons than Father Byrne supposes.

The question is: Will you follow the lead of an out-of-touch firebrand and take up the cudgel? Or will you take up the right cause: support our community, the lace makers, women we've known all our lives, our daughters and friends, who are only trying to better their craft and themselves—and us too?

I think you know the answer. I know I do.

"Such eloquence," Niall chuckled. "Perhaps you should run for office."

"Might have to run for my life, more like it," Denny joked, though there was a bit of truth to the concern.

Just then, they heard the sound of Oona's car laboring up the lane.

"I'd know the sound of that engine anywhere," Denny said. "The sound of judgment."

"Has she seen it yet?"

The car screeched to a halt. Oona got out and slammed the door. (It wouldn't shut otherwise, and yet she might have done it with more force than necessary that morning.) She marched toward them, a stern expression on her face.

"She must have by now," Denny said. "I'll probably be getting an earful." He sat up straighter, ready to face her down. He'd only said what needed to be said.

She stood before him, not speaking. It was only then that he saw she was fighting back tears. It had been years, years and years, since she'd hurled herself into his arms and buried her face in his neck and cried with sorrow or joy, that tiny red-haired girl, all arms and legs and temper. Even when things were bad with the cancer, she hadn't broken down, not in front of him, being strong for everyone.

Niall patted Denny's shoulder, letting Oona take his place. He would wait for his friend at the pub.

Up at the vicarage, a curl of smoke rose from the chimney as the priest tried, unsuccessfully, to burn every copy of the *Gaelic Voice* he could get his hands on.

Chapter 27

A Turn in the Road

The house felt right now that Finn had returned, her Finn, home at last—his mac hanging on the peg by the door, his boots below, his fisherman's cap on the shelf above. The salmon pegged on the line to dry. (Colleen had given him his own pegs so that he wouldn't take the laundry pins—how many times did she have to tell him she didn't like her clothes smelling of fish?) The nets laid out to be dried and mended in the days to come. The boat in its slip on the dock.

Everything where it should be. Him too.

He insisted on cooking dinner that night, picked a bouquet of primula and columbine for the table.

"What are you making?" she asked, leaning over the pot.

"Cioppino," he said, slipping a hand around her waist.

"Cioppino? What do you know about cooking? Oh, I see. You

traveled all the way to the Meditteranean on your last trip, did you? No wonder you were gone so long."

"Wouldn't you like to know?" He smiled, holding up a spoonful of broth for her to taste, cupping a hand underneath.

She closed her eyes and savored it. "Delicious."

"Surprised?"

"A little."

"I'll have to see what else I can do to keep you guessing and spice things up." He shook some pepper into the pot with a flourish.

"Look at you. Such culinary prowess."

"Culinary and otherwise." He winked at her.

"I'd better watch out," she said. "Soon you'll be hosting your own cooking show."

"Captain Finn's Table." He saluted her. "I'm serving a special dish for you tonight."

"You're a terrible tease."

"Am I making you hungry?"

"Yes." She kissed him before putting on her coat.

"Love them and leave them, eh?"

"I'm only going for my evening walk. I'll be back soon enough."

"Mind you are. The soup—and I—won't wait."

She walked the cliff road as she did almost every evening, breathing in the salt of the sea, feeling its mist on her face. It's come out well, hasn't it? she thought. The lace growing more lovely each day—who knew what they'd make next? Denny giving Father Byrne what-for in the *Gaelic Voice*. (The priest would no doubt have a fiery reply that weekend at mass.) Finn home safe. The two of them would have another special evening together when she got home. She was wearing the lace. She'd learned that anything could happen with the lace.

Seabirds quarreled over bits of cockles and clams, abandoned by diggers that afternoon, the tide higher now, the ocean keeping its secrets once more. Seals rode the silvered waves, heads bobbing, regarding her with limpid eyes. It wasn't hard to imagine Cuculain's horses galloping in the surf, or the merrows swimming in the shallows, the men bestial, rarely seen, the women achingly beautiful, hair festooned with shells. The birds joined in, swirling now, in a great spiral; they made it look easy, the gift of flight. If she spread her arms, she might soar with them toward the far horizon. She used to dream of doing so when she was a girl, when she wanted to get away, be part of something greater than herself.

Not now. Her needs and wishes were simple. She was a fifty-five-year-old woman who wanted nothing more than to take an evening stroll and go home to her husband.

The way twisted and turned as it climbed to the high ridge, no guardrails, no mileposts, just the road and the drop to the beach below. She wouldn't go the entire length as she did some evenings when Finn was away. He was home now. He was waiting for her, making stew with mussels and clams from the docks, from the fish he'd caught in the sea, the sea that had returned him to her. In her mind's eye, she saw him knocking about the kitchen, bumping his head against the copper pots hanging from the ceiling. She laughed at the thought, would have teased him if she were there—her tall, ungainly husband, in some ways still awkward as the teenager he'd once been.

She glanced at her watch. She should head back soon. He was expecting her. He'd worry; he wasn't used to waiting at home while she was away, the roles reversed. It was tempting to linger, so that he'd know what it was like, but the thought of him pacing the length of the room in anxiety stopped her. She'd go partway up the cliffs, then turn around at the pullout, just past the graffiti kids had painted on the rocks on the right side of the road. "Ronan was here." And the little sign with the words "Panoramic View," the arrow pointing. It wouldn't take long. Lord knew, she needed the exercise. The climbing was good for the heart, that's what the doctor said at her annual checkup. She felt her pulse quicken as she tackled the incline. Finn sometimes came along on her rambles when he was home. He could join her more often now. He said he wouldn't put out to sea again. He'd promised.

The sea hit the coast hard there, drowning out all sound but itself. "I knew you hadn't forgotten me," she said, thanking it again. Its voice had always given her solace. It did then, too.

The waves crashed so fiercely that she didn't hear the car approaching from behind as she stepped onto the road to avoid a pothole, the sunset on the water, blinding, brilliant, her feet leaving the ground, and she was flying at last, flying, though she was past feeling anything by then, past feeling the rush of air, the impact of her body against rock and sand, the waves caressing her skin, welcoming her home.

Chapter 28

A Soul of the Sea

It was an accident, the Garda said, a terrible accident, a convergence of unforeseen events: the time of day, the glare on the water, the hairpin turn, a tourist unfamiliar with the road. "She didn't feel a thing," he assured Finn, as if the knowledge would lessen the pain. "She died instantly."

A shroud of quiet settled over the village, the clouds standing vigil overhead, mourning too, casting everything into shadow. One day passed, then another. The women couldn't bring themselves to take up the lace. The minutes, the hours, ticked by in a fog of disbelief, until they found themselves in the candlelight procession, winding up the road to the McGreevys' house, the shuffle of their footsteps on the path, the rhythmic sound of their breathing in time with the sigh of the wind in the reeds and grasses, the candles flickering in the darkness before being set in votives inside the room where the coffin rested, Colleen there, as if she'd just fallen asleep, dressed in a blue gown and velvet slippers, a rosary wound around her fingers, the women whispering that she didn't look broken at all, that her skin had the glimmer of pearl, the scales of the sea creatures rising, that the braided kelp cord was her merrow's bridle, placed there by an unknown hand. Her baptismal candle burning at one end, the mirrors turned to the walls, the room smelling of fresh flowers, flowers everywhere, the priest saying the decades of the rosary, them replying with the Prayer of Eternal Rest: *Requiem aeternam done ei Domine; et lux perpetua luceat ei. Requiescat in pace. Amen.* Colleen's mother weeping in her wheelchair, because it was her right, the sobs sharpening until she keened, long and piercing, with the violence reserved for the death of a young child, but Colleen was her child, wasn't she, the bonds of mother and daughter the hardest to sever. "Her father wanted to name her Niambh, after the god of the sea, but I gave her a good Irish name, didn't I?" Colleen's mother wailed. "A name of the land, thinking it would save her . . ." The women held her hands and prayed with her, took up her cry, their voices carrying through the open window and across the deserted fields to the place where the waves battered the rocks, the place where Colleen's body lay that night, before they brought her home and washed her and brushed her hair and dressed her in her best clothes.

Some stayed all night, the lace makers among them, watching over Colleen, drinking the ale and the tea, eating the cakes and sandwiches and salmon and soda bread, the priest too, wishing he hadn't whispered those words the day Colleen left the church in a huff: "Fine," he'd replied. "Let these be the last notes you sing." He hadn't meant for her voice to be silenced permanently, not like this. He wasn't the sort to say he was sorry, to take anything back, but the others saw the regret on his face and let him lead them in prayer without protest. To stand against him then would have been cruel, and Colleen would not have wanted that, for though she had a temper, she was also the most forgiving of them all.

They went to the chapel as the sun rose, spreading a golden light across the horizon, the larks and swallows darting across the lanes, the priest already there, wearing his black cope, greeting the coffin at the door, sprinkling it with holy water, intoning the De Profundis and the Miserere. They read from Thessalonians and John, took communion, said the Libera Me and the Kyrie, sang "In Paradisum" as they followed the body out of the church and to the cemetery, where their parents and grandparents and Bernie's baby daughter and husband were buried, now Colleen, taken too soon, her sons carrying the coffin on their shoulders, her only daughter, Maeve, walking behind: *May the angels lead you into paradise: may the martyrs receive you at your coming, and lead you into the holy city, Jerusalem. May the choir of angels receive you, and with Lazarus, who once was poor, may you have everlasting rest*, their words hanging in the air like smoke.

And after, they gathered at the house, in the garden, Rosheen too, finding Aileen at last, burying her face in her neck as she had as a child, eyes brimming with tears, voice a trembling whisper, "I heard about Auntie Moira, Mam, and that a village woman had been killed on the cliff road and I know you go walking there, and I thought it was you, Mam, I thought it was you." Aileen kissing her forehead—"No, love. I'm here. I'm right here."

Even William was there, playing the fiddle and singing, William who had known Colleen in the old days, accompanied her at the dances and in the pub when she sang in her glorious voice, the others sharing the stories, the memories, too:

I remember how she swam to the island and no one could catch her; nothing could touch her, not even the cold.

I remember she had the voice of an angel, bringing us closer to heaven each time she sang at mass.

I remember she could beat any man at arm wrestling, any man at all. She wouldn't take guff from anyone.

I remember how she helped me when the twins were born and I thought I'd lose my mind.

I remember how she taught me to make the lace. Her patience, her grace.

I remember the color of her hair when the sun caught it just so.

I remember how she could read the wind and the tides.

I remember . . .

Kate gazed up at the clouds, blinking back tears. *No more deaths, please. There have been too many deaths.* Only a few days before, there had been a party at the McGreevys' house, welcoming Finn home—and another now to send Colleen on her way. How could this have happened?

William touched her arm.

"That was beautiful, what you were playing," she said.

"It was part of her repertoire when we were young."

"You must have known her well."

"It was a long time ago," he said. "But I never forgot her. I came as soon as I heard."

"Finn looks so lost without her."

"They were kindred spirits. When you find a love like that, you shouldn't let it go. It's one of those things in life worth fighting for," he paused. "I know. I know. You're thinking here's William, a man on his own, talking about commitment. Hindsight, my dear. Hindsight."

Kate wondered if he'd heard about her and Sullivan. She felt

Sullivan's eyes on her. He stood across the lawn with the men, with Padraig and Denny and Niall and the rest, neither of them able to bridge the distance. She noticed that Finn and Sullivan were deep in conversation as well, casting occasional looks in her direction.

"Perhaps they're having the same talk, eh?" William squeezed her hand before crossing the lawn and taking up the fiddle again. Finn joined him this time, singing the words to Colleen's favorite tune, closing his eyes, and Kate knew that he was imagining her there beside him.

The children played on the lawn, the teenagers resting their backs against the fence, Rosheen too, the strap of the bra Aileen had redesigned for her sliding down her shoulder. Kate joined the lace makers huddled a short distance away, the space Colleen once occupied next to Oona, always next to Oona, empty.

Oona, who took it hardest of all. "It was me who was supposed to go. Not her. Never her. She was the strong one. She was—" She put her head on Bernie's shoulder and sobbed. Bernie stroked her hair.

"I can't believe she's gone," Kate said.

"Neither can I. I keep thinking she's going to walk out the door any minute," Aileen said, taking her place with the women once more.

"I know. I know." Moira squeezed her sister's hand. She'd insisted on coming to the funeral against doctor's orders—"How can I rest," she'd asked him, "when our friend has died?"

"She was truly a soul of the sea," Oona said. "Just the other day, she told me the sea gave Finn back to her. And now it's taken her instead." The tears came again. "It named its price."

"Maybe it was embracing her in its own violent, inexplicable way." Bernie blotted her eyes.

"Maybe. I just wish it hadn't taken her from us so soon," Oona replied. "I'm not ready."

"None of us are," Aileen said.

"He's coming," Bernie said. They wiped their tears. They must not add to Finn's grief. The stoop in his shoulders, the pain in his eyes, were almost more than they could bear.

His daughter, Maeve, was on his arm. She'd flown from London the night before. "Colleen's home now," he said, swallowing hard, eyes red from his own private weeping, running water in the washroom so no one would hear. "That's what she'd want us to know, hard as it is to let her go."

They nodded, dabbing their noses with tissues. If he could be strong, they would try to be too.

He looked out toward the sea for a moment, the sea he'd sailed for years, hundreds of terns circling in unprecedented numbers, as if to see Colleen off. "You must start again," he said finally, "with the lace."

"Yes," Maeve said, Maeve who looked so much like her mother when she was a girl. "You must."

"How can we," Oona asked, "now that she's gone?"

"No, she isn't," Finn said, joining each of their hands together in turn, until the women formed a circle once again. "She's there in the very center of things. Don't you see?"

And indeed, at that moment, there was a brief shimmer in the space between them, a shimmer that could have been a trick of the light, a play of the sun off the church windows, or a part of her spirit, with them still.

Chapter 29

A Word, Please

Two days later, Kate saw Sullivan coming up the walk, hands in his pockets, head down. She didn't know what had alerted her to his approach, but something made her turn and look as she dried her hair with a towel, skin prickling from the cool air coming in the open window. She pulled on a sweater, wondered if there were time for her to leave out the back door, if he would see her hurrying over the curve of the hills rising behind the cottage, if he would follow her this time, if it mattered. She'd already spent hours trying to sort it out with no success.

One moment, she told herself that it was simply that reality was setting in, as it had to, eventually. Better it happened now than later, when the pain would cut too deep. She'd only suffered a scratch. It hadn't even broken the skin, had it? If he didn't want to see her anymore, it was for the best. What could have come of it, really, if she'd stopped to ask herself, taken the time to contemplate, rather than letting down her guard? Being with him might have been a mistake, and if so, she would learn from it. Maybe one of these days she'd stop picking the wrong men. She'd stop letting such things matter so much.

The possibility of escape beckoned: She could be out the door before he reached the threshold. She could take to the road again and be gone.

The next, she considered all she'd be leaving behind:

Bernie.

And Oona, Moira, Denny, Niall, William, Aileen, yes, even her, the memory of Colleen.

And Sullivan. Yes, Sullivan Deane.

She looked at her things in the bag—in the three weeks she'd been there, she hadn't moved them into the dresser. The arm of her hoodie dangled from the zip compartment, begging to be taken out and folded neatly. She wouldn't do it, but she didn't force it inside either.

She listened for his knock, even though she felt shaky and unsure. Bernie's voice, a low murmur, Sullivan's reply in a deeper timbre. She couldn't make out what they were saying. A pause. Footsteps coming upstairs. Not his, Bernie's—she moved briskly, lightly. His would have been heavier. A tap on the door. "Kate? Kate, you have a visitor." As if they both didn't know who it was.

He waited for her in the garden near the tulips, red petals spattered on the pavers as if there had been an explosion, when the only blast had come from the wind, the wind that seemed to stir everything up—the ghosts, the memories.

He had his back to her. Her eyes lingered on the line of his shoulders, his spine. The sun cast his shadow toward her, as if he were the arm of a sundial and she the number, marking time. It changed again when the breeze dragged the clouds over the sun, extinguishing the light, the shadow play between them gone and the chill settling on them once again.

"We need to talk." He turned toward her, hands in his pockets, fingering loose change.

"So now you're ready? You weren't when I stopped by the other night." She moved neither toward him nor away. She would stay where she was, keeping a margin of graveled earth between them.

"I didn't expect to see you there."

"That much was clear."

"You don't understand," he tried again, a note of impatience creeping into his voice. "Everything's been happening so quickly. Us too."

"Yes." That was true. She'd felt it herself.

"Kate—" He made a futile gesture with the hands that had touched her just days before. "Do you want to walk? I feel like we're stuck in one place, standing here like this."

"All right."

It would be better to have some privacy if they were to continue the discussion. She sensed Bernie hovering at the kitchen sink under the pretext of doing dishes, the window ajar to let in the air—and their conversation.

"We'll stay away from Greegan's Face," he said with a hint of the old teasing. "I'll never forget the first time I saw you there."

"It must have been quite a view." She smiled in spite of herself.

"It was."

In the silence that fell between them, the land asserted itself again—the clatter of broken rock and shell on the path, the hum of bees in the field daisies, the cries of goshawks overhead.

"It can't be all fun and games, you know," he said.

"It doesn't have to be—but we shouldn't shut each other out when things get hard either," she said.

"I know." He paused.

"You can tell me anything. I thought you knew that."

He searched for the right words. "You see, last year, I lost someone very dear to me," he began. "And I—"

"Yes?" she asked, her voice almost a whisper.

"I didn't know if I could ever feel that way about someone again," he said.

He told her about London. She listened, watching his face. He kept his eyes on the hills as he talked.

She touched his arm when he was done. "I'm sorry."

"There's still a part of me that's struggling with what happened," he continued. "I thought I was getting past it, but then when I started to feel closer to you, it all came up again, the nightmares too. And yet, after everything that's gone on over the past few days, the one thing that is clear to me now is how much I want to be with you. Does that make any sense?"

"Yes," she said after they'd walked a certain distance. "I lost some people who were important to me too. It's been hard for me to trust again. I guess I have a fear of being left." She told him about her father, her mother, and Ethan. She nearly lost her footing on the scree, adding, "It seems like we're both trying to regain our balance."

"Maybe we can help each other find it. Can we be patient with each other? Can we try making it up as we go along?" He stopped and turned her toward him.

She looked into his eyes and nodded. She didn't feel the chill of the wind any longer or hear the calls of the hawks hunting in the fields below, low green hills that seemed to go on forever, one after another, into the very heart of the country.

Chapter 30

On the Mend

The women turned Bernie's detached garage into a workshop. It would do until they could afford to open a place in town. They scrubbed the floor and gave everything a new coat of cream-colored wash, swabbed the windows, swept away the dirt and cobwebs, thinking of Colleen with each dab of paint, each dusted shelf, each clear pane. They hauled in battered tables, destined for the junkyard, made a sign for the door: "Sheer Delights, International Headquarters." Colleen would have done the lettering if she was alive—she had the best hand. Oona did it instead, feeling as if her friend were guiding her. They hadn't had any orders except Mrs. Flynn's yet, but they kept sewing. They'd start small, making samples in different sizes, selling at regional craft fairs, and take it from there. Their spirits were low, but they tried to rally for Colleen, for Finn and Maeve.

The lace makers encouraged Moira to take some time off. Signs of the beating she'd taken from Cillian last week remained: the yellowish bruises on her face, the limp, and the sling on her arm. "I won't be a mascot," she said. "I want to work. My fingers aren't broken, are they? I owe it to Colleen." And she did, resting her arm on the table, a determined set to her mouth. The doctor had given her pills for the nightmares and anxiety. Cillian had left marks that went deeper than her skin.

Her children played outside, jumping off the stones, flapping their arms, pretending they could fly, the younger ones sure they'd done it, Sorcha not telling them otherwise for once, letting them think they could do the impossible. She didn't want to be alone in the house, and Moira didn't want to leave her, leave any of them. Sometimes Sorcha sat with the women, learning the stitches, working on a lace shoulder bag patterned with daisies—because, she said, daisies were happy flowers.

"Will we have enough done by the end of the week?" Oona wondered. That was the date of the next craft fair, held in conjunction with the celebration at the end of the Saint Brendan's festivities.

"Enough to pique people's interest," Bernie said. The shelves began to fill with knickers, camisoles, and bras. "To show them what we can do."

There was the sound of footsteps outside on the gravel. Moira jumped, her body tensing.

But it was only Aileen, arriving late. She met her sister's gaze, shook her head slightly. Moira looked away to collect herself before turning back, as if nothing had occurred.

Aileen's face was pale.

"What happened?" Moira asked. "Is it Rosheen again?"

"I thought we'd patched things up at the funeral, but she's too used to being on her own. At some point, I have to let her go. I wasn't thinking it would be so soon. She's only sixteen."

"Of course you're worried," Oona said. "It's the mother's lot."

"I made some lace for her a few nights ago. I meant to tell you about it, but then—" She fell silent.

"It's all right," Bernie said. "Tell us now."

She did.

"Skulls? With the lace?" Oona said. "I hadn't thought of that. You're not turning into a Goth, are you?"

"Ailey went through a punk phase in the late seventies. Remember the short skirts and torn fishnet tights?" Bernie said.

"That was a long time ago." Aileen stood next to the shelves. The only open seats were Colleen's chair, painted as a memorial to their departed friend, and one next to Kate.

"The fashions come around. Leggings are in style again, ankle boots too," said Kate.

"Please tell me that horrible polyester double knit material isn't returning," Bernie said. "That's something I could do without."

"I still have a picture of you in those mod flowered pants," Aileen said with a half smile.

"Those awful rust-colored things?" Bernie hid her face in her hands and groaned. "I can't believe Mam let me buy them. And to think they came from that fancy shop in Galway."

"You thought you were hot in those pants, if I remember correctly."

"I *was* hot. I was sweating. The fabric didn't breathe," Bernie said, adding, "What colors did you use for the skull?"

"White with silver threads, pearls for the eyes. I thought about rhinestones, but that seemed too tarty."

"Sounds punk-Victorian," Kate said.

"I hadn't thought of it that way, but yes, exactly." Aileen stared at the younger woman as if seeing her for the first time.

"That's brilliant. I bet she loves it," Moira said. "Both because of the style and because it's from you."

"I just hope we can find a way to talk to each other again," Aileen said. "I keep thinking one of these days, she'll be gone for good."

"No, she won't," Oona said.

But sometimes the teenagers did take flight, like Susan Kelly's son, up and gone after a big row two years ago. She hadn't heard from him since. Her marriage broke up after that, and she moved away, no one knew where, her family scattered like dust.

Aileen took the empty seat next to Kate. Usually, she did everything she could to avoid sitting there, going so far as to pointedly pull a chair to another spot around the table. But this time she didn't. Bernie gave her a little nod, which Aileen didn't acknowledge. Her expression seemed to say, *It's only an empty chair, isn't it? And I need to sit down.*

Kate remained wary, focusing on her work, Aileen careful too, and yet as the morning went on, they seemed to grow easier with each other, the atmosphere in those few inches that separated them tension-free for once. They might never be the closest of friends, but perhaps they didn't have to be at odds, looking for slights and insults at every opportunity.

"Ailey," Bernie said in a coaxing voice, "we haven't forgotten about you: it's your turn."

"Oh, no—"

"Too late. It's already done." Oona pulled out a bundle wrapped in tissue. "Go on, open it."

Aileen snipped the string and pulled back the paper, revealing the deco-patterned lingerie. "But how—?"

Bernie smiled. "Rourke gave me the knickers and bra he thought needed embellishing. We figured the flapper look would suit you."

"I don't know what to say," she said, tears welling up in her eyes. "No, yes, I do: Thank you. Thank you, for everything."

All that day and into the evening, their fingers flew. The patterns of the lace were everywhere, if the women opened their minds and looked past the sorrow: in a horse's mane, butterfly's wings, blades of grass, sprigs of ivy, spiderwebs, drops of rain, the waves of the sea, the feathers of a lark, the lines on a face, in their very own hands. The lace could be anything they wanted it to be. It was the lace of dreams, the lace of their imagination. At the end of the day, they looked at their callused fingers, amazed they'd made such extraordinary things, the threads connecting each woman to the one beside her, and out into the wider world. "It's about all of us, isn't it?" Oona said, touching the back of Colleen's chair. "All of us, together, still."

Chapter 31

Market Day

From the front window of his cottage, the priest saw the visitors gathering in the village below, the lines of buses and cars, backed up to the junction, the excitement building. They hadn't just come for the Saint Brendan's Day festival. They'd come for the lace, the story of the women, the town. It was nothing short of an invasion. He nearly ran down to the road to ward them off. He would have done so even two weeks ago, before everything changed. Before Colleen died. Before he'd lost his place, his position, his way.

The telephone had rung that very morning, another representative from the bishop's office on the line: "Father Byrne, have you received the letters?"

Not the familiar form of address. Not Dominic, no. "Father Byrne," indicating serious matters.

"Yes."

"And did you read them?"

"Yes."

"And yet you haven't responded."

"There have been important matters requiring my attention."

"You do understand that the parish is closing? That Glenmara will now be served by a circuit priest. He will be there next week—"

"I do. I could offer my services—"

"We thought we'd made ourselves clear: the parish, as such, is now subject to consolidation. It's the only way we can keep it open. One man will serve it on a part-time basis, Father Byrne," the voice said. "You are needed elsewhere."

Elsewhere. What did that mean? "I see."

"There is, however, an assistantship in—"

A demotion. He couldn't bear the thought of it. He stopped listening to the voice on the other end of the line. He looked out the window at the framed view of the church and its steeple, to which he'd opened his eyes every morning for more years than he could count.

No more.

It was done. He was done.

A circuit priest would take over within days. He'd be young, energetic, hopping from parish to parish. He'd be from Kenya or Cameroon. Or perhaps he'd be older, having found his vocation after working in advertising or law or some other profession, a worldly man, the Church calling him to a new mission. He would be anyone but Dominic Byrne.

Dominic Byrne wasn't wanted. That much was clear.

He must go.

The world was changing, and he hadn't changed with it. He was an artifact, destined for a museum, the basement of the

Vatican; he could already feel the dust settling on his clothes. He packed his things in the car. Clothes in a suitcase. Books in a box. He would visit his cousin first, to get his bearings; or maybe he'd drive until the road ended, find a ferry to take him across the water. He didn't know where. He hadn't thought that far ahead, a strange sensation for a man who had lived such an ordered life. His world, so solid, so set, a few days before, had gone soft at the edges, no more than a delicate membrane easily torn away, leaving him floating in ether, a specimen unworthy of study.

Only the narrow road behind the chapel was free, the one he would take, shedding his robe like a chrysalis. The gestation had taken years, but the time had come. Time to leave this place. Leave his vocation. Though he hadn't seen it coming, not at first, it felt inevitable now, ordained by God, by nature itself.

He watched the birds go, heading north to their summer feeding grounds, the beaches, the islands, released from the ice, warmer days coming. He too, away, away. Mrs. Flynn at the festival with the rest of them, selling the lace, dancing, singing, celebrating. He left a note for her to find later. No one would notice at first. No one would see the Mini buzzing up the hill road, diminishing to nothing, Father Byrne gone at last.

Aileen scanned the crowd for Rosheen. (She'd left Rosheen's dancing shoes on the bed where she could find them, in hopes she'd show up for the *ceili* after all.) Rourke waved to her from his post on the road, directing traffic. He looked official in his cap and orange vest. "A man in uniform," she teased as they left the house that morning. He liked the new lingerie, especially the tassel. One night didn't fix everything—far from it. Aileen still felt as if she were playing a role, though there was an interlude that night when her troubles receded and she allowed herself to be consumed by the moment. That might be enough, for now, a reminder that they could still find their way toward each other in the dark, that it was possible to rediscover the passion they'd once had, if they tried. That she wouldn't be starved for conversation, for attention, after the children were gone.

Moira watched the road too. For Cillian. Keyed up, she was, saying it was the excitement of the visitors. Aileen knew better. They all did. The women kept an eye out, just in case.

Sile sat by Aileen, wearing her dance costume. Her troupe would be performing soon on the small stage at the end of the lane. The round and long dances: "Rince Mor na Tine," "Staicin Eorna," "An Rince Mor," and "Ionai na hInse," the Siege of Ennis. "Come on, Mam. It's time for the dancing. She'll be here. She will." Sile took her mother's hand.

And so they danced. The visitors, the women. Sile, her hair in ringlets, lace on her collar and cuffs and hair band, her white bawneen with green ribbon, embroidery around the openings. In the center of the bodice, Aileen had embroidered the cross with the four cardinal points of the world, the fifth rising in a vertical from the center. The cosmic quadrangle, the sign of life—the life they shared, the family, the village, bound together, in spite of everything that had come between them, the tragedies they'd suffered. Her shoes struck the stage, the beats pure, throbbing to her mother's pulse, her heart; Aileen joining in, and Oona and Bernie, Sullivan, a hand on Kate's waist, Rosheen there too, perhaps, on the fringes, just beyond Aileen's sight, the music of the willean and William's fiddle skirling over the village. "Put your hands together," the cruit player called. "Hands together now."

More people arrived, jamming the streets. The chip man had to send for additional filets. The pub did a booming business. The jewelry and trinket stalls had brisk sales; so did Oona's husband Padraig with his honey, and Denny, who played his accordion for an enthusiastic audience other than the chickens, coins and bills filling his case.

The women worked the lace table, taking a break from the dancing, Colleen's daughter Maeve with them, the line stretching down the lane. Bernie tugged Aileen's sleeve. "Look, just look! I don't think we've ever had so many people in town, not since—"

"Not since ever." Aileen laughed in disbelief.

"Father Byrne must be having fits. It's the modern world, laying siege to the village."

"Haven't seen him all morning," Oona said.

"He's probably barricaded himself in the vicarage."

"How do you think people heard about the lace anyway?"

"It was the mention on *Wear in the World*, wasn't it? You know, that fashion program? Everyone watches it. Word's been spreading fast. It's all over Dublin, all over London," said a woman who was ordering the Celtic cross pattern. "Did you see the reporters coming down the hill? They want to speak to you. It's big news."

"*Wear in the World*? But I didn't send anything to them," Bernie said. "I mean, I never thought they'd—"

"Wait a minute," Oona said. "Isn't that your show, Maeve?"

"Yes." Colleen's daughter could no longer suppress a smile. "It was me—or rather, it was Mam. She sent me the lingerie for a birthday present a couple of weeks ago. She said you've been making lovely things with the lace. She knew I'd see how special they are—and my producers would too. 'Leave the door open,' she used to tell me, 'and see what comes in.' I told her I'd like to do a piece on the lace—on all of you. There's a camera crew up the road, waiting for my signal. What do you think of that?"

"It's mad—and wonderful!" Bernie said.

"Mam told me the details, but swore me to secrecy. She wanted it to be a surprise. She was going to tell you today. And that's why I waited until now to let you know. Because it's what she wanted. It's her gift to you."

"And what a gift it is," Bernie said.

Oona shook her head, laughing and crying at once. "Oh, Colleen. Colleen McGreevy. You really are something."

Chapter 32

Fame & Fortune

The website, which they managed to launch with Sullivan's help (he asked a friend at the bar in Kinnabegs to monitor it until they worked out a better system), received so many hits, the server jammed. The electronic mailing list swelled into the thousands. The women called an emergency meeting at the workshop the next day.

Bernie rubbed her forehead, reviewing the paperwork. "I wish Colleen was here to help us with the figures. She was always good with numbers."

They nodded, exchanged somber glances.

"How can we possibly meet the demand?" Aileen spoke next. "We never expected anything like this."

Bernie thought for a moment. "People need to realize this is a cottage industry, that our pieces are manufactured on a small scale, that handmade items are special. They take time, but they're worth it."

"Still, we can't handle it all ourselves," Moira said.

"No, and perhaps that's the beauty of it," said Bernie. "We'll form sewing circles along the coast. Think of the women we know in the area whose families can't make a living from the fishing anymore. Oona, you and I will make the calls tomorrow. We should be able to get this off the ground within the next couple of weeks. We don't want to lose our momentum."

"What about quality control?" Oona asked. "We don't want anything shoddy going out."

"We'll have everything go through the shop. Nothing leaves without our approval," Kate said. "We'll have set designs, as well as limited editions."

"What about special orders?" Moira asked.

"Yes," Kate said, details of a business plan taking shape in her mind. "But only for those who can afford the fee."

"Let's put a gold-edged card in each package, written in Gaelic and English, 'Made for You by Sheer Delights,'" Bernie said. "I'll place an order with the printers this afternoon."

"I hate to mention this," Aileen said, and for once she seemed truly loath to be the one to point out a problem. "Where will we get the seed money? We don't have any funds coming in yet."

"I'll talk with McClaren at the bank. He must have seen the news. He'll see the potential," Bernie said.

"Not without someone to guarantee the loan," Aileen said.

"Da and Niall have been taking up a collection. You wouldn't believe how many people from the village have been chipping in."

"It won't be enough—"

"We're getting ahead of ourselves," said Bernie. "Let's take it one step at a time. It will work out. I know it will."

"I can help," Kate said. She thought of her mother's house, which she'd yet to put up for sale, the modest inheritance she'd hardly touched.

"We can't ask you to do that," Bernie said.

"It's what my mother would have wanted." She felt Lu there with her in the room, beautiful once more, the scars of the cancer gone at last, showing her how to sew the straightest seam, tie the strongest knot to keep everything from unraveling. *This way.* "She would have loved being a part of this, and this way she can—" Kate brushed away tears.

She didn't have to finish. The women put their arms around her, understanding now, even Aileen laying a hand on her shoulder.

They wouldn't consider Kate's offer seriously until she let them design a set of lingerie for her. They didn't allow her to contribute a single stitch. When they were finished, it was as if there were something magical in the thread. It was the color of light, woven into the most complex and delicate of Celtic patterns, a story of her life, in America, in Ireland, everything that had been, everything that would be. How could they have known? And yet somehow they did, their fingers guiding them with a knowledge, a creative instinct, they didn't know they possessed.

When Kate put the pieces on, she felt her mother there too, her essence, a flash of radiance in the room, one last time.

And she knew, finally, what she would do.

Chapter 33

Finishing Work

"I'll have to fly to Ireland, won't I?" Ella said over the phone. She hated to fly, but for Kate, she'd make an exception. She'd have to. "You're not coming back. I can hear it in your voice."

"Of course I am, eventually," Kate said. It was good to talk to her, really talk. E-mailing was quick and convenient, but it wasn't the same. Kate pictured Ella in the shop, the display case of costume jewelry and accessories glittering beneath her: the rhinestone peacock, the Lisner and Coro necklaces from the 1940s, a Schiaparelli brooch, a Hattie Carnegie bracelet, Pucci and Hermès scarves, treasures from the golden age of design.

"But not to stay," Ella said. "You've gone all Irish on me, haven't you? Next thing I know, you'll be speaking Gaelic and I won't be able to understand a word you say."

"I'm learning." She didn't ask about Ethan, the way she used to any time she communicated with Ella. She hardly thought about him now, only sometimes, a small tug, the anchor still catching, every now and then, on the sinking wreck of the past. But she was pulling free, finding, if not calmer waters, at least another place to call home. "About so many things."

"I miss you," Ella said. "The shop isn't the same without you. Everything is full of holes."

"Everything?"

"The sweaters and the gowns."

"You only like me for my needle."

"You're using it for far better things than alterations these days from what I hear," Ella said. "Who would have thought modest you would go in for designing thongs and panties—when do I get a pair, by the way? It's all over the Internet. You and the Lace Makers of Glenmara, that's what they're calling you in the news."

"It is? We knew there was coverage in London, but—"

"No, it's international, honey."

"We'll have to enjoy our fifteen minutes of fame."

"I have a feeling it's going to be more than that," Ella said. "What is it about the place that made you want to stay? The creative inspiration? The lace?"

Yes. No. How could Kate describe her journey from one place to another, one self to another? "Come visit. You have to meet everyone. There's Bernie, Oona, Moira, Aileen, Denny, Niall, William, Mrs. Flynn," she said, "and Sullivan."

"I thought there'd be a Sullivan," she said. "He doesn't have any eligible friends, does he?"

"He might." She laughed.

"I've heard Irishmen are charming."

"They certainly aren't dull," she replied.

"There must be something in that Irish rain."

"There must be," Kate said, thinking back to the day she first arrived in town. "You never know. You might like it here too."

"Would I?" Ella mused. "Starting a reverse migration to the old country, are you?"

Yes.

Maybe you'll find yourself on a deserted lane and a man driving a colorful cart will offer you a ride and bring you to a village where the land runs down to the sea, a place where everything is waiting to begin. It doesn't have to be perfect. You don't have to be perfect. All you have to do is be.

You'll take up the same needle and thread and see that they're magic, or could be—if only you let them, if you try—that the women, who gossip like sparrows and bite like midges and laugh so hard they cry, will teach you something new and you will teach them too, and it won't be all bitterness, not all, no, and the man walking up the road to see you is someone you could spend time with, make a life with, if you take a chance.

It all remains to be seen.

Acknowledgments

To those who have offered help and encouragement along the way: Kyle Lindskog, from the time we were children, the best friend a girl could have; Jeannie Berwick, for years of laughter, adventure, and good counsel; Juan Alonso, for his artistry and soulfulness; Monica Prevost, for sharing the stories, old and new; Maura Hayes, for her free spirit; Marcellina Tylee, for her creative flair and friendship; the Doran and Barbieri clans, including my dear sisters, Tessa Effland and Robbi Anderson; parents, Bob and Michelle Doran, Kay Barbieri, Jan McAvoy, and Letty Pericin; the members of the Red Shoes Gardening Society, Jeannie, Tina Albro, and Korina Layne-Jones; Bob and Paula Rohr, Carol Carlson, Grace Van Zandt, the Fridays at Vic's crew—Kit Bakke, Mary Guterson, Randy Sue Coburn, Garth Stein, and especially Stephanie Kallos, for her kindness and support, and Jennie Short-ridge, who was so generous with her time, reading early drafts and offering sage advice and reassurance when I needed it most. Special thanks to Sara Nickerson, for being such an excellent reader and friend; J. J. Cariaso-Hughes, for making me look good; my miracle worker of an agent, Emma Sweeney, for her unwavering belief in and passion for this book; her associates, Justine Wenger and Eva Talmadge, for connecting the dots; and Jennifer Barth, for helping me find the heart of the story and being the best editor a writer could ask for.

And with love to Mark, Sian, Connor, and Sera, most of all. Every day begins with you.

P.S.

Insights,
Interviews
& More...

About the author

2 A Conversation with
Heather Barbieri

About the book

11 The Story Behind
The Lace Makers of Glenmara

Read on

14 Author's Picks: Favorite Books

A Conversation with Heather Barbieri

Tell us about your childhood.

Books were very much a part of everyday life in our Pacific Northwest household. My mother, who studied political science and opera in college, is an avid reader who made the extensive living-room bookcase available to me from a young age. My dad was an attorney and a judge, and one of my favorite things to do as a child was sit with him at the breakfast table, reading the paper (there's a family photo of me "reading" the paper solo at eighteen months, trying to follow his example), and accompanying him to the state law library with its marble halls rows upon rows of leather-bound books.

When I turned six, we moved into an early-'70s style house in a southeast Olympia subdivision. The neighborhood was surrounded by woods, and my friends and I would be out all day, climbing thirty-foot-tall trees, building forts, and trying to put ourselves into trances from which we'd emerge as pirates or queens or ghosts. Nights were made for reading, and read I did, often not closing the pages of a favorite book until dawn.

How long did it take you to write The Lace Makers of Glenmara?

Start to finish, including the editing process, about nine months.

When did you first know you wanted to be a writer?

I was an avid reader and imaginative from a young age, staging plays and various adventures, scripted and unscripted, with neighborhood friends, so acting or writing were natural childhood dreams. I was also fortunate to have influential teachers—especially Rich Martin in sixth grade and Barbara Hubbard in eighth—who saw something promising in my writing assignments and encouraged me to follow my dreams.

Did you study creative writing in college?

I started out as a journalism major, but ultimately found the discipline too rigid and switched to English, where I did indeed study creative writing, as well as literature. Then, naturally, upon graduating, I needed a job, and got one as—you guessed it—a journalist, albeit one who specialized in the arts and profiles. ▸

A Conversation with Heather Barbieri
(continued)

How did you first get published? Was it a difficult process for you?

I was a practicing journalist and magazine editor for a few years before starting a family. By the time our first daughter was a toddler, I found it difficult to keep regular hours and talk on the phone. In my sleep-deprived condition, I thought I might try pursuing a lifelong dream of publishing fiction. I tried short stories first, eventually publishing in small literary journals and winning a few prizes. Getting a novel published took a greater commitment of time and energy, obviously. To use a running analogy, writing short fiction versus novels is something like running sprints versus marathons. I wrote a novel or two that didn't go anywhere other than the bottom of the file cabinet drawer before deciding to focus solely on voice and craft, rather than publication, telling myself it didn't matter if I never got published as long as I loved what I was doing, viewing writing as a lifelong apprenticeship, just hoping to get better and learn from each piece I wrote. My agents sent out the manuscript, and again, I told myself not to expect too much, but when the news finally came that

66 It didn't matter if I never got published as long as I loved what I was doing . . . just hoping to get better and learn from each piece I wrote. 99

Snow in July (Soho), my Irish-American–themed first novel, had been accepted for publication, it was the perfect fortieth birthday present.

Both of your novels have Irish or Irish-American themes. Tell us a bit more about that aspect of your background.

Every summer when I was growing up, we'd travel to Butte, Montana, my dad's hometown, to visit family. Since we lived in the Pacific Northwest, the difference between the landscapes was dramatic, to say the least. Butte is a former mining town and iron frames still dot the landscape above the old town, which looks like something out of a Capra movie set. The Doran-McGeehan side of the family would tell colorful stories during these family gatherings, much in the Irish oral tradition, and were pros at the form. Though our ancestors left Ireland in the 1870s after the Famine, a hint of a lilt survives in their accents. (Butte had the largest Gaelic-speaking population outside Ireland at the turn of the century.) I owe my love of the spoken word, and storytelling itself, to those long afternoons in the shadows of the Rocky Mountains. ▶

A Conversation with Heather Barbieri
(*continued*)

What was the inspiration for your first book, Snow in July?

Because Butte spoke so strongly to me, I'd been drawn to setting a novel there for some time, but hadn't found my way in. It wasn't until I saw a photo in the *New York Times Magazine*'s "What They Were Thinking" feature that the pieces clicked into place. The picture featured a young woman, looking pensively out the window and two young children playing next to her. She wasn't the mother of the children, she was their young aunt, who had come home to help care for them while her sister, their primary parent, was in drug treatment. I was interested in playing the idea of a family's disintegration and resurrection off against that of a town struggling to survive as well. And yes, it really can snow in Butte in July—and I had firsthand experience with the phenomenon on a summer visit when I was eight years old, having packed only Heathtex shorts and T-shirts and square-toed red Keds. (I wore some of my four-foot-eleven, ninety-pound grandmother's clothes around the house, including her high-heeled mules and mohair sweaters.)

Where do you do most of your best writing?

The ideas flow in inconvenient places—the shower, on walks, and driving (sans kids). When I'm ready to get serious about getting things down on paper— or the computer—I go to my office, which isn't exactly private (no door, right off the kitchen), but it has wonderful light and if I'm focused enough, I really don't need to be closeted away.

Describe the objects on your desk.

I'm an inveterate beachcomber/ collector, totally enchanted with the process of discovery, whether on the page or out in the world at large. There's a perfectly round, smooth rock I found on the beach at Ebey Landing on Whidbey Island, two pieces of honeycombed wasps' nests, a red-winged blackbird feather, a carved jade ram (I'm an Aries), a snail shell from the tip of South Africa, cockle and clam shells from the Strand of Inch in western Ireland, a dried urchin and starfish from Baja, Mexico, and a stone Buddha head. ▶

> " I'm an inveterate beachcomber/ collector, totally enchanted with the process of discovery, whether on the page or out in the world at large. "

7

A Conversation with Heather Barbieri
(continued)

To which author would you compare your writing?

I wouldn't dare! I'll let readers draw their own conclusions.

Are you writing another novel? If so, what is it about? When will it be published?

I'm not quite ready to talk about it yet. That magical/scary gestational phase, when one has to jump off the diving board and believe.

What's the craziest thing you've ever done?

Here's one, which is somewhat in keeping with the *Lace Makers* theme. Some years ago, when we were going boating with acquaintances, the rather obnoxious "captain" insisted that only women in bathing suits could board. (I was in a T-shirt and shorts.) I took off my shirt and sat down in a bra and shorts, saying, "Will this do?"—figuring a bra wasn't much different from a bikini top—and wanting to teach him a bit of a lesson. Result: He turned bright red and didn't say another word about it.

What's your favorite hobby other than writing?

There are several, including travel, yoga, gardening (I went overboard with the rare seed catalog this year, planting purple snow peas from France, yellow peas from India, winter squash from Italy and France, and green apple cucumbers from Australia, among other things; gardening seems to partner well with writing, both in its creative and editing phases), and playing the piano—especially Debussy and jazz pieces.

What's your favorite travel memory?

From Ireland: strolling the Strand of Inch in Ireland and having people speak to me in rapid Gaelic as if I were a native and might actually understand them.

Are you a cat person or a dog person, and why?

I like animals in general, which is why a cat or dog usually finds its way into my novels (Webster, a tabby, in *Snow in July*; Fergus, a Labrador, in *The Lace Makers of Glenmara*). Currently, we have a cat who thinks she's a dog. ▸

A Conversation with Heather Barbieri
(continued)

What are some funny things people don't necessarily know about you?

A few silly ones: I can wiggle my ears, screech like a chimpanzee, and Russian dance (Cossack style).

What advice would you give aspiring writers?

Embrace the process, keep trying, and never lose heart. ◞

The Story Behind
The Lace Makers of Glenmara

WHEN I WAS A CHILD, my Irish-American grandmother loved to tell stories, pulling tales from memory or making them up as she went along, a master of the form, me listening, mesmerized, at her feet. Despite a hardscrabble upbringing in the shadows of the copper mines of Butte, Montana, she was an elegant woman, fond of the theater and partial to velvet coats, high-heeled mules, and jewelry. She taught me the value of style—and the art of storytelling, myth and reality woven together in the most tantalizing ways, bringing the streets of Butte and the hills of Donegal, where her parents were from, to life. So vivid were her words that I knew I had to go to Ireland someday.

Years later, I fulfilled her dream, discovering that the Gaelic Ireland of her imagination still existed in small villages scattered along the west coast, away from major roads and tourist attractions. One rainy summer evening, my husband and I passed a crafts museum while motoring along those narrow lanes, and I remembered a short piece in the *New York Times* fashion supplement about a group of Polish lace makers ▶

> 66 When I was a child, my Irish-American grandmother loved to tell stories, pulling tales from memory or making them up as she went along. 99

who had run afoul of their village priest for designing lace undies. He went so far as to threaten them with excommunication.

Eureka: The plot for *The Lace Makers of Glenmara* was born, those two threads of setting and plot converging, leading me to a cast of colorful, memorable characters who lived in my imagination before finding their place on the page—and in the fictional village of Glenmara.

With *Lace Makers*, I wanted to explore the healing and communal qualities of craft. (I have a crafts background myself, thanks to a patient step-grandmother, who taught me to crochet, and mother, who gave me her childhood sewing basket in the shape of a bee skep, filled with an embroidery hoop, floss, and transfer patterns.) I was interested in the idea of lace making itself as a means for women to forge stronger interpersonal connections at the same time they literally join one thread to the next. As *Lace Makers* unfolds, each woman has her "lace moment," as the others design lingerie especially for her, and is transformed by the process.

I took daily long walks as the leaves began to fall and the weather turned cold—the perfect time for settling in

66 I was interested in the idea of lace making itself as a means for women to forge stronger interpersonal connections at the same time they literally join one thread to the next. 99

to write. And on those walks, the characters that would inhabit the pages of *The Lace Makers of Glenmara* began to talk to me, dialogue which eventually found its way onto the page. In a burst of inspiration, I wrote and revised a draft of the novel during the fall and winter, then began searching for an agent and signed with Emma Sweeney within a week. A week later, Jennifer Barth at HarperCollins signed on as editor. I am eternally grateful to both of them. A magical ending for a writer indeed. ∾

Author's Picks:
Favorite Books

You mentioned a deep love of reading. Who are some of your favorite authors?

I have towers of books in my home office. It's like a miniature book metropolis, really, with skyscrapers made of novels, memoirs, poetry, and cookbooks. Some are mine, some are borrowed. I've tried to convince my family that they are a form of public art; they're not buying it.

How wonderful it is to be surrounded—literally—by literature! Some of the books come from my favorite local bookstore, others from the neighborhood library branch. (I've been a card holder, in one place or another, since the age of five, when I prowled the stacks at the old Olympia Public Library, once housed in a slope-floored Carnegie structure worthy of Lemony Snicket.) One of these days, I might have to resort to wheeling the treasured tomes to and fro in a red wagon or hand truck. There's so much to read! The hold slips also come in handy for jotting down thoughts for my current projects, which are also scattered around the office.

Here's a sampling:

West with the Night by Beryl Markham. As evocative a memoir as one can imagine. Totally transports the reader to another time and place—and into the life of a truly remarkable woman.

The Size of the World by Joan Silber. A pitch-perfect collection of linked short fiction. Utterly captivating and exquisitely crafted. Definitely a writer to watch.

The Shell Collector by Anthony Doerr. Short fiction at its finest. The title story is especially breathtaking. I'm envious of Doerr's command of craft.

Light Years by James Salter. I often reread the opening passages of this book. They never fail to inspire. Absolutely gorgeous, uncompromising prose.

The Woman in White by Wilkie Collins. Gothic novels don't get much better than this. Suspense, romance, tragedy, it's all here. Impossible to put down.

The Story of Lucy Gault by William Trevor moved me to tears. There is none finer than Trevor for illuminating the depths of the human condition. Brilliant and tragic, as is the rest of his impressive body of work. A master.

100 Years of Solitude by Gabriel Garcia Márquez. To read the first line of this novel is to enter another ▶

world, fully, magically, and irrevocably. Simply astonishing.

The White Bone by Barbara Gowdy. One of her very best. Daring, moving, and surprising in the very best way. This novel and *Watership Down*, which I read as a child, are my favorites of the genre.

Jonathan Strange and Mr. Norrell by Susan Clarke. Endlessly inventive and enthralling. Who knew footnotes could be so full of life.

The Star of the Sea by Joseph O'Connor. A riveting drama of the Famine and transport to the New World with a cast of characters you won't soon forget.

To Kill a Mockingbird by Harper Lee. It simply doesn't get any better than this—and as a lawyer's/judge's daughter and oldest/tomboy child, this book had special meaning for me.

The Assault by Harry Mulish. The first chapter alone is worth the price of admission. Shattering and deeply moving. ❧

Don't miss the next book by your favorite author. Sign up now for AuthorTracker by visiting www.AuthorTracker.com.